Columbus' Last Journey

Columbus' Last Journey

∞

-SANTA CLARA-
-KADDISH-

Steven Derfler

Copyright © 2015 by Steven Derfler.

Library of Congress Control Number:		2015913819
ISBN:	Hardcover	978-1-5144-0144-6
	Softcover	978-1-5144-0143-9
	eBook	978-1-5144-0142-2

All rights reserved. No part of this book may be reproduced or transmitted in any form or by any means, electronic or mechanical, including photocopying, recording, or by any information storage and retrieval system, without permission in writing from the copyright owner.

This is a work of fiction. Names, characters, places and incidents either are the product of the author's imagination or are used fictitiously, and any resemblance to any actual persons, living or dead, events, or locales is entirely coincidental.

Any people depicted in stock imagery provided by Thinkstock are models, and such images are being used for illustrative purposes only.
Certain stock imagery © Thinkstock.

Print information available on the last page.

Rev. date: 08/26/2015

To order additional copies of this book, contact:
Xlibris
1-888-795-4274
www.Xlibris.com
Orders@Xlibris.com
723302

Contents

Prologue xi

I:	Miami International to Havana Jose Marti	1
II:	La Isla Bonita, 1492	22
III:	Valladolid, Spain, May, 1506	25
IV:	The mystery deepens…. and a revolution interferes	29
V:	Havana, the present	32
VI:	La Habana, 1795	43
VII:	La Habana, the present	45
VIII:	Santa Clara, 1957	55
IX:	Havana, the present	62
X:	La Habana, 1795	72
XI:	Santa Clara, 1957	78
XII:	Havana, the present	91
XIII:	Havana to Santa Clara and back, 1795	99
XIV:	Santa Clara, 1957	104
XV:	Guanabacoa to Havana to Santa Clara, the present	114
XVI:	Santa Clara, the present	125
XVII:	Back to Havana	163

DEDICATION

The history of the human experience is a journey shared by all of us in one way or another. The hopes and dreams, aspirations and doubts, joys and sorrows, loves and hates, all link us together in some way.

Important figures in our collective past link us together as well- viewed by some as heroes and by others in more negative ways. However, their roles still shape our present and future. In some ways we wish to 'own' their influence; whether it means sharing in their achievements or honoring their memory by bringing back their remains to a 'native land' as a final resting place.

This explores the 'what ifs' of the past in a quest to clarify present possibilities.

Thank you to my friends and colleagues for their support and assistance in this third adventure. Thanks to my friends in Cuba for sharing their lives. Thanks to C.S. and E.S. for their editorial skills.

Special thanks with love to my family, for experiencing parts of the world that serve as the background of this adventure.

-KADDISH-

Part of the mourning rituals in Judaism in all prayer services; often referred to as *The Mourner's Kaddish*.

Mourners say Kaddish to show that despite the loss they still praise God.

יְהֵא שְׁמֵהּ רַבָּא מְבָרַךְ לְעָלַם וּלְעָלְמֵי עָלְמַיָּא

(Yehei shmëh rabba mevarakh lealam ulalmey almaya) "May His great name be blessed for ever, and to all eternity"

ANTIQVISSIMA ORBIS DELINEATIO.
MARE CRONIVM.
MARE EOVM
Mare Erythræum
OCEANVS
ANTICHTHONES VETERVM
SEV ALTER ORBIS.

PROLOGUE

'*L*ECH, LECHA! GET *up and go!*' This is what our ancestors told us, the young Spaniard thought. Ever since the days of Abrahan our forefather, we were born to explore, to travel, to lands far away... seeking peace, security, a home away from murder and violence. Who would have thought in this year 1492, that our community's homeland for over a millennium would so radically turn against us, torment and persecute us, murder us- all at the behest of the Catholic Church and our beloved el Rey Fernando y la Reina Isabel. Our sages taught that our history seemed to truly be in evidence whenever those opposing us imposed edicts upon us. They made mention of the Council of Elvira, around 305, that issued edicts against good Catholics marrying Spanish Jews. Our fate was sealed.

Rodrigo de Triana knew his people's history. It had been taught to him, handed down l'dor v'dor, from generation to generation, by his ancestors- proud Jews. He could recite the stories by heart, with pride and dignity.

Yes, there was a time of relative peace and prosperity, surprisingly, under the rule of the Moslems. It was Spain's Golden Age, the 9th-13th centuries, and it bode well for her Jews also. The inauguration of the Golden Age was closely identified with the career of the Jewish councilor of Abd ar-Rahman III, Hasdai ibn Shaprut. Originally a court physician, Shaprut's official duties went on to include the supervision of customs and foreign trade. The community prospered, and took advantage of its unique relationship with the Moors that afforded wonderful opportunities. Shaprut brought a number of men of letters to Córdoba, including Dunash ben Labrat, innovator of Hebrew metrical poetry and Menahem ben Saruq, compiler of the first Hebrew dictionary, which came into wide use among the Jews of Germany and France. Celebrated poets of this era included Solomon ibn Gabirol, Yehuda Halevi, Samuel Ha-Nagid ibn Nagrela and Moses ibn Ezra.

But it wouldn't last. As Catholic Spain entered into a period known as the Reconquista, Jews who prospered under the Moors were horrifically slaughtered for decades until the Spaniards realized that they could ill afford to turn the Jews against them. By the 13th century, Alfonso VII, who assumed the title of Emperor of Leon, Toledo and Santiago, curtailed the rights and liberties which his father had granted the Jews. He ordered that neither a Jew nor a convert might exercise legal authority over Christians. Crusaders began the "holy war" in Toledo by robbing and killing the Jews, and if the knights had not checked them with armed forces, all the Jews in Toledo would have been slain.

There were about 120 Jewish communities in Christian Spain around 1300, with somewhere around half a million or more Jews, mostly in Castille. In the beginning of the fourteenth century the position of Jews became precarious throughout Spain as anti-Semitism increased. Jews were forced to wear badges that set them apart from the community. The Jews no longer dared show themselves in public without the badge, and in consequence of the ever-growing hatred toward them they were no longer sure of life or limb; they were attacked and robbed and murdered in the public streets egged, on by those who said that they spoke en el nombre de Dios y de Cristo Jesús, 'in the name of God and Jesus Christ.' The year 1391 formed a turning-point in the history of the Spanish Jews. The persecution was the forerunner of the Inquisition; which, ninety years later, was introduced as a means of watching the converted Jews.

Synagogues were converted to cathedrals, tens of thousands of Jews were massacred, and tens of thousands others endured forced conversion. As soon as the Catholic monarchs Ferdinand and Isabella ascended their respective thrones, steps were taken to segregate the Jews both from the "conversos" and from their fellow countrymen. Though both monarchs were surrounded by Neo-Christians, such as Pedro de Caballeria and Luis de Santangel, and though Ferdinand was the grandson of a Jew, he showed the greatest intolerance to Jews, whether converted or otherwise, commanding all "conversos" to reconcile themselves with the

Inquisition by the end of 1484. An Edict of Expulsion was issued against the Jews of Spain by Ferdinand and Isabella on March 31, 1492. It ordered all Jews of whatever age to leave the kingdom by the last day of July. It was no coincidence then, that Christoforo Colon set sail from Spain on 3 August of that year.

It was now October 27th, and by Rodrigo's reckoning this made it the 28th of the Hebrew month of Tishrei in the year of 5253, Baruch HaShem, 'praised be God's name'.

The wind whipped around the pantaloon leggings of the young man high up the mast as the sea spray drenched him; the salt stinging his eyes mercilessly. As he held on for dear life, there was a brief lull as the clouds perceptibly thinned. Rodrigo uttered a *'mishseberach'*, a thanksgiving prayer, in Ladino, the language of his ancestors, and wiped the spray from his eyes with the tail of his *camisa*, now tattered after months at sea.

He couldn't believe it! Was it an illusion? The clouds closed in again. But now with renewed strength, he clung to his precarious nest 13 m above the deck. There was still 2 m of mast above him, but he certainly wasn't going to climb outside his small platform and shinny farther up to get a better glimpse- this was enough. But he did wait impatiently for the clouds to allow themselves to be pulled apart by the stiff breeze. And suddenly the sun broke through! There, not more than a dozen leagues away, was an island shrouded in mist; hazy, but nevertheless still there! His commander would call it San Salvador.

1

Miami International to Havana Jose Marti

WHOEVER SAID THAT LAX was the most congested, chaotic airport in the U.S. must have never set foot in Miami International, I thought as I weaved my way through the throngs along Concourse D. As I listened to the cacophony of sound that marked travelers rushing from gate to gate, or to hopefully retrieve their luggage from a carousel far away and on another level, I had a hard time imagining that I had not landed in a foreign country.

In an airport that served as the gateway to Latin America, English speakers could easily become disoriented. Even though there was no passport control, it felt as if I were in some southern Spanish-speaking nation like Argentina, with a similar standard of living and way of life. I kept from being run over by trolleys whose metal frames seemed to bend beneath the weight of enormous, green shrink-wrapped pieces of luggage. *Don't they know that they can't fold a 52 inch flat screen LCD so that it can fit in the overhead bin?* But I couldn't let my frustration show. After all, soon I would be among these passengers on a flight to *La Habana*.

As I waited in line to check-in for the nonstop charter to Jose Marti Airport, I thought back to how I got here. It seemed that everywhere I went internationally over recent years, a revolution broke out. I recalled January, 2011. I had just returned from Cairo with a bunch of students and 'real people' (okay, non-traditionally aged students!). The funny thing was that, although there had been rumblings and grumblings throughout the land, pretty much no one saw a full-blown uprising in the cards for the nation. Many were as surprised as I was. In Morocco, the situation was similar but much milder. Moroccans staged demonstrations against their democratically elected officials, but *not* the monarch, Mohamed VI. And there's Israel, where my work has brought me frequently over the past years. Regrettably, the situation between Israel and her Palestinian Authority and Syrian neighbors has been one of consistent confrontation with uneasy lulls in between bouts of fighting. The same, on a lesser scale, occurred on the northern frontier with Lebanon; oftentimes itself at the mercy of big bully brother Syria and its surrogate, *Hezbollah*. So, in the past couple of years, it seemed like my presence was the 'kiss of death' purely by coincidence.

However, this time around, it was not due to Arab-Israeli conflicts but rather internal Arab world politics, that ignited the situation. In December, 2010, a Tunisian fruit vendor became sick and tired of the undue taxation and government harassment of small-time entrepreneurs. Twenty-six year old Mohamed Bouazizi had been the sole income earner in his extended family. He operated a purportedly unlicensed vegetable cart for over seven years in *Sidi Bouzid*, 300 km south of Tunis. When Bouazizi tried to pay the 10-*dinar* fine (= $7), the policewoman slapped him, spat in his face, and insulted his deceased father. He went to the provincial headquarters to complain to local municipality officials but was refused an audience. Within an hour of the initial confrontation, Bouazizi returned to the headquarters, doused himself with a flammable liquid and set himself on fire. Public outrage quickly grew over the incident, leading to protests. By January 14, 2011, President Zine el Abadine Ben Ali would flee the country, with Prime Minister Mohamed Ghannouchi assuming power, only to resign in February.

So why did this seemingly small incident provoke the entire eastern Mediterranean Basin? The time was ripe for people to assert their rights as free citizens in a region known for its limited democracy and brutal repressive methods. The key motivations for the popular uprisings that would ensue were the governments of dictatorships or absolute monarchs, human rights violations, and government corruption. Internet-savvy youth of these countries studied in the West, where autocrats and absolute monarchies are considered anachronisms; and they would return with democratic 'stars' in their eyes. Another reason was an economic decline (increasing food prices and global famine rates), unemployment and extreme poverty. A large percentage of educated but dissatisfied youth within the population saw a concentration of wealth in the hands of autocrats in power for decades, with insufficient transparency of its redistribution of wealth, leading to corruption. The refusal of the youth to accept the status quo simply needed the tinder necessary to ignite the firestorm. Bouazizi was literally the spark.

The first country outside of Tunisia to feel the heat was Egypt. On January 25, 2011, the 'Arab Spring' as it was now called exploded in Cairo. My annual group of students and 'real people' had just wrapped up a marvelous two week journey to the land of the Pharaohs. We left the country on January 24. Although we were aware of the sketchy details of what had occurred in Tunisia weeks before, there was only the slightest sense of unease- certainly nothing compared to the explosion of sentiment in *Tahrir* Square the very next day.

Since it was a non-stop Cairo/New York flight, with scarcely 3 hours between landing, baggage claim and customs, to the next connection, none of us knew what had transpired until the following day. I then frantically called my friends Sobhy and Hythem in Cairo to make sure that they were safe. Once certain, I told them that I was shocked that so many people were upset to see me leave the country! At that time, they didn't think that it was funny. Now, however, it's part of the mythology of the Egyptian Spring!

Anyway, this was the back story to my first visit to Cuba. The travel agency that I had worked with on a couple of dozen trips to the Mideast shut down its programming to the area until things 'blew over'. Unfortunately, even today, in some parts of the region they're still waiting for the 'blow over'.

So, I was a bit surprised when I heard from the agency that handled all of my study-tours suggesting that I add my name regarding educational licenses, People to People missions, to Cuba. The Obama Administration began to ease American citizen travel to Cuba, by allowing for strictly licensed and regulated groups to travel to the island as long as they 'didn't have any fun.' Okay, that's a stretch. Just look at Beyonce and Jay-Z! But the licenses granted were designed to re-introduce Americans to a people just 90 miles from our southernmost point, while maintaining the ridiculous embargo (called *el bloqueo,* 'a blockade', by Cubans). This would allow for a gentle transition into re-establishing full relations with the island; most likely equally desired by both states.

I have an unwritten rule; that I never take people on study tours to destinations where I've never been. So, I was sent on a 'fam' or 'familiarization' trip, to *La Isla Bonita*. Boy was I in for an unexpected, wonderful surprise. Since then, six journeys have only heightened my respect for the Cuban people, and strengthened my feelings that the embargo should end. (There's only one 'good' thing about the situation... as of now you can't legally bring any Cuban rum back to the States, so you have to drink it all there!)

Meanwhile, as I waited in line patiently and respectfully (that could have been my *biggest* mistake) I thought back as to how similar this all felt to checking in to Mideast destinations. The noise, the press of people, the pushing, the shoving- did I mention the noise?- It seemed all too familiar.

I was reminded of flights to Cairo, Casa or Tel Aviv. Well, not so much Tel Aviv. Yes, the pushing and shoving and noise was all inherent in the check-in process; but at least with the Tel Aviv flights they *apologized* before pushing and shoving and yelling. Here in Miami there was nary a *'permiso'* to be heard. But I let it all roll of my back.

When I finally got to the head of the line, there was yet another 'roll of the dice' regarding check-in. It's a crap shoot whether the charter company, Sky King, would charge for checked bags. (Okay, so where's niece Penny when you need her? Give up? How about 'out of the blue of the western sky comes.... Sky King'? No? It was a '50s TV show that any boomer recalled with fondness, and all boys developed a crush on the niece) Since it's a charter, they are not bound by the same laws of disclosure; so sometimes they charge for the bag, and sometimes they don't. It's Miami. I got lucky this time around, no fee. So rather than *shlep* my bag onto an already over-TV'ed overhead bin, I opted to check. This was good in several ways. I didn't need to worry about the 3 oz. liquid rule since it was all checked- more so because I was bringing some stuff for friends that was in limited supply on the island.

The other reason had to do with scissors. I had learned my lesson the hard way on the last trip. The Cubans, ever security-conscious, have an X-ray machine inside the terminal after passport control. (As if you smuggled something between U.S. security and the plane on the way to Cuba, like U.S. water). I had traveled all over the world for years, and had taken with me a very small pair of foldable nail scissors. Israel, Egypt, Jordan, Greece, Morocco, Turkey, England.... and nowhere were they confiscated. However, the first time to Cuba, and after going through this security screening in *Jose Marti* Terminal before getting checked bags, the security officer pulled me over and asked to see my scissors. Apparently he really liked them, because they were gone in a flash into a pocket, all the while he smiled at me and said that they were a sharp object and security risk. So now, everything that possibly could be scrutinized went into the checked baggage and was safe and secure. I hoped.

So, once in that 'never-never land' after passport control, I sat back and awaited my flight with only my smartphone, Kindle and small carry-on containing a change of clothes 'just in case.' You never know when a bag can get a mind of its own and decide to go to another destination. This had happened to me once. But it was on the way home, not outbound. I was coming back from a previous adventure in the Mideast, one that 'rediscovered' a couple of Elephantine Papyri that had been 'acquisitioned' by the Germans prior to World War II. Even though I was flying a nonstop to Atlanta from Tel Aviv, my bag opted for a brief sojourn in Paris on the way back to the States. Four days later it finally arrived home, reeking of stale cigarettes and cheap perfume. But, to its credit, it never gave me any of the apparently racy details of where it was and what it did while in the City of Lights. (Much to my chagrin)

Only one other time was there any trouble with bags, and, in an unreal way, it happened twice with the same group on the same flight. During a previous journey to Cuba two bags from two group members never arrived in *La Habana*. It's only a five minute tram ride from the ticket counter to the gate, and then only a forty minute flight from Miami. HOW can bags get lost? Well, it wasn't just two bags. Apparently, one entire cart of baggage, totaling over 20 pieces, was never brought to the plane by the ground crew. At least my folks weren't alone in this.

However, once in Cuba, with lines of communication sketchy at best, we were never sure if and when the bags might arrive at *Jose Marti* International. Agents from *San Cristobal* Travel, one of the government-owned agencies, would call, be put on hold for dozens of minutes, and then find the line mysteriously disconnected. (They never told me if the canned 'on-hold' music was Buena Vista or not!) So, after two days of trying to call, we opted to get the people out to the airport with a rep. And it was a good thing. After trying to speak with three Sky King agents and one airport porter, the group was led to a left luggage storeroom and, lo and behold, there were the pieces of luggage. You never saw two happier faces. We never did find out when the bags arrived; whether it was later on the same day, or a day later. Nor did we care. The simple fact made the rest of the trip an incredible experience for all.

So I sat back and awaited the next great adventure.

* * *

I closed my eyes, and sort of drifted off. The sound of Spanish voices lulled me into a semi-conscious zone, something that I had learned from my Israeli 'brother' Eitan. As a member of the IDF, the Israeli army, he had learned the knack of falling asleep anywhere, everywhere, while in the military. After all, there, you never knew when your next downtime of shut-eye might come.

But this was different. The sometimes harsh, guttural sounds of Arabic and Hebrew are absolutely *nothing* like the lilt of Castilian/Canary Island-influenced Spanish, to softly enfold you and send you off to the never-never land of dreamscapes. I was just entering that state when, from the gate desk, a jarring PA blasted the area around me, announcing the start of the boarding process. It needed to be overly loud out of necessity, in order to drown out the myriad of conversations in several languages that were going on in the gate area.

I picked up my carry-on and made my way to the ticket scanner where the gate agent took my boarding pass and scanned it; with the usual 'beep' that signified that I wasn't a threat and could proceed down the jetway to 21C, on the aisle.

It was stiflingly hot and steamy, and the screaming kids, waiting-to-be-checked strollers and their moms slowed the process to a crawl. Did I say 'crawl'? How about rush-hour traffic standstill? Beads of sweat popped out on my forehead; and just ahead of me, a man looked as if he had just exited a swimming pool in his *guyabera* and jeans. I silently hoped that he wasn't going to be the one seated next to me. As I recalled, I thought that I saw his picture on Wikipedia under the entry entitled "*Schvitz*: Yiddish word for uncontrolled perspiring".

Upon arrival at the plane's door, a wave of coolness washed over me. Thankfully, the crew had fired up the AC a few moments earlier, and the cabin was a refreshing oasis. I actually felt chilled for a minute until my body temperature settled down. Oh what a relief.... I hurried down the aisle, unburdened by LCD TVs or rollerbags, and plopped down- unbuckled- as I waited for my row-mates to arrive.

Thankfully, they were 'normal-sized' people, with relatively stable body temperatures, and quite pleasant. It made for an uneventful short hop to *La Isla*. We chatted briefly before the flight attendants began their *spiel* about safety and security and what to do "in the unlikely event of...". It reminded me of some of those pharmaceutical commercials on TV, that list about 100 things that *may* go wrong with you as a side effect. Thank goodness the very last one mentioned is "with the possible occurrence of .....death!" Okay, I've never actually heard that one on TV before, but I'm certain that it will be coming someday.

Speaking of flight attendants, one look made you feel like you were on the set of a *Univision* soap opera. Both the man and woman were poster children for advertising models. They were nearly perfect in physique; with their uniforms apparently just about ½ size too small- designed to accentuate certain...... assets agreeable to the opposite sex. However, their informal presentation of the safety features was both accurate and solidly delivered; assuring all of their competence in the air. I thought that I heard a sigh of relief from one of my aisle-mates. I guess you never know when paying attention might become necessity. We all sat back, enjoyed our small bottled waters, and waited for the almost immediate descent into Havana.

As soon as I heard the double ping used by the cockpit crew to warn the cabin crew that the descent had started, I moved my seatback into its 'upright and locked' position. I knew that we were only ten minutes out. I turned off my Kindle and savored the quiet; in a few short minutes chaos would hit the Sky King cabin. And sure enough, as soon as the twin puffs of dust trailed behind the wheels on contact with the runway, all sorts of dings and chimes and pings and other cell-tones that defied definition filled the previously quiet plane. These sounds also shared the 'earways' with a smattering of applause from passengers scared to death of flying- now eternally thankful to the Almighty for a safe landing at *Jose Marti* International.

I girded myself for the inevitable- the quiet security agent at the airport who would pull me aside and grill me as if I was *pescados asado*. I wasn't disappointed. He asked to see my passport and began with the eternal lead-in, "Have you ever been to Cuba before?"

Well, based on years of international travel, and years of carefully accumulated bits of wisdom, the smart-ass responses remained tucked in my carry-on bag. Gone were the days of my impetuous youth, when an out-of-line answer put me in a whole lot of international hassle and, looking back, embarrassment. Such was the case in the Hashemite Kingdom of Jordan in the years before the peace treaty with Israel.

* * *

I was the American director of an excavation in Israel, and, as a result, was responsible for arranging group travel for students and 'non-traditionally-aged' students. It never ceased to amaze how average everyday people would pay a good sum of money to work as volunteers on archaeological sites in the hot desert sun of Israel. I guess that it was the biblical connection. Several years earlier, a mentor, friend and colleague, Frank Anniston, wrote a scholarly article entitled "Compulsory Slave Labor Gangs in Ancient Israel". Someone got a hold of it, and 'rewrote' it; removing the "Ancient" from the title and creating a parody of life on an archaeological field school. It went over really well with the volunteers and staff- not so much with Anniston. But he eventually came around... weeks later.

Anyway, the travel agency that I worked with made an innovative suggestion as they searched high and low for the best possible airfare package. They discovered a multi-airline deal that incorporated Royal Jordanian Airlines, Alia, with a codeshare partner, SwissAir. The package was a great price, provided that you flew into Amman International and out of Tel Aviv/Ben Gurion.

They went on to discover that an overnite and tour of Petra before crossing into Israel could be included *with the price still cheaper than flying into Tel Aviv!* This seemed to be an opportunity that couldn't be resisted. It was a win/win, and the incredibly beautiful Nabatean Arab city could be visited as well. I got on board with the opportunity for the group.

A few weeks prior to the departure, as I was preparing, I got out my dog-eared, well-worn passport. As I idly scanned through the pages, all of the

Israeli visa stamps suddenly jumped out at me. Technically, Jordan and Israel were still 'at war' at that time. All Arab states except Egypt were; this was back in the 1980s. I knew that the stamps ran the risk of creating a problem so I called the U.S. State Department for advice. This was a mistake.

I spoke with three people, all progressively higher up the food chain, who all gave me the same answer with the same infinite wisdom. 'Wisdom' by a political appointee in the State Department is an oxymoron.

"You are a U.S. Citizen, and the U.S. is not, I repeat, is not in a state of belligerency with the Kingdom of Jordan. They are our allies. It does not matter at all what kind of stamps you have in your passport." This was the 'final' answer afforded to me. I couldn't even 'call a friend' or 'poll the audience'.

By now it was too late to get a new passport because of the bureaucratic nightmare called 'passport application' so I saved a copy of a letter received from the government agency and finished preparing for the journey.

Travel day came, and the group was bursting at the seams- excited to go on this adventure that would answer all of the burning questions about archaeology, the bible and ancient Israel's history. (Needless to say, the lecture about 90% boring grunt work on the dig with only rare flashes of extraordinary discovery seemed to have passed by all the participants) Since we were flying to Amman first, and this was before the age of non-stop travel from the east coast of the U.S. to the Middle East, we were faced with three legs of the journey. When we finally landed at Amman International, over 17 hours of minimal comfort had passed. I handle jetlag better than most, but still suffered a bit from lack of rest. This would come back and bite me somewhere with pain and anger.

As we all deplaned, we dragged our carry-ons down the flight of stairs and onto a sizzling tarmac. It may have been 95 degrees air temperature, but the concrete runway thermometer was hovering around the 115 degree point. We entered the terminal and were greeted by a 'chilly' temperature that may have been 90, but we welcomed it as we wiped the perspiration from our brows. Once inside, it was a mere hundred steps to Passport Control, manned by red-and-white-checked, *keffiyahed,* Arab Legionnaires. The nightmare would begin.

Of course, even though two international flights arrived within moments of each other, there were only three control booths open to handle a couple of hundred passengers, although there was one dedicated to the flight crews- perhaps eighteen all told. This obviously riled a lot of people in the lines and tempers combined with jetlag led to lots of grumbling.

Finally, as I approached the window, the officer inexplicably left. I was left standing there for another several moments until another soldier entered and sat down. (Apparently it was tea break time. Well, as we say in the Middle

East, 'blame it on the British!') He fussed a bit, logged on to the old computer terminal, and gestured for my passport. I handed it over, with a smile.

"From where are you staying in Amman?" was the first boring question that he asked.

"Amman Hilton, sir," I responded.

He then looked at the passport more closely and frowned, typed a few strokes on the keyboard, looked at the passport, looked at me, and frowned some more.

"What am I to be looking at here?" he tapped my passport.

"I can't see, what are you looking at" was my reply. (Pleasant, not sarcastic, eh)

"Is to be looking at *Is-rah-ay-lee-a* stamp," was his reply to my reply.

I looked at him, perplexed a bit, with as calm an expression as possible. *Remember our State Department conversations, and the letter, if need be,* were the thoughts running through my head. But I was tired, needed some sleep and needed a bottle of the locally brewed *Petra* beer. It is licensed by Amstel, and is only available in hotels that cater to foreigners- after all, as an Islamic nation, alcohol is (wink-wink) forbidden. Its informal slogan is "If a visit to the ancient city of Petra doesn't knock your socks off, this bottle of beer will!" At over 8% alcohol- no wonder!

I was shaken from my reverie as the guard was making a statement- "*Habibi,* my friend, there is no *Is-rah-ay-il* but only *Falesteen,* Palestine."

I tried to process. Israel was created in the same year as the Hashemite Kingdom of Jordan, but I certainly wasn't going to give this Legionnaire a history and political science lesson when he had an AK-47 leaning against the wall of his cubicle and a Webley Break-top Revolver strapped on a Sam Browne belt. So I opted to be as non-confrontational and friendly as possible. Remember, I was jetlagged and a bit cranky.

"Well, if Israel doesn't exist, I suppose that this stamp isn't 'real'", was my reply. If Richard Dawson had polled his 'Family Feud' audience for the answer, this would not have been one of them.

The guard looked at me, I looked at him. He looked down at the passport, his eyes turning flinty (maybe it was the caffeine). "You will to be coming with me!" he shouted while he pressed a buzzer mounted below his desktop. Suddenly, two more Legionnaires came through the door that led to baggage claim- and freedom- not so gently taking an arm each and led me outside the terminal to a dun-colored military Toyota tender. They walked me up the ladder and onto the back benches under the canvas top. The temperature matched that of the tarmac, until we started to move.

"Where are we going?" I asked the guardian of the Kingdom.

"To your hotel", was the terse response as he lit a Palace Filtered cigarette.

When we arrived at the hotel, in advance of the rest of the group (since I wasn't allowed to pick up my bags, and flashing lights on the truck sped us through the city), I was escorted up to my room and told not to leave. Of course, the two soldiers positioned outside my door convinced me not to try otherwise.

Around dinnertime, a knock on the door revealed a room-service trolley with extremely edible food. In addition, there was a note from one of my colleagues stating that the group was fine, checked-in and a bit concerned about my well-being. I hastily scribbled a note which one of the soldiers determined could be delivered to the group.

The next morning at 5am there was a pounding on the door. I groggily opened up to discover another soldier (apparently they had changed shifts) with a breakfast tray. He said in extremely broken English that I was to go to the U.S. Embassy with them in a quarter of an hour. I hastily shaved and dressed in the only set of clothing I had. Another knock indicated that it was time to go. We descended to the same Toyota truck and drove, in a more sedate fashion, to the U.S. Embassy. Once there, I was escorted to the Marine guard booth at the compound's drive. A note was given from the Jordanian officer to the Marine, who then escorted me into 'U.S. Territory' and one of the offices.

I was then issued a new U.S. passport. Remember the saying that you must be sick if you look like your passport photo? Well, I must have had a terminal disease, the picture was so bad. But now, I had a clean passport, with no stamps from non-existent or illegal nation-states. I could proceed as a well respected member of the international community. With new passport in hand, the Jordanian accompanying me politely asked for it once I stepped off of "U.S. soil" and back onto Jordanian land. I must have had a fearful look in my eyes. He smiled warmly and told me not to worry. He then ceremoniously stamped my passport with a Jordanian entry visa, and said, rather pleasantly, "Welcoming you, dok-toar, to the *Hashemi* land of our beloved King Hussein. Wishing you a happy visit here. Thank you too much!"

In the back of the pickup truck were my bags. I was taken back to the hotel. I breathed a deep sigh of relief once I shut the door to my room. Then I started shaking. I suddenly realized that for nearly 24 hours I didn't 'exist' anywhere on this planet. I could have been made to disappear and no one would have been the wiser. I could envision the scenario.

"What, an American? As you can see by our meticulous Passport Control records, no one of that name was logged into our country on that day."

From then on, I tried to curb my tongue whenever I found myself in a potential situation like this. But, knowing me, well......

Needless to say, we never got to Petra that year, but I did get my socks knocked off by the beer.

* * *

I snapped back to the world of *mojitos* when the agent asked me the same questions again. I smiled and responded as best I could. I gave a copy of the governmental travel license, the itinerary, and the contacts on the island. After about ten minutes, I was waved off with a desultory *gracias,* passed through security and entered the baggage claim area.

I felt like I was in the checkout line of Sam's Club, given the number of incredible large shrink wrapped flat-screen TVs, computer towers and 'ginormous' suitcases laden with anything imaginable from the unbelievably 'rich' Cuban-Americans living the good life in the United States. Ever since the loosening of travel restrictions, this one-way flow of commerce dazzled the mind. The presents must have stunned the poor relatives in Habana who had just this side of nothing in terms of luxury goods.

Thank goodness I could proceed through the 'nothing to declare' exit to the relative 'calm' of the covered patio area where hundreds of relatives waited noisily for their long-lost family members triumphant return to *La Isla*. But first, I needed to stop at the *Cadeca* for some CUCs.

Cuba is an economic mystery- not about *how* it works, but *how* it continues to work. Its currency system is based on a dual-peso scenario that could only have been dreamed up by Hollywood, or a delusional politician, or both. It's part of the weird 'dance' being played out by Cuba and the United States in the 21st Century. But in addition, it is also a direct result of the partial reversal of the lukewarm economic reforms enacted by the government back in the 90s to combat the loss of, well, *everything* with the collapse of the Soviet Union, who for years had been the primary partner/ supporter/ 'propper-upper' of Cuba itself. Remember, over 90% of all economic trade and support came from the U.S.S.R. and her allies. The dark days after the fall brought on hardships never seen before on the island- including the days immediately following the Revolution. Castro and Company were hanging on by the proverbial thread and needed some sort of immediate reform to keep the people from 'counter-revolutionizing'. This led to a loosening of governmental regulations, a beginning experiment in privatization and greater freedom for Cuban entrepreneurs.

However, with a very slight rebound bounce internally, and the desire to slap the Bush Administration in the face due to its overwhelming support of anti-Castro Cuban expats (who just also happened to be live-the-American-dream-strike-it-rich Republican supporters), a major currency reversal was in the offing.

Two Cuban currencies had been in existence; the Cuban Peso (CUP) and the Cuban Convertible Peso (CUC). The CUC was on a par with the

U.S. Dollar, and would be used by tourists. The CUP was used in everyday life by Cubans to buy necessities. It was loosely based on 25 CUP equaling 1 CUC. However, the USD was also widely accepted as a currency of exchange in this sector as well. Loosely linked, with exchange rate fluctuations, both the Cuban government and individuals could 'bank on' a bit of extra funds depending on the market.

This radically, dramatically, painfully, came to an end in July 2003. The Cuban Government made the first big move against the circulation of the dollar in Cuba. From this point forward, all transactions in the dollarized network would have to be conducted in CUC. Deposits and banking accounts of Cuban firms also would have to be denominated in CUC. In addition, all operations by Cuban firms demanding foreign currencies would require approval of the Cuban Central Bank. A decree passed in November 2004 designated the CUC as the only currency accepted in the dollarized network of goods and services. At the same time, the Government established a 10% tax on the U.S. dollar. By taxing the USD, the Cuban Government was supposedly encouraging remittances in other foreign currencies. In essence, it was a form of currency extortion. U.S. restrictions on the use of USD by Cuba were allegedly the reason for implementing the tax. Cuban economists claim that this measure has succeeded in slashing the share of inflows in dollars from 80% to 30%. But then they were voices of the government; what else could they say. Finally, the CUC was officially appreciated against all foreign currencies in April 2005.

The true end result though is that tourists are feeling the heat, and the pinch, economically- especially with the opening the door a crack to American 'humanitarian tourism' during the Obama administration. (This simply meant that you could now visit the island as long as 'you weren't having any fun'- *snicker, snicker*)

So, with no use of American-based credit cards, debit cards, traveler's checks or the like, it meant that a pain-in-the-butt hard cash relationship was in play. Clearly, it was a 'different' kind of *baisbal* game. So, I reluctantly changed $300 USD and, with the added standard extortion, er, exchange rate fees, got 261 CUC. Talk about a rip-off.

I took a deep breath, then headed past the final pale-blue uniformed officers and into the steamy sunlight.

I heard him before I saw him. A tumultuous roar of delight filled the air as hundreds of Cuban family members anxiously awaiting their long-lost relatives from Miami suddenly caught glimpses of familiar faces pushing loads of goods on trolleys that seemed to have their steel frames visibly bend under the weight. But, over all that cacophony of sound I heard a calm, yet strident voice arguing with a police officer- politely yet firmly.

"*Jefe*, boss, but the flight is *in*! My mobile just got the text that my *companero* has just left the *Cambio* and is on his way out! I can't move my car because if I walk away now he'll miss me and I'll miss him and we'll miss each other and then he'll presume that I wasn't here…"

"*Mas que suficiente!* That's more than enough from you! Just because you San Cristobal Agents think that you own the airport and can park anywhere and at anytime…"

I made like Moses parting the Reed Sea as I hurriedly bulled my way past dozens of arrivees and shouted out my friend's name.

"*Berto! Amigo! Com' esta?* Boy am I happy to see you!" I studiously ignored the officer standing next to him. I bussed him on both cheeks as we embraced, he with that patented smile that lit up half of Havana. He grabbed my roller-bag from me and we proceeded quickly down the ramp to his waiting ride, leaving the officer in the dust with a big frown on his face. Apparently there was to be no citation issued, *nor* a "token of esteem" in lieu of the ticket. The policeman lost out in either case.

Berto slapped me on the back again, grinning like a madman. As we got into the car he tossed me a bottle of *Ciego Montero* spring water. Did I say "car" when I mentioned his vehicle? Well, that certainly didn't do it justice. It was a fairly mint condition '59 Chevy Impala- a deep purple hue. The color accent was white on the roof- thus serving to compliment the body tone. The chrome gleamed, I could see if my hair was combed in its reflection. The twin rear fins sparkled in the hazy Havana sunshine. The white sidewall tires (yes, white sidewalls!) were almost spotless. The rear fins were splayed out horizontally and it looked as if the car could hold its own against a Chris Craft motorboat in the Florida Straits. The cloth interior was without blemish as well, although not in as pristine a condition. Cubans notoriously were possessed with the idea of a clean ride on the outside- not so much on the inside. When he turned the key, however, it was a slightly different story. As he turned the key, the engine ticked over with a much more gentle purr than the roar that Americans associated with 'muscle cars' of the 50s; when gas at 25 cents a gallon was cheap, thrills even cheaper and American youth prowled the streets on warm summer nights in their rides, with their girls, without a care in the world. The local carhop where you could get a burger, fries and malt for about 45 cents was the place to be on Saturday night. And the sounds and smells of American made cars set your heart afluttering!

But in spite of its looks, Berto's car was a far cry from its pedigree. With the initiation of the Embargo by the U.S. after Castro's rise to power, all of the glory and greatness of American industry just 90 miles north was cut off. As retaliation, Castro hastened the nationalization of many industries, thus adding insult to injury. With thousands of U.S. imports on Cuban roads, drivers suddenly found themselves without, well, *everything* compared to the abundance that they were used to just months earlier. Gas was severely rationed, and the American-made guzzlers began to sit idle out of necessity. In addition, *El Bloqeo*, as the Cubans called it, turned off the flow of auto parts that were so sorely needed. This increased the number of idled vehicles. However, the ingenuity of the Cuban people rose to the top of the pyramid. As other foreign auto companies saw a great opportunity for their vehicles, Cubans saw the opportunity to improvise. Ford drive trains would be matched with newer Toyota engines, brackets would be realigned and re-welded. The American muscle car of the past became a hybrid of 'Heinz 57 Varieties'- and kept running down the road. With the influx of Soviet gear, this became a really weird combination of things as *Lada* and *Moskvitch* parts became blended into the mix as well. Can you imagine- a communist/capitalist road warrior?

But that was Berto's vehicle, and whatever was under the hood, he was damn proud of it and kept it pristine on the outside. Of course, he didn't use it much for a couple of reasons. The first was the obvious one; with the price of gas hovering around the equivalent of $4.85 a gallon, and rationed, it was an incredibly steep price for anyone. But for a Cuban, it was almost, as they say in *baisbal*, 'out of the ballpark!' The second reason was his employer. As the chief of guides for San Cristobal Travel Agency, he was able to get around on their *centavo* most of the time and needn't worry about transportation. So this was a luxury for him, and for me. I knew that it also came at a great cost for him, and vowed to make it up to him as best I could. A *mojito* or two in one of the world's most famous bars, the Bay View, in the Hotel *Nacional* would be a fitting start.

However, as I also understood the man, his privacy was of the utmost importance to him. When you work in any service industry that deals with people almost all of the time in public, you cherish, you *hoard* your personal time more than the average person. In that regard, the travel industry and education are similar. When you are working, you are 'on'. You project a certain image, you work with people, you try your best to be as professional as possible even if it means biting your tongue on more than one occasion. (Or not, when there is one too many stupid remarks or actions that are made by insensitive tourists) Then, when you are done for the day, you absolutely crave your quiet, down time. I have been accused of being a quiet, retiring person more than once when it came to my personal life.

For Berto, the nature of the communist way of life in Cuba would dramatically infringe on his personal down time if he were to drive his car on the roads very often. After the Revolution, many private cars and other vehicles were forced off the road, and the public transportation system was simply not up to speed to meet an increasing demand. Because everyone worked in Cuba and had a job created for them (unless they didn't want to work and would suffer the consequences), ride-sharing on the highways became a necessity. The government created a job position to ensure that people would get picked up by government-owned vehicles (which were the majority on the roads). So men would work for the government as *amarillos*, yellow-jumpsuited men stationed along the roadways in Cuba. People would congregate around them at intervals alongside the berm. If a government vehicle was coming by and had empty places in it, the *amarillo* would stop the car and order it to take on passengers. It was felt that this was a government responsibility and that the driver, a government employee, needed to follow the law. This might to extend private cars as well and, to Berto, this was simply too much of an inconvenience should it happen. So, his *belleza púrpura*, his purple beauty, would sit at home and be lovingly dusted off every once in a while.

We threw my bag in the trunk, and I sat back and watched as I was transported to a highway scene that was 60 years in the past. We exited the airport and immediately a roadside billboard could be seen; announcing *Ano 54 de la Revolucion*! I idly wondered how many years of revolution were necessary until it was deemed a success. I must have been telegraphing my thoughts, because Berto suddenly was talking to me.

'You know, *amigo*, although the times here on the island have radically changed over the last decade, we still believe that *revolucion* and all that it entailed needs to be constantly minded after. We too can roll with the punches and modify and change for the betterment of our citizens, but we must always be mindful of the events that shape us."

Wow, talk about being psychic!

"So my friend, were you reading my mind and am I that easy to read?" I laughed and punched his arm. At least I had the Cuban answer to what I was thinking.

The road was somewhat sparsely populated at this hour, but gradually began to fill as we swallowed up the 12 miles from airport to the heart of *La Habana*. It was a vision of paradise for all of those 'back to the 50s' car aficionados; in the current calendar system, that would be considered to be BC- 'Before Castro!' We passed by 100s of what American would call 'vintage' motorcars that harkened back to the heyday of Detroit's auto industry. Hollywood had nothing over Havana. Who needed a stage set for a movie when you could be living it right on the spot. We could have been on the set of the movie, Cuba, where Sean Connery played a British mercenary in the late 1950s during the turmoil. Or my other new favorite, the Redford/Olin/Julia film, Havana; set in the city in 1958.

In addition, as we progressed into town, we passed scores of newer vehicles, *Ladas* and *Moskvitchs* of the later 60s, 70s and early 80s- a throwback to the heady days of Soviet support and, to a high degree, control of her western hemisphere surrogate.

We headed northeast and crossed the *Almendares* River into the district of *Nuevo Vedado*. This area was called *Vedado*, meaning 'prohibited' because of a Spanish government decree banning the creation of paths to the beach in that area of Havana. It was a warm, pleasant day and we rolled through the suburb without a care in the world. Berto seemed at ease, in part because he had just finished up with a group of British tourists the other day, the last of 3 weeks of back-to-back-to-back groups; and was off for 10 days. A bit of RnR was just what the doctor ordered. The river formed a natural boundary between *Miramar*, meaning 'sea-view' to the west and *Vedado* proper to the east, along the shoreline. Both were well established residential areas, leafy and green.

As we passed the Colon Cemetery to our left, it gave me the ideal opportunity to explain the reason for this visit. Yes, it was humanitarian as required by the U.S. government. And yes, it fulfilled all of the requirements necessary for continuation of the licensure. After all, I would be visiting a number of religious agencies while on the island. However, in addition to the fulfillment, I was planning to follow up on scholarship that seemed to indicate literary evidence that Christopher Colon, aka Columbus, was of Jewish ancestry.

"You know, amigo, that there is still a great debate raging about Columbus' roots." "*Por supuesto*, of course I know that", was his reply. "They don't call me 'the encyclopedia' for nothing!" He roared with delight almost as loud as the traffic surrounding us.

I ignored him and went on. "Simon Wiesenthal felt that Columbus was a *Sephardi*, concealing his Judaism- yet eager to locate a place of refuge for his persecuted countrymen. Wiesenthal argued that Columbus' notion to sail west to reach the Indies was less because of geographical theories and more of his religious belief in Hebrew Biblical texts—in particular, the Book of Isaiah. He repeatedly cited two verses from that book: "Surely the isles shall wait for me, and the ships of *Tarshish* first, to bring thy sons from far, their silver and their gold with them," (60:9); and "For behold, I create new heavens and a new earth" (65:17). Wiesenthal claimed that Columbus felt that his voyages confirmed these Biblical prophecies."

He shot me that 'don't I know it' look but asked me to continue.

"Estelle Irizarry, in 2006, argued that Columbus was *Catalan*, claiming that he tried to conceal a Jewish heritage. In "Three Sources of Textual Evidence of Columbus, Crypto Jew," Irizarry noted that Columbus always wrote in Spanish, and occasionally included Hebrew in his writing, and referenced the Jewish High Holidays in his journal during the first voyage."

"So he never wrote much in Italian? That I didn't know," replied my Cuban friend.

"Finally, there was the argument by Jane Francis Amler, that Columbus was a *converso* (a *Sephardi* Jew who publicly converted to Christianity). In Spain, even some converted Jews were forced to leave the country after much persecution; it is known that many *conversos* were still practicing their Judaism in secret. So, with these major points, it's now up to me, er, rather, us to track down any other leads that might give us more clues." I sat back.

"So as you Americanos say, 'who's buried in Grant's Tomb?'" He laughed again. He was lightly humming to himself as he drove on; a wide grin on his face. I had him hooked...

* * *

We headed past the *Teatro Nacional*, the National Theatre, and the university area. Just as we turned onto *Calle 21* I called out to Berto, "STOP!!!!!!!"

I must have scared the hell out of him for he jammed on the brakes and looked frantically around. "Where are they!?" he demanded sharply.

"Where are who?"

"The State police, that's who!" He was nervous as an American tourist trying to bring a bottle of Havana Club Rum back into the States.

"There are no officers a-....... Wait a minute! We were just passing *Coppelia* and I wanted an ice cream! That's all." I said, a bit sheepishly.

"You mean that you screamed at me because of an ice cream stand!" The veins were bulging from his neck, and I thought that he was going to have a stroke. "*Cálmate! Por favor*! Calm down my friend." Now I really felt bad.

"*Sus madres ojos! Hijo de puta!* I should put on my emergency brake, reach over, and strangle you a slow death!" He reached to unclip his seatbelt. Suddenly, he snapped it back on and drove ½ a block and got a parking space and pulled in. "My emergency brake is broke," was all that he said as he got out. "But you're buying!"

I smiled again, getting out a few CUCs as we headed across the street. On *Calle 23* in the area known as *La Rampa* in the *Vedado* district, it is a flying-saucer-shaped building that takes up the entire city block between *Calles* 23 and 21, and *Calles* K and L. As one of the largest shops in the world, the ice cream store has been a major landmark for both Cubans and visitors since its opening in 1966; but acquired an even greater reputation when it was featured in one of the most widely viewed Cuban films, released in 1994, 'Strawberry and Chocolate'.

Even at this time of day, the line of customers ran ¼ of the way around the block- attesting to the enormous popularity of this Cuban phenomenon. While we waited, 'The Encyclopedia' recited one of 'his' entries for me.

"Did you know that *Coppelia* was originally built as a project led by Fidel himself in order to introduce his love of dairy products to the Cuban masses, creating the *Coppelia* enterprise to prepare those products? Fidel's longtime secretary, Cecilia Sánchez, named *Coppelia* after her favorite ballet, *Coppélia*?" He asked slyly, knowing that I indeed did not know.

Who am I to argue with an encyclopedia.

From there, it was a short 5 minute drive to one of the most iconic hotels anywhere in the world- the Hotel *Nacional*.

The hotel is located in the midst of *Vedado*, the center of Havana. It stands on a hill just a few meters from the sea and offers a great view of the Havana harbor, the sea-wall and corniche, here called the *Malecon,* and the ancestral fortress called "*El Morro*".

On December 30th 1930, the Hotel *Nacional de Cuba* opened its doors. Its architecture shows a mixture of Art-Deco features, Arabic artistic influences, and Spanish-Moorish architecture; becoming the most interesting and unique hotel in the Caribbean region.

It has a large garden with two big cannons of the former artillery battery called Santa Clara; named "*Krupp*" and "*Ordoñez*"- the last one was considered the biggest cannon in the western hemisphere at the time. The names are derived from the artillery manufacturers, Krupp in Germany and the Spanish armorer, Salvador Diaz Ordoñez. Both were declared, together with the historical center of Old Havana, to be a World Heritage Site in 1982 by UNESCO.

In December 1946, a great meeting of the mafia took place in the hotel and its doors were closed to the public to accommodate the heads of the most notorious families of crime in the United States when they gathered- including Santos Trafficante and Meyer Lansky. Entertainment was provided by Frank Sinatra. Other notables who stayed there (obviously at another time!) included: Johnny Weissmüller (Tarzan), Edward VIII (Prince of Wales), Jack Dempsey, Tom Mix, Buster Keaton, Errol Flynn, George Raft, Betty Grable, Jorge Negrete, Pedro Vargas, the Duke of Windsor, Karol II of Romania, Mario Moreno (Cantinflas), Tyrone Power, Lucky Luciano, Rita Hayworth, Ali-Khan, Ernest Hemingway, Fred Astaire, Cesar Romero and Gary Cooper. Pictures from each personality are on display in the "Bay-View" Bar, also known as 'Hall of Fame'; with the aim to show all the distinguished guests of the hotel since 1930.

But now, before dropping me off (and promising to meet me for breakfast the next day), it was Berto's turn to educate me, for I had little knowledge of the life of the *Nacional* in post-revolution Cuba.

"It's what Fidel has done with the hotel since *La Revolucion* that is more impressive, given the nature of Cuba", he said. "At first, there was a noticeable change in the type of guest activity; more Cuban guests and, can you imagine, small farmers! Reflecting changes in the revolution, in October, 1960 the hotel served as the setting for the foundation of the National Revolutionary Militias and the Committees for the Defense of the Revolution (CDRs). Remember the 'American' Missile Crisis of October '62?"

"How could I forget? Wait... what? The *American* Missile Crisis?" I let it go. "I was an elementary school student in Ohio and we suddenly had drills where we got under our desks and put our arms over our heads.... as if that could protect us from a missile strike!" Even though I laughed, I was sobered by my memory of those quite scary times, when the world was at its first 'brink' since the Korean War.

"Anyway, anti-aircraft gun emplacements were installed on the hotel's hill, and walled trenches and tunnels were excavated below the gardens that faced the Florida Straits- an unbelievable engineering feat."

I interrupted, "*This* I do know. I have been in the bunkers before. As part of the hotel's history tour, they take you into the network and explain those dark days from a Cuban standpoint. The woman who conducts the tours was a 17 year old girl serving in the militia at that time. Now she's come full circle."

Berto smiled, "You mean Estrella, don't you." See, he still had all the answers.

"That's her, now go on and tell me something else I don't know."

"Some of the more recent guests have included Jean Paul Sartre, Simone de Beauvoir, Josephine Baker, and Gabriel García Márquez. In 1992, the *Nacional* was fully restored and was given the status of serving as Cuba's flagship hotel. Since then, Pierre Cardin, Geraldine Chapman, Harry Belafonte, Arnold Schwarzeneggar, Robert DeNiro, Hank Aaron, Mohamed Ali and Francis Ford Coppola have all stayed there. And of course, you!" Now he laughed.

In 1998 the first historic rooms were inaugurated, including Room 235, the one used many times by Errol Flynn.... and me!

* * *

The first visit to Cuba was a 'working fam' for me, a familiarization trip. The travel agency had me counting noses and serving as liaison with *Transneco*, the Cuban travel agency, and its guide from San Cristobal Travel Agency, one of its subsidiaries (remember, they are all owned by the government anyway). I had no idea what I was in for. As the *Transgaviota* Tour Bus (another subsidiary!) pulled onto the enormous drive of the *Nacional*, I was forced to pick my lower jaw up off the bus floor. I was amazed. It looked like The Breakers Hotel in Palm Beach, Florida....*exactly*! I would later find out that the same architects designed the two.

Once inside, the agent assigned to the group checked us all in. I was handed a key-card to room 235. Boy, was I in for a shock. I proceeded to the bank of elevators, and rather impatiently, waited for the bronze doors to part. The main block of 4 lifts turned out to be on the opposite end of the building, so I hoofed it along the main corridor. It seemed a bit seedy, and I was girding myself for a nominal stay, not at all luxurious as I had envisioned when we approached the hotel. The floor was old, with white and green checked tiles. I would find out that this floor was considered to be one of the 'historic floors;' and that the tiles dated to 1930. I worked my way down and suddenly noticed pictures and plaques on the walls adjacent to a majority of the rooms. Pictures of Nat King Cole, Stan Musial, Rita Hayworth, Tyrone Power; and then, just off one of the wings, *the honeymoon suite of Frank Sinatra and Ava Gardner!* Wow! That was all that entered my mind. Then, across a small lobby at the junction of the wings, there was Room 235. I looked at the picture. *It was Errol Flynn!*

Talk about a show-stopper! I wasn't all that familiar with his work, but I did know of some of the tales surrounding his career- checkered and otherwise. A great actor, but an even greater 'playboy', Flynn would come down to Havana for 3 months at a time in between films. That's what Hollywood types did in the 40s and 50s, when Havana was the playground of rich and famous Americans, with their share of 'wild and crazy guys' as the saying goes- Flynn included on the short list.

In 1940 he was called the 4th most popular actor in the U.S. But Flynn also had a reputation for womanizing. His freewheeling, loose lifestyle caught up with him in 1942 when two underage girls accused him of statutory rape. Flynn was cleared of the charges. The incident, though, served to increase his reputation as a ladies' man. It is believed this is the source of the phrase "in like Flynn." It was also rumored that he had gay proclivities as well. By the 1950s, Flynn had become a parody of himself. Heavy alcohol and drug abuse made him almost unrecognizable as the swashbuckler of just a decade earlier. He died in 1959. Or did he?

I opened the room and was really pleasantly surprised. The room, at the junction of the 2 wings, was irregularly shaped as it 'bent' around the corner a bit, and enormous. The kingsized bed was dwarfed. A large window overlooked an even larger wrap-around balcony that overlooked the gardens and the Florida Straits to the north. It was a stunning view. The refurbished furnishings were vintage. But inside the armoire was a 32-inch flat-screen TV with a limited number of satellite channels. Remember, this is Cuba- none of the mainstream U.S. networks could be seen. CNN was out of Hong Kong of all places. But you could get TNT and some of the other cable networks, as well as ESPN's Spanish speaking channel. In addition, there were five local Cuban stations. Adorning the walls were more photos of E.F. himself- one with Papa Hemingway. The bath was redone as well.

But the real shocker came that night. Since we were to be in Havana for 3 nights, it made sense to unpack a bit, at least hang up the shirts. So into the closet they went. After a good dinner, and orientation with the group that I was tasked with herding over, I went back for an early night. I turned in after watching a bit of Cuban baseball on TV. It was the *Habana Industriales* v. *Cienfuegos Elefantes*. No matter what language, a hit is a hit and an out is an out. I was surprised at the level of play. It put a few major league teams in the states to shame- like the Chicago White Sox (sorry, Sox fans!). Because I was so impressed with the *Elefantes* and their level of play, I would press our guide to hurry some touring up just a bit so that we could catch one of their games later in the week. I learned, with my broken Spanish, that the announcer noted that the team would be back home in Cienfuegos in 3 days' time.

But I digress. After the game, I crawled into bed and slept like a log... until around 3am. I was unexpectedly awakened by the slow opening of the closet door, and *the closet light coming on!* It scared the hell out of me. I sat up ramrod straight and stared at the closet intently. Then it hit me- it could be none other than good old Errol himself! He was coming in from another late night out on the town.

"Errol, er, Mr. Flynn," I said to the closet. (So I'm talking to closets now?) "You aren't staying in this room right now, I am. And if you insist on coming in at such an ungodly hour, please have the courtesy of coming in much more quietly, AND DON'T TURN ON THE DAMNED LIGHT IN THE CLOSET!"

I got up enough courage to go over to the closet and shut the door. I discovered that it was an automatic light that went on and off with the door opening and closing. I quickly got back into bed and pulled the covers over me. It took a while, but I finally fell back to sleep and wasn't bothered anymore.

As a matter of fact, I have been back to the hotel 6 more times, requesting and getting Room 235 each time for a total of 23 nights; and Errol has never bothered me since.

* * *

II

La Isla Bonita, 1492

*T*HE CREW WAS *unbelievably excited; after all, it had been months since they had set foot on land. But it was a bittersweet landing for the men of Colon's fleet of three small ships. Several men had either died of illness, washed overboard in one of the violent storms or simply chose to end the agonizing uncertainty of the seemingly endless ocean crossing by stepping off the ship in the middle of night.*

After finding suitable anchorage, and sending out a small reconnaissance team, Colon was satisfied that for the time being the beachfront was safe and secure. He ordered the majority of the men ashore, with the remaining skeleton crew to be relieved the second day as a crew rotation was established.

Besides Colon, one of the first to slosh his way through the surf onto the shore of San Salvador, Saint Savior, as the land was aptly named, was the Sacerdote Catolico, the Spanish priest who accompanied the voyage. Apprentice sailor Rodrigo idly wondered what on earth that man had done to God to be given this mission.

Although weakened by the long voyage and extreme physical inactivity, the priest found a renewed vigor as he triumphantly plunged the base of the 2m high wooden cross into the sand. As he invoked the glory of God and king in Latin, his acolyte hastily translated into Spanish for the rest of the crew.

In nomine Patris, et Filii, et Spiritus Sancti, Quod ego loquor in nomine terrae et omnium Hispaniae Isabella et Ferdinandus!

En el nombre del Padre, del Hijo, y del Espíritu Santo proclamo esta tierra en nombre de Dios y en nombre del rey Fernando e Isabel y toda España!

In the name of the Father, the Son, and the Holy Spirit, I proclaim this land in the name of Queen Isabella and King Ferdinand of Spain!

'Where did they ever find the strength,' the priest wondered, as the men cheered and roared with delight. Wine flasks that had been filled from the barrels onboard were passed around and the men drank with enthusiasm.

However, Rodrigo was more pensive. He remembered the dead, and the missing presumed dead, whose sacrifices allowed the remainder to celebrate their good fortune. He stepped to one side, a few paces removed from the others, and silently murmured the Kaddish, the prayer for the dead. Although his two Jewish comrades were still alive, he felt that someone ought to remember the souls of the departed. In spite of what the Inquisition had said about God and his abandoned relationship with the Jews, Rodrigo was certain that the Almighty took no sides when it came to honoring the deceased.

As he recited the age-old prayer, he was reminded of the uplifting nature of Judaism's relationship with God. There was no morbid fascination with death, or mournful approach- but rather a celebration of life as a gift from God to be enjoyed to its fullest. The prayer's words were full of hope and life; not like the fear that the priest instilled if one didn't toe the Catholic line.

The words flowed freely and compassionately in his mind… 'Yitgadal, v'yitkadash, shemay rabba…'

> May the great Name of God be exalted and sanctified, throughout the world, which he has created according to his will. May his Kingship be established in your lifetime and in your days, and in the lifetime of the entire household of Israel, swiftly and in the near future; and say, Amen. May his great name be blessed, forever and ever. Blessed, praised, glorified, exalted, extolled, honored elevated and lauded be the Name of the holy one, Blessed is he- above and beyond any blessings and hymns, Praises and consolations which are uttered in the world; and say Amen. May there be abundant peace from Heaven, and life, upon us and upon all Israel; and say, Amen.
>
> He who makes peace in his high holy places, may he bring peace upon us, and upon all Israel; and say Amen.

Suddenly the Spaniard's head snapped up and he looked frantically around- but no one noticed him as they were all gazing in awe as the priest intoned his blessings. Rodrigo was certain that, in his own religious reverie, he had inadvertently voiced his prayers aloud. After all, only El Capitan knew his true religious belief. This led his mind to wander. He pondered the rumor that had been 'afloat' since the weeks before the journey had begun; that Cristobal Colon himself was a Jew who took on this endeavor as his own means of escape from the torture of the Inquisition. Tall tales were the fuels that stoked the hearths of every waterfront taverna along the Mediterranean and Atlantic shores. Sailors thrived on gossip, at times they were even worse than scullery maids and bar wenches. And when it came to gossip about other seafarers, well, there were no holds barred. All were fair game on the docks.

The word on the waterfront was that Colon had an ulterior motive for sailing west… to the end of the world. If he was in fact a hidden Jew, could he have desired to find a safe haven for his co-religionists? Would that in itself be an incredible motivation far beyond the mortal wealth and fame offered by his monarch? If this was true, then El Capitan was putting more faith in biblical texts than this sailor would care to admit. It was a known fact that the Book of Isaiah was his favorite passage that gave him strength. In his addresses to the crews of his ships, he repeatedly cited two verses in particular– "Surely the isles shall wait for me, and the ships of Tarshish first, to bring thy sons from far, their silver and their gold with them" (60.9). The other he read to them was "For behold, I create new heavens and a new earth" (65.17). He was certain that God had confirmed these prophecies through the voyage that they were on.

That could explain why Rodrigo was included in the roster. Why else? His own admission to his family that he was a 'competent' but not outstanding seaman was proof, at least to him, that there was another motive behind his inclusion. Did Colon secretly want to have a fellow Israelite with him on his journey? Was the God of Israel truly looking to establish a safe haven for the persecuted? Would Rodrigo become one of its Patriarcas, founding fathers, in a New World that might be free of prejudice?

"Venir aquí a mi hijo", "Come here my son!" The young sailor was shaken from his reverie by the words of the priest. He jumped up, alarmed at the thought of suddenly being caught out to be offered as a sacrifice to the God of the Catholics.

"Help me over to that rock so that I might sit a bit and rest." The Father smiled benevolently at him and held out his arm for support. Rodrigo breathed a sigh of relief and quickly hurried over to the man in the cassock. He guided him to a flattened boulder and eased him down gently. As the priest arranged himself, the sailor grabbed a flagon of mulled wine and bade him to drink a bit. The sweltering, steamy climate of the island was debilitating to say the least.

Rodrigo also took a drink, and wondered how he was going to survive without slipping up- unless Colon himself showed him the way.

III

Valladolid, Spain, May, 1506

*S*ADNESS EMBRACED THE *villa, the mirrors that once reflected the gaiety that was so often felt here were covered with black mourning cloth. It was just a short 2 years since the great man's final voyage. According to the son, Fernando, his father suffered from gout, and that this was the cause of death. Colon was a relatively young 54 when he died. He desired to be buried in the Americas, but there was no cathedral with great enough standing for the great explorer, so Valladolid would have to do. The other brother, Diego, was in such shock that he tasked some of the burial arrangements to his wife. The young woman was confused at her father-in-law's written instructions upon his death. To her, they were a mixture of blasphemy and, it seemed, witchcraft.*

The document clearly stated that no priest come to the aid of the family, nor was a priest to oversee the burial practice. The body underwent excarnation; the flesh was removed so that only his bones remained, and then wrapped in a plain burial shroud. In addition, it was stated that a candle be lit immediately after interment as soon as the family returned home. It needed to be either of paraffin, or olive oil- nothing else would do. This candle needed to burn for precisely one week- not longer. Even though she was opposed to her father-in-law's instructions, the daughter-in-law saw how distraught her husband was, and being a strong presence, she forced herself to carry on and not question Colon's wishes at this time. After all was said and done, and a proper time had passed, she might go to the priest at La Catedral de Nuestra Señora de la Asunción, the Cathedral of Our Lady of the Holy Assumption. After all, she had her own soul to worry about as well and the Church was quite adamant about salvation and the path that one needed to take to ensure that the journey to Heaven would be a safe one.

She had clearly questioned, but to herself alone, the instructions of her complex father-in-law and his ideas of belief. He seemed so pious, so devout. But he turned his back on celebrating Mass and attending church services. He didn't seek out the blessing of the padres before his numerous departures across the great sea to the west, only that of the monarchy. Yet when pressed about this around the dining room table, Colon made it clear that he strongly believed that God would watch over him, his family, his crews; and that the way that he chose to worship God was a path known to him and God alone. It was not something to be shared by humanity- even his immediate family.

But Colon did eloquently express his wishes; and try to explain as best as he could, what the preparations were all about. Colon noted that the candle was the symbol of a human being. The wick and the flame symbolized the body and soul, and the bond between them. The flame is the soul that strives ever upward, and brings light into darkness. However, the location of the candle was important as well. It should not be placed in the main salon, or the dining room, of the villa. The focal point of life at this time of mourning was... life itself. We should remember the deceased, and mourn them; but we should not be consumed by death. She remembered being distressed at all the talk of his impending death, but his gentle smile reassured both her and his sons.

He told them all of a prayer, and, as he stated, it was one that they were not familiar with because it was extremely old and no longer considered to be a part of Catholic liturgy. (After his passing, the daughter-in-law inquired of the Sacerdote about the prayer, and he said that he truly had no knowledge of it and planned to ask the Cardinal the next time that he was in Valladolid. Colon had hastily scribbled it in Spanish. Every so often the family would take out the notation and read it again. It was comforting and hopeful- something totally alien to many of the prayers and

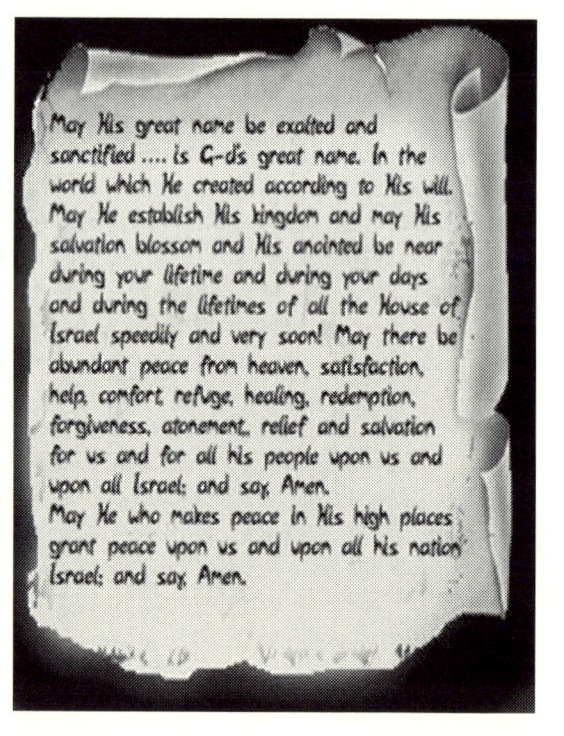

> May His great name be exalted and sanctified .... is G-d's great name. In the world which He created according to His will. May He establish His kingdom and may His salvation blossom and His anointed be near during your lifetime and during your days and during the lifetimes of all the House of Israel speedily and very soon! May there be abundant peace from heaven, satisfaction, help, comfort, refuge, healing, redemption, forgiveness, atonement, relief and salvation for us and for all his people upon us and upon all Israel; and say, Amen.
> May He who makes peace in His high places grant peace upon us and upon all his nation Israel; and say, Amen.

attitudes presented to them by the clergy. And, most amazingly, it didn't even speak of death! How refreshing, she thought; how uplifting it was. It was nothing like she had ever heard at the La Misa Funebre, the Requiem Mass designed to save the soul of the departed.

Unfortunately, her husband could shed no light either. Years of being apart from his father had made him more devout, but in the traditional, Catholic sense. He could make neither heads nor tails of these wishes- nor was he ultimately concerned. The period of estrangement simply led to an apathy when it came to his father.

However, in a bizarre twist, an old, wizened man knocked on the door one evening in the first week following Colon's death. He said that he came to pay his respects to the family of the great adventurer. A servant ushered him in to the central court, its fountain burbling faintly.

As he sat on a bench, admiring the greenery, he noted with satisfaction that the mirrors were covered. As he murmured a prayer under his breath, family members approached him. He humbly stood, bowed slightly, and offered his condolences.

"How did you know my father?" asked Diego of the gentleman.

"Senor, I had the honor of knowing your father when he was just a young child," was the respectful response.

Diego Colon was a bit confused. "This is not possible. We were always told by my father that he came here later in life."

The old man simply smiled, but offered nothing further. Diego chose to let it pass.

"I have heard that you are somewhat confused as to some of the instructions of your father."

"But how...." The amazement was clear on the faces of both Diego and his wife.

"Words filter their way onto the street. Suffice it to say. I have come to answer any questions that you might have. But once I leave, tell no one, por favor, of our conversation. That is all that I ask of you." The old one looked at them beseechingly. The Colon clan acceded to his wish, and then the questions began to flow freely.

"I am more than happy to answer you. I know that things seem quite alien to you, almost like witchcraft. But I assure you, they come from a spirituality that is more ancient than you can possibly imagine. Man was created in the image of God. That resemblance is the vehicle for his dignity and value. The death of one of God's creatures diminishes the very image of God Himself. It disrupts the relation between the living world and living God and anything that reflects man's 'image' should not be used at a time when this tear in the fabric occurs. When death has entered a household, one needs to focus on the relationship between Creator and creature. A mirror simply allows us to dwell on our own earthly vanity. It is almost comical at this moment of tragedy. We should all concentrate on the painful loss that confronts us."

The old man went on. "It is obvious that the individual, if he were isolated from society, would have little need of the precious reflecting glass. The mirror is the means of achieving social acceptance by enhancing the appearance. In this spirit of mourning, however, the attitude is one of loneliness. The mourner should dwell silently, and in solitude, on his personal loss. Social etiquette and appearance become terribly insignificant. The covering of the mirror symbolizes the sense of withdrawal."

To the family, this seemed to make very good sense. But no one had ever been counseled in this approach by any member of the Catholic clergy. Diego looked hard at the fellow, trying to place him. No luck. But he seemed, well, different. Aside from his astute answers to the many questions that they had, every so often, a nervous glance towards the door betrayed his unease.

"How do you know these things? Are you an 'alquimista?' An alchemist or dabbler in black arts?" The tension in the courtyard now was palpable. Colon's son was ready to call a member of the Tribunal created by Torquemada that dealt with blasphemers- notably the Jews. He had his suspicions…

"Senor, I come to you not as a blasphemer, nor alchemist. But as a humble member of the Jewish community whose faith is as fervent as yours when it comes to worshipping God."

"But how can this be? It is well known that all Jews who didn't convert to the true religion were expelled by Archdeacon Martinez in 1483."

"That is true senor, but I am a Crypto Jew, and beg you not to turn me over to the authorities. I simply wished to convey my condolences, put your minds at rest, to allow your father the peace that he so deserves- and clear the air privately. I am at your mercy."

* * *

A few years came and went, and the wanderings of Cristobal Colon did not cease. In 1509, the great man's sarcophagus was taken to Seville. The primary reason for this, according to the family, was that he deserved to be buried in a much more prominent, and worthy, location. The place that they identified was the Monastery on La Cartuja, a river island adjacent to the city.

Not too long after, in 1526, Diego, Colon's oldest son, and first heir, died as well. He was laid to rest alongside his father. However, Diego's widow, Maria de Rojas y Toledo, was haunted by her father-in-law's fervent wish that he be buried in the new world. Her late husband also expressed that desire from time to time. Maria took matters into her own hands. She began to make plans to fulfill these wishes.

It wouldn't be for some time though. It would take a decade of planning, for the daughter-in-law to finalize plans to ship the bones of Cristobal and Diego to Haiti. However, a problem arose. There was no location suitable to inter the remains of such great men. As a result, the actual movement wouldn't take place until 1541. That was the year that the great Cathedral of Santo Domingo was completed. A special place was reserved adjacent to the right hand side of the altar. There they would finally rest in peace, father and son, at least for two centuries.

IV

The mystery deepens…. and a revolution interferes

MATTERS WERE GOING to take an interesting turn when Spain officially lost control of Hispaniola. It was 1795, and the French would take possession of the island. The two nations had been dueling for control of the New World for quite some time, with the French finally beginning to gain the upper hand. The loss of several colonies across the ocean had left an incredibly unpleasant taste in Spanish mouths. After all, they truly felt that the Americas were an integral part of Spanish rule.

This was exacerbated by the fact that one of Spain's greatest heroes, Colon, was considered to be a treasure of the realm. There was no way on earth that his remains would fall under foreign rule.

As the Spanish prepared to leave Hispaniola, they followed the original set of instructions regarding his burial place. The officials 'liberated' the remains from the ground, carefully packed them up, and took 'the national treasure' with them as they escaped the French. The destination was Cuba. Most assumed the remains were interred in La Catedral. Eventually, within a few years, by 1806, a sarcophagus found its way into Cementerio Espada. It would eventually become known as Cementerio de Cristóbal Colón. However, by this time, there most likely was nothing more than powder with a few tiny bone chip fragments inside.

It seemed that the great man's remains would be at peace for nearly another century; then the new world would once again be in a state of upheaval. Cuba would find itself in the throes of a democratic revolution.

* * *

The heady days of the expansion of the United States' influence throughout the western hemisphere was just becoming realized. Political and economic dominance were the rules rather than the exception. American capital began flowing into Cuba, mostly into the sugar and tobacco industries. Mineral exploration was beginning as well. By 1895, investments surpassed the $50 million mark. This was an incredible feat for the end of the 19th century. Although Cuba remained Spanish territory politically, economically it started to depend on her neighbor just 90 miles to the north across the Straits of Florida.

However, the plight of Cuban workers was still dire. Working conditions, wages, and the overall attitude that focused on exploitation, rather than local development, meant that conditions were ripe for revolt. The new, relatively peaceful, vehicle for change that was evolving was the labor union. By the end of 1894, the basic conditions for launching the revolution were set.

Jose Marti, an essayist, poet and political activist, would motivate Cubans in their quest for freedom and democracy- but out of necessity he would focus not only on Spain but the United States as well. Martí's impatient drive to start the revolution was affected by his fear that jingoistic elements in the United States would succeed in annexing Cuba before the revolution could liberate the island from Spain.

One of the great proponents of this attitude was the U.S. Secretary of State, James G. Blaine. His view reflected much of American citizenry at that time. A decade earlier, he had loudly proclaimed "That rich island, the key to the Gulf of Mexico, is, though in the hands of Spain, a part of the American commercial system… If ever ceasing to be Spanish, Cuba must necessarily become American and not fall under any other European domination". His arrogant stance went as far as insisting that all of Central and South America would become part of the United States vision of the western hemisphere. Independent Cuba? Not in his world.

For Marti, he was alarmed when he heard about the movement to annex Hawaii; viewing it as establishing a pattern for Cuba- the next U.S. 'victim'.

Marti's plan included mobilizing exiles in Ybor City, central Tampa, and Key West, Florida, to help foment a revolution against Spain before 'imperialist US forces' would move to annex the island. On March 25, 1894 Martí announced the Proclamation of Montecristi, an outline of the policy for Cuba's coming war of independence.

The ensuing war was designed to not only liberate Cuba, but provide for a true democracy that would be created by blacks and whites in unison, creating a new *political and economic life for all. Sadly, Martí was killed in the military action shortly after his landing at Dos Rios on May 19, 1895,.*

As the war progressed, the U.S. administration of President McKinley became increasingly alarmed at reports coming out of the island of Spanish terror waged against both Cubans and U.S. citizens. The battleship Maine set sail for Havana Harbor as a show of American resolve. On Feb. 15, 1898, the Maine was sunk by an explosion of indeterminate origin; nearly 300 crew losing their lives. The battle cry that was voiced by millions of Americans was "Remember the Maine, to hell with Spain!" And so began what on the island has been called the 'Cuban-American War' (to hell with the Spanish!).

Spain would lose both the Philippines and Puerto Rico, and with no hope of maintaining a grip on Cuba, she would find that her only avenue would be to sue for peace on July 17, 1898. On August 12, the United States and Spain signed a peace initiative. Spain would agree to relinquish all claims of sovereignty over Cuba. By December 10, 1898, the United States and Spain would sign the Treaty of Paris, which recognized Cuban independence.

But herein lay 'the rub' as they say. Although Cuban representatives had participated in the revolution, the United States made certain that Cuba would not participate in the Paris peace talks and be a signatory to the treaty. The treaty set no time limit for U.S. occupation. Although the treaty officially granted Cuba's independence, U.S. General William R. Shafter refused to allow Cuban General Calixto García and his rebel forces to participate in the surrender ceremonies that took place in Santiago de Cuba.

By then, a de facto form of 'sainthood' was bestowed on Jose Martí. Ever since, he has been considered to be one of the great turn-of-the-century Latin American intellectuals- not to mention the 'father' of Cuban independence. His written works consist of a series of poems, essays, letters, lectures and even a novel. After his death, one of his poems from the book, "Versos Sencillos" (Simple Verses) was adapted to the song, "Guantanamera;" which has become the definitive patriotic song of Cuba.

* * *

And now, the mystery deepened. In 1877, workers in the Cathedral of Santa María la Menor in Santo Domingo, Dominican Republic, found a heavy leaden box inscribed with the words "Illustrious and distinguished male, don Cristobal Colon." Inside were fragmentary human remains that everyone assumed belonged to the legendary explorer. Columbus was returned to his resting place and the Dominicans have claimed ever since that the Spanish hauled the wrong set of bones out of the cathedral in 1795.

On the other hand, to this day, you can see the 'grave' of Cristobal Colon in the Seville Cathedral. Or can you?

V

Havana, the present

THE NEXT MORNING, rather early, I woke up fairly refreshed and ready to go. No nocturnal visitors put away any clothing, and the hall was devoid of typical morning hotel sounds yet. I turned on the flat screen TV and surfed until I got to *ESPN Deportes*. After all a *beisbol* score is a baseball score, no matter what language. The Twins were still languishing in the lower half of the division, the evil empire in New York had lost A-Rod to the ongoing steroid controversy, probably for the rest of his career, and the *Tigres* in Detroit maintained their domination. Nothing had changed during my journey.

I went down to *La Veranda* Restaurant on the lower level for breakfast. I greeted the *maitre d'* and gave my room number. The buffet tables spread out before me- long lines of hot and cold items that would put Old Country Buffet to shame back in the States. I usually opted for the omelets, made precisely to order. (Something that you *wouldn't* find back home.) The coffee was thick and aromatic, or as Guy Fieri would say, "from Flavortown!" The usual one cup as part of my normal routine was transformed into 2 whenever I was abroad. If you look up 'bad coffee' on Wikipedia, a map of the United States is highlighted.

As I scrolled through a couple of documents on my Kindle, I once again lamented the fact that the embargo was still, irresponsibly, in place. No U.S.

32

cellular carriers were allowed to operate here. That also meant that internet access was quite limited as well. Since I was quite familiar with the routine, I had come prepared by downloading as many articles and bits of material onto my e-reader that I felt I needed so that they could be readily available. If I needed to read any emails, or try to get some further data, I could always go up to the mezzanine level and use one of the hotel *terminales de computadoras* in the business center. As I savored a third, yes, *third* cup of Cuban coffee, a plaid-shirted gentleman sat down and took my cup and sipped from it.

"Berto, *tu ladrón de café*, you coffee thief, *com' esta?*" With him, my attempts at feigned anger never worked. He saw right through me from the moment we had met a couple of years ago. His infectious smile and laugh set everyone at ease.

"So, *amigo*, I take it you slept well, and are ready to tell me all, yes?"

"*Por supuesto*, of course, but first… GET YOUR OWN DAMNED COFFEE!" I glared, then started laughing, almost choking on what was left of my own cup.

He got up and went over to the machine and poured his own, stirring in lots of sugar and milk. I grimaced at the process that I witnessed- destroying an exquisitely well brewed cup of java that was meant to be savored to its fullest, devoid of any and all additives. Even *I* didn't bother to add any sweetener while drinking Cuban coffee.

He sat down, drank, smiled to himself, and then leaned back and waited to hear more of what would be in store.

"So, as I told you on the ride in yesterday, I'm looking at Columbus' background. But I am just as interested in the rumors of his final 'residency.' As you well know, the possibility of two burial locations, the Dominican Republic and Spain, are more than real. In fact, some even feel that the Spaniards screwed up in 1795 and actually sent his son's, Diego's, remains back to Seville. They got the wrong sarcophagus disinterred!"

"Well, they never got things right as far as I am concerned. Dead reckoning and a magnetic compass was slightly more accurate than what was called New Navigation in the 1500s."

"And that was…?" I was intrigued.

"Some of the earlier cosmographers, who were land-locked, began to use what they referred to as 'celestial observations.' Eventually, they were sent along on the voyage to determine the latitude of the destination. The latitude was needed so these geographical landmarks could be located on the master chart maintained by the Spanish monarchy. This master chart was not for navigation, but primarily for use by geographers and cartographers to establish sovereignty rights to new discoveries for Spain."

"So the 'modern science' of its day was *not* an advance over the earlier system used by sailors for centuries." I was amazed at that revelation.

"Ample evidence shows that Mediterranean navigators developed dead-reckoning to a fine art and accurate science", Berto explained. "Andres Bernaldez, a historian, was a close confidant of Colon. He seemed to confirm the accuracy of dead-reckoning navigation used at this time when he reported that *A good pilot or master is not considered such if, in traveling over a great distance from land to land, out in the open sea with no indication of any land, he is off by ten leagues even when the trip is a thousand leagues long.*' I feel that Cristobal felt more comfortable in time-tested methods than relying on landlocked theorists."

"So, he wasn't the innovator that most assumed that he was?"

"Apparently not, but that in no way diminishes his feat. But here, check this out."

Berto got his shoulder bag from under the table, and took out a folio. He pushed aside some plates and opened it. A beautiful reproduction map of the world *before* Colon's journeys was laid out before me. It was an awesome sight.

"It's difficult to imagine half a world, only 500 years ago. We have come so far and our knowledge has multiplied exponentially at such an accelerated pace." We both sat back, quietly; pensively sipping our coffee for a few moments.

* * *

Cups drained, we plotted our next steps and exited the restaurant. I quickly ran up the mezzanine stairs to the business center to check my email to make sure that there was nothing earth-shattering. But even at this early hour, I had to wait a several minutes. There were three groups of people that I could immediately lump together. First, there were the visitors to the island. It was easy to spot them, most sporting clothing that was well above 'the pay grade' for 90% of the Cuban population. Nothing flashy or over the top, mind you, but of a cut and quality that hadn't been seen here since 1959. The next group that I could see were Cuban businessmen and women. Since the internet was so severely limited to the general public, the guest hotels and their access points were 'surreptitiously' visited by them. I use the word obliquely because, as everyone is aware, people constantly look the other way, and the 'backwards palm' is the rule rather than the exception. Unless they have legitimate business in the hotels, or are visiting guests, they are usually turned away at the door. Again, I say 'usually.' The keepers of the gate, the doormen, would often shake hands with locals that they knew, casually folding bills and slipping them into deep pockets. Finally, the last, and smallest, group were younger Cubans. These kids were not unlike youth all around the world- connected electronically. They would slip into the hotel in whatever way they could, and sit in the lobby of the business center- not quite entering its well-staffed confines. (Those employees were often beyond the reach of the 'handshake'.) One would go in and pay for the day's code for WiFi access, and relay it to the friends sitting in the nearby lounge. The access was not sophisticated enough to be a 'one-off' used only by one computer. So the procedure worked. As expected, the western world was still sadly intact, the status quo maintained; at least according to my email.

I then rejoined Berto outside the grand *porte-cochere* of the hotel. Out front were half a dozen vintage 1950s Cuba Taxis, waiting to take *turistas* on *Habana* tours. The few *Ladas* also parked were waiting for local Cubans (less stylish, but *way* less expensive). He waved off the drivers who began swarming us, and we made our way to the car park just off to the left side of the drive.

We got settled and headed to the location of *Habaguanex* SA, where we could find the offices of the City Historian, Eusebio Leal Spengler. Spengler was appointed to be the Havana City Historian and director of the *La Habana Vieja* Restoration Project- part of the acceptance as a UNESCO World Heritage Site that was designated in 1982.

We left the hotel grounds and made 2 right turns around the hotel property until we were heading east on the *Malecon*. It was a beautiful, clear day and the Straits of Florida off to our left were very calm; several small fishing boats dotting its surface. For those without boats, a short hop over the sea wall and a few steps took them to the water's edge, and dozens of lines were cast by Havanans in anticipation of catching the evening meal. As we rounded the western headland of Havana Harbor, and the fortress of *Castillo de San Salvador de la Punta*, the Castle of the Tip of San Salvador, the road changed names to *Avenida del Carlos Cespedes*. Our destination was San Francisco de Assisi Plaza, *Plaza de San Francisco de Asis*. Because of the incredible lack of parking space in the Old City proper, this area was the nearest to our destination. Along the frontage road, there were precious few spots. However, being the head of guides for *San Cristobal* had its perks. Berto always seemed to have someone waiting with a space saved for him! Of course, a little bit of *proteccion* never hurt. He pulled into the spot and slipped a couple of CUCs into the handshake of the self-proclaimed 'parking lot attendant' in this part of Havana. By the time that we would return, the vehicle would shine with a fresh coat of wax- just saying, just one of the perks.

I shook my head in amazement. "So much for the notion of total equality for all of the people as foreseen by your founding fathers of the revolution," I quipped. He simply hit me with that 1000 watt smile and lightly punched my shoulder. We crossed into the plaza and made our way past one of the Old City's many famous landmarks, "The Conversation," installed on 25 May 2012. *La Conversacion,* the work of French sculptor, Etienne was donated to the city of Havana by Vittorio Perrota as a gesture of friendship between France and Cuba. I paused for a moment, as it was one of my favorite pieces. It seemed to be a natural for the space- with an openness that allowed it to be an integral part of the square without a context. From any direction, you could see 'through' it into all corners of the plaza.

From there, we proceeded down *Avenida Amargura* toward the Hotel Raquel, a Jewish oriented hotel, located only a block away. Dating back to 1908, Venezuelan architect Naranjo Ferrer designed the building. However, it was not inaugurated as a Jewish hotel until June of 2003. Hotel Raquel today is known for its references to Jewish tradition and faith; which consist of various decorative items including stained-glass panels and mezuzahs. Rooms are named after biblical figures. A stone engraving of a menorah dedicated to Jerusalem can be found at the reception. This stone was imported from the Judean Hills outside of Jerusalem. Created in 2008 by the artist Tuly Bauman, is it a replica of the menorah inscribed on the Arch of Titus in Rome- that celebrated the destruction of Jerusalem by Rome in 70 CE.

The lobby bar is called *L'Haim,* 'to life.' The dining room, called *Jardin del Eden,* 'Garden of Eden,' offers meals that hearken back to the European Jewish heritage of most of Cuban Jewry.

A couple of more minutes, and we arrived at *Lamparilla y Amargura,* where in suite #110 were the offices of the city historian. As we entered the reception, Eusebio Leal Spengler exited his interior office with a wide grin and outstretched hand.

"*Hola, Senor Enciclopedia*!" First, the handshake. Then, an enormous bear hug. I stood back, slightly amused at the director's nickname for Berto. Apparently, *everyone* on the island knew to whom it referred. A moment later, my hand was 'two-handedly' pumped with a vigor that belied the man's 70+ years.

"*Muy encantado, mi amigo.* It is a pleasure to meet you finally. I have heard a great deal from our friend here about you and your work. Your exploits in the MidEast have intrigued me- based on what Berto described. And now here you are, in *Habana,* with another mystery as you put it. I am at your disposal, as are the resources of my office, as humble as they may be. As you know, we also have 'folded in' a department called the *Gabinete de Arqueologia* under the umbrella of the city historian."

Where to start? I guessed that Spengler was very well informed about the traditions surrounding Columbus' many burials. I quickly outlined the official 'government lines,' from Cuba to Spain to the Dominican Republic and back. He smiled, aware of all the 'facts behind the rumors.' However, I filled him in on my suspicions regarding the many bits of conflicting data. It was entirely possible, to me at least, that Colon had never left Cuba once interred. Things then began to become very interesting.

He interrupted my line of thought. "However, you should also know that we will have to consult with another of my colleagues- at the Havana Heritage Office. The *Colon* Cemetery is considered to be a national monument, and is listed as such. So it doesn't only fall under the jurisdiction of my office. We need to bring in that office's expertise as well. It's a territorial matter, just like everywhere else in the world," Eusebio explained.

"*Perfecto*! The more the merrier!" Berto was clearly relishing this opportunity to continue any kind of intellectual pursuit in the search for accurate information about his beloved island. And if Columbus was really still here, well, what a coup for Cuba.

I left a dossier of material with the city historian for his review, and Berto and I left after thanking him. On the way out, I thought that I heard a rumble.

"Are we expecting a bit of rain this afternoon?" After all, Cuba's weather was identical to that of Southwest Florida, with pm showers always in the forecast in this month.

"No, I don't believe so, why?" Berto grinned a bit sheepishly. Then he came out with it. "I think that it was my stomach. I guess that I'm ready for lunch, how about you?"

I laughed and mimed a back-handed slap across his face. We clasped shoulders and proceeded to one of our favorite hangouts in *Havana Vieja- La Bodeguita del Medio*. We turned left on *Cuba* and headed north a couple of blocks to *Empedrado*, then turned right and headed ½ block toward the *Plaza de la Catedral*. The yellow and black sign was just off to the right. My mouth started to water, not for the drink, but for the *tapas* and *Morros y Christianos*, the local black beans and rice.

* * *

Although its main claim to fame was as a favorite watering hole of Papa Hemingway, (and he needed lots of 'watering') *La Bodeguita* was equally well known for its 'walls of fame' (and not so famous!) In 1942, Angel Martinez bought out the small *Bodega La Complaciente* on *Empedrado* Street, in the old Havana district. On April 26, 1950, the name *Bodeguita del Medio* was officially adopted. Tourists and locals alike continue to go there to drink an authentic Cuban mojito. Numerous celebrities were regulars of the *Bodeguita* : Pablo Neruda, Gabriel Garcia Marquez, Nat King Cole, Marlene Dietrich and Ernest Hemingway. "My mojito in La Bodeguita, My daiquiri in El Floridita" can still be read on a stained placemat, in Hemingway's handwriting. It is framed and mounted on the wall behind the bar today. Since that time, thousands of people have scribbled their name and date on the walls, covering them from edge to edge- even reaching 'beyond reach' at 15 feet or more high.

Because Berto had some *proteksia*, we were able to get a table upstairs in the open air room fronting the building that overlooked the street. With what seemed like a thousand people packed wall-to-wall, the idea of a fire-marshal's occupancy rating was ludicrous at best. The noise was enough to deafen one permanently. As we walked toward the back stairway, I motioned up and to the right in the stairwell.

"See there, about 2 feet to the right of the corner and 6 feet above our heads?" Berto scanned the wall intensely.

"Oh, you mean 'Cher 2003'?" he asked not so innocently. I punched his bicep.

"OK, OK, just to the right of that!" I laughed.

"Aha! I should call my friends in the *policia turistica* and have you arrested for defacing a national treasure." He mimed a cellphone call. We continued up the narrow flight and into the balcony room.

At the small table that was reserved for us, a petit woman sat and sipped a *Buccanero* Beer. She projected a somewhat exotic air. It most likely was because of the high cheekbones and slightly almond shape of her dark eyes. When she saw Berto, her smile filled the room with a dazzling light. She got up and embraced him, kissing him on both cheeks warmly. I stood off to the side, shuffling my feet a bit. They broke off and as she sat back down, Berto introduced us.

"This is one of my colleagues, and good friends, Yolanda, we call her Yoli for short. When I retire, she may become the newest version of 'The Encyclopedia' for *San Cristobal*!"

I looked at her with a greater appreciation. Those were strong, supportive words from someone who was renowned in Cuba and the guiding world in general as being *the* font of knowledge when it came to information about the island. And on top of this, he had fluent delivery in English and German.

"Wow!" is all that I could muster. "A recommendation like that is almost better than one from Raul!" I smiled and grasped her hand with both of mine. "It is an honor to meet someone like you." She smiled again, and colored a little.

Apparently Yoli was not accustomed to hearing such praise in public. "Please take this as a great compliment, but you have a certain look about you. It's quite mysterious and, well, *oriental*. I understand fully now why some of your friends and colleagues refer to you as *la muchacha China*. And again, meant in only the most positive of ways."

She blushed again, but just a bit, clearly flattered by the compliment. Apparently she was unaccustomed to all the attention paid to her. But it was taken in the right way.

"I too have heard a lot about you as well, *El Loco*!" There was a certain mischievous look in her eye.

I spluttered a bit, and then spit out, "How did you ever…" Then it dawned on me. In one of our late evenings a year ago, I had mentioned in passing to Berto the nickname given to me in Egypt and Israel, *el Majnoon*, 'the crazy one.' It was based on some previous exploits regarding statues and papyri, that had taken me throughout North Africa, the Mideast, and even Germany.

"I thought that the discussion was a private one, between friends, not for general consumption," I hissed between clenched teeth as I pulled the chief guide aside. I wasn't as much upset as slightly embarrassed.

"Are you sunburned, or is that a rash on your face?" Yoli asked with a bemused, not-so-innocent look on her face. Then she and Berto burst out laughing. I joined in, suddenly knowing that we had a bright, sharp ally who was ready to aid in our quest. (And that I had been 'had' by the two of them. Revenge would come some day.) It was my turn to smile… but they had no clue!

'*Salud*!' We clinked glasses and set about devouring our lunch. Over the meal, we outlined our thoughts and our research plan. It seemed to be solid, but Yoli mentioned a couple of avenues that we hadn't considered. Berto had made a very wise choice in asking for her assistance. Our 'attack' would commence the following day. She would head into the archives at the Havana Heritage Office, while we would visit the *Patronato*, the Bet Shalom Synagogue, and speak with the president there.

"Can we give you a ride somewhere?" I asked as we left *La Bodequita*.

"Thanks, but my father lives only a few minutes away from here, and I'm off to visit him. He's only a block or so from *La Museo de la Revolucion* on *San Juan de Dios*. By the time we walked to Berto's 'limo' and drove all the way around the old city, I would have already been there 20 minutes earlier. But the offer is appreciated. Besides, I need to walk off lunch."

With that, she pecked Berto on the cheek and shook my hand, and headed off down *Empedrado*. She had a good idea, about walking off lunch, so the 2 of us decided to do the same in the old town. A short half-block took us to the *Plaza de la Catedral*, and one of the most impressive religious buildings of the New World.

The *Catedral de la Virgen María de la Concepción Inmaculada de La Habana* (Cathedral of The Virgin Mary of the Immaculate Conception) is the seat of the Cardinal Archbishop of Havana. On Cathedral Square, it was constructed by the Jesuits between 1748 and 1777. However, it took years to get permission to build such a magnificent edifice. The Society of Jesuits relations with the authorities in Havana were contentious at best and for decades they did not have the blessing of the Spanish authorities. Finally, in 1727, a site was chosen for their cathedral and convent - a swamp. Apparently the 'peace treaty' between Church and State didn't need to be equitable, or amiable.

However, things did not bode well for the Jesuit order in the midst of the 18th Century. Throughout the world, they were persecuted and expelled from scores of locations around the globe- Cuba included. The Society had a reputation back in Europe. The Jesuits were seen as greedy, and, through their ties with members of the different royal courts, liable to meddle in politics (something that was the rule rather than exception for any clergy at this time in history) in order to further the special interests of their order and the Papacy.

Kings in Europe grew more wary of what they saw as undue interference from a foreign entity. The expulsion of Jesuits from states and their territories had the added benefit of allowing governments to seize the Society's vast wealth and possessions.

The building project was brought to its knees and the work was suspended. But Havana still needed a major religious structure; all of its other churches were in a terrible state of repair and none were considered to be worthy of God. So, the authorities grudgingly allowed for the Jesuits to complete the cathedral in 1777. Final consecration as The Cathedral of Havana would take place in 1789.

We passed a couple of hole-in-the-wall shops selling T-shirts, 'Cuba' license plates and other souvenirs, and suddenly we were in the plaza adjacent to the monumental church. But, even though we entered the open space immediately next to the building, we were not overwhelmed by it. It was never designed to be the major religious house of worship for the city. Its footprint was only 34 x 36 m. So, we walked a few steps into the center of the plaza to take in the view for a moment.

'The Encyclopedia' assumed his role and gave me the '25 *centavo*' spiel about the wonderful building.

"You know the Jesuits, always considered themselves to be stylish! They designed the building in the relatively modern Tuscany Baroque style of architecture and many architects consider it to be the most outstanding Baroque building in all of Cuba. It is not overly ornate, gaudy, like a majority of the buildings of this style. But it is harmonious, pleasing to the eye in spite of its asymmetry."

"So why is it lacking in balance?" I had never gotten a good answer.

"As you know, the area was swampy with poor water drainage. The mismatched towers were constructed in that way in order to allow for freer water flow to remove the standing water that accumulated during heavier rain in the plaza. In addition, the right hand bell tower is taller than the left. According to legend that grew, the bells in this tower, when cast, had some silver and gold added to the mix. This seemed to make their tone sweeter to the ear."

I was dazzled by his knowledge. The sun was really beating down on us now, and we hastened into the cool interior. To many, after the purge of excess interior decoration, the austere interior was refreshing serenity. It was flooded with light entering from the vast wooden doors studded with bronze medallions. Wooden vaults rose in a lofty fashion above 3 naves. A simple black and white marble tile floor enhanced the coolness of the interior. The unique building material consisted of coral. It was cut and hauled in from around the coast of Cuba by slaves. We looked closely, and actually could see fossils embedded in the surface. To me, it was fascinating. We proceeded toward the altar area. In the corner was a dedicatory tablet, inscribed to honor the first archbishop of Havana, Don Jose Felipe de Trespalacios.

The extraordinary fresco-work around the altar area was begun by Guiseppe Perovanni. He was brought in to execute the work by Bishop Espada, said to be a man of unusual sensitivity. These three frescoes were *La Ultima Cena* (The Last Supper), *La Asuncion de la Virgin* (The Assumption of the Virgin Mary) and *La Potestad de las Llaves* (The Key Holder). We approached the main altar, of Carrera marble. A fine sculpture of Saint Christopher, patron saint of Havana, dated to 1632 and was made by Martín Andújar in Seville.

I sat in one of the first rows of pews, mesmerized by the art. But, I have to admit, part of the trance was due to the filling meal that we just had. That's where the Mediterranean notion of siesta originated and then was extended to the New World. Good food deserves an equally good rest to follow. How else could anyone then feel refreshed to continue the afternoon's work? And of course that would only lead to the evening repast; recharging the batteries for a music filled evening.

I must have dozed off a bit, because I got a gentle nudge that shook me from my dreamless state of semi-awareness.

"You know, according to tradition, soon after the Cathedral was consecrated in 1789, in 1796, some of Columbus' remains were kept here before being transferred in 1895 back to Seville." I heard the faint whisper. Almost ghostly in its delivery, the voice seemed to come out of the deep recesses of the nave of the church.

Suddenly I was fully conscious.

"What did you say?" I demanded of Berto. "Did you say that Colon's remains were kept in this very cathedral before transfer?"

He looked alarmed. Apparently I was more forceful in my question than he deserved. And apparently I was louder as well. A few of the faithful seated in pews surrounding us looked up, startled, at the sudden vocal intrusion on their own prayers. I took a deep breath and calmed myself. Berto's hand on my shoulder was reassuring. I lowered my tone a million decibels.

"*Lo siento amigo*, sorry for the outburst. You startled me awake, then continued to startle me with your statement. So our friend Colon was an itinerant corpse?" I said as quietly as possible. Apparently it worked, as everyone surrounding us resumed their meditations and paid no heed to us now.

"Well, er, yes. His body was in transit in several stages. After all, we're talking 16th and not 21st century now. It's well documented."

This I found fascinating, as it meant that this location would play a role in precisely what I was seeking- the truth about Columbus' final 'journeys' after his death.

VI

La Habana, 1795

*F*ATHER MANUELO HAD just finished matins in the small chapel within the recently finished and consecrated Cathedral complex in La Cienaga. He was still a bit upset at his posting here in La Habana, not so much because of being Cuba- no, that suited him just fine. In general, the climate of the island was much more preferable than that of Europe. No, it was being a part of the clergy here at La Catedral de la Virgen María de la Concepción Inmaculada that irritated him. Who would have ever thought of building a house to God in a swamp! The irritation came from the physical discomfort that Manuelo felt. Apparently, he was highly sensitive to a dank, damp, mold-infested environment.

This part of the city was a lowland, prone to flooding; with standing water that refused to filter between the cobbles of the plaza for days on end. This crept into the atmosphere of the church as well. It assailed his senses, triggering a fit of coughing and sneezing at the most inopportune of times. On top of that, he had a headache that would not quit. His meager supply of laudanum had dwindled, so he hoarded it. Not even the cannabis brought by the Spaniards from South America seemed to alleviate the pain.

He quietly stole into one of the small confessionals and lay down on the cool tile floor. Relief washed over him, the darkness a welcome escape from the throbbing pain. Now that he could think clearly, he contemplated the news that had been given to him. It seemed that the French had nearly completed their occupation of Hispaniola, just a few miles from them. The last of the Spaniards to flee the island were transporting a very precious relic back to La Isla- the bones of Colon the Explorer. He was considered to be a national treasure, and, of course, simply could not fall into the hands of the French dogs- Spain's mortal enemy.

La Habana should be honored to be the recipient of this great man's remains, and serve as his final resting place. Everyone that the Father spoke with was enthralled with this. However, he was uncertain. For centuries, rumors had swirled about that Colon was a hidden Jew, a member of that perfidious race of people who not only rejected The Lord, but actually killed him as a direct result of their actions. Would it not be an insult to Mother Church, and to his Lord Jesus Cristo, to have his remains buried in hallowed, sanctified ground.

As he pondered this dilemma, he was reminded of a discussion that he had with the Superior General of the Jesuit order, Father Alexandro. Manuelo had delicately broached the subject when he heard of the impending transfer. Alexandro's answer was carefully balanced, and as politically correct as possible. He stated that, regardless of the rumors, Colon was a Spanish adventurer of heroic proportion, and his possible Jewish origins in spite of his conversion still made his first faith that of 'People of the Book'; more akin to Catholicism than the pagan natives or Moors. And, as a result, he deserved a place of honor and dignity.

This is with what Manuelo grappled. Even if Colon was Jewish, his belief in one God should afford him a dignified rest. But to be buried in a cathedral? He felt that it would be blasphemy. So what to do. Then it came to him.

There were Jews scattered across the landscape of the island. Many of them had come fleeing the Portuguese reconquista a century earlier. They had settled on the island and began to develop a thriving trade as go-betweens for Europe and the United States. Some moved inland to smaller communities, like Santa Clara. Founded in 1689 only, this new ville lived up to the great city planning standards of Spain, with a perfectly square Plaza Mayor and governmental buildings surrounding it. And from what he understood, the few Jews lived quietly and were accepted.

The thought struck him that he could have things work out for all concerned, Jew and Spaniard and Catholic alike. If Colon were indeed Jewish, then it would be a sin to desecrate the grounds of any Christian institution or cemetery with a Jew's body. Yet, as the Church argument went, it would be almost equally as horrendous a crime against God should the corpse of a 'Person of the Book' simply be tossed aside for the feral animals to devour. And what of desecrating the remains of a national hero? That certainly wouldn't play well.

His plan that would give honor to all began to take shape. In the end, the rumors wouldn't even matter.

VII

La Habana, the present

AFTER LEAVING THE Cathedral, Berto and I walked to the harbor area. We passed one of the fortresses that used to guard the harbor entry on the western side, the *Castillo del la Real Fuerza*. Partially excavated, cleared and restored by the office of the city historian, the Castle of the Royal Force is a star-shaped fortress built for the King of Spain, Philip II, in the 1560s. Today it serves as the Maritime Museum.

As we neared the water's edge, I remarked on the cleanliness of the area. Berto took great pride in his city, and its bold attempts to move into the 21st century almost directly from the 1960s. However, the pace was slow, and progress even slower. The Cubans had to contend with so much, both internal and external, as they strived to 're-enter' the international community after having been isolated for so long. They had to contend with the worst of so many worlds in their recent, past history that it was almost impossible to keep up with the surrounding world.

Tourism was a great way to gain the international community's confidence. Send everyday people to visit the island, have the infrastructure to welcome them, and they will surely spread the word back home.

In the case of Cuba, this was easier said than done. There have been four major periods of evolution of architectural style and technique. First came the Spanish Classical architecture of the 18th-19th centuries. This would be followed by the 'Americanization of Cuba,' during the first half of the 20th century. Architectural giants like McKim, Mead and White would begin the process of turning the island into America's southern playground, only 90 miles from Key West. But with the rise of Castro's Cuba, the spigot of American dollars would be turned off; ushering in the era of the Soviet Union. Totally dependent on the communistic bloc, the drab, utilitarian 'architecture of equality' turned the island into either massive fortress-like concrete structures or boring, uniform 'shoe-boxes' of housing. And finally, with the collapse of the Soviet Union in the early 90s, entrepreneurs from western nations began the process of rebuilding the island slowly. One notable example was the Melia chain of Spanish hotels now dotting the island.

For centuries, construction on the island was of limestone, easily degraded in the Caribbean. Architects had to learn to contend with the climate. This soft stone succumbed to the vagaries of the salt air and wind erosion that were architecture's greatest enemies. Only on rare occasions, like with the Cathedral, were more rugged materials such as coral used. Thus, this type of Classical Spanish architecture of the 18th-19th Centuries actually has withstood the elements far better than later construction. Decay and decadence abounded everywhere the eye could see at the turn of the millennium.

But now, a building and restoration boom was on. The *Malecon* was a beehive of activity with the road being repaved, and buildings restored at a breakneck pace. This also meant that traffic snarls were a rule, rather than exception. And for a people not used to having so many cars on the roads for decades, the boom in tourism and vehicular traffic was now seen in some ways as a nuisance.

On one hand, Berto took obvious pride in the restoration of the Old City; yet on the other, the noise, inconvenience and added pall of dust hanging in the air upset him tremendously. I could sense it as we got to his '*proteksia*-parked car.' He immediately took out an old handkerchief from the glove box and started wiping down its surface.

"*Amigo*, we can wash and wax your baby when we get back from the cemetery," I started to explain.

"*De vertad esta loco!* You really are crazy. You live up to your nickname!" He glared at me and wiped the surface even faster. "It's all a matter of perception, don't you get it? I remember once, when I was in Montreal, I was watching your Saturday Night Live TV show. By the way, that was outstanding comedy…"

"Get to it, *senor*," I said.

"Right, anyway, it was that actor Billy Crystal who…. Hmmmm…. I could use a *Cristal* Beer right about now…."

"Berto……" I was growling at him now, in no mood for his side journeys at the moment. I wanted him to get to the point, so that we could get on the road.

"OK, OK. He portrayed a Latin actor with such a hilarious, exaggerated accent. He would say at the end of his routine, 'Ju know, ees not how ju feel, but how ju look- and ju look mahvelous!' How can I take my baby out on the streets of Havana like this?"

So okay, he got me. I was laughing so hard that tears started to flow. I got out my kerchief as well and together we made short work of the dust. From there, we headed away from the construction/paving, around the southern edge of *Habana Vieja*, and then west to *Vedado* and *Colon* Cemetery.

I must admit, the admiring looks were an ego boost; even if it was a secondary ego boost by association.

* * *

We wove through small streets until we got to a main east/west artery, *Avenida Salvador Allende*. Soon it turned into *Calzada Zapata*, or Zapata Roadway, as it curved its way toward the northern perimeter wall of the cemetery. After about ½ hour we found ourselves outside of the monumental 3-storey gate entry. Once again, the familiarity of the tourist industry personnel all over Havana with my colleague paid off. *No one* gets to park within the grounds of the cemetery unless they are 1) staff/personnel, 2) attending a funeral or 3) *the reason* for the funeral (meaning the hearse). A couple of CUCs in a surreptitious handshake with an attendant sealed the deal. Plus, he didn't even have to leave the keys (God forbid!) should the car possibly need moving. (Which the attendant assured Berto would not be the case). He even steered us to an ancient banyan tree that offered a wonderful amount of shade. The car was parked at a very slight tilt, however, as the roots of this enormous tree had buckled the pavement just a bit. But best of all, nothing would drop on it!

As we left the car, and turned back to the small administrative office, we looked up to appreciate the massive gateway and entrance. Only about 1½ centuries old, the beautifully crafted inscription by Cuban sculptor Jose Vilalta de Saavedra, said it all-

"Pale death enters the palaces of kings and the cabins of the poor the same."

One of the local guides, Andreas, greeted Berto effusively.

"*Senor Berto!*" he acknowledged with a smile as he clasped our mutual friend's shoulder. He inquired as to his health, the health of his family, the health of his neighbors, the health of his co-workers at *San Cristobal*, ad nauseum. I know that it is part of the culture, but one could grow old and die by the time that introductions and greetings were concluded. It reminded me of the Bedouin in Israel, and their obsessive, yet respectful, insistence on decorum.

As you may recall in earlier adventures, living with the Bedouin meant an introduction to one of the most noble of societies in the world. A place

where honor and respect meant everything. It seems that no matter where you are on the planet, traditions of age-old cultures are mostly the same when it comes to interacting with others. I mentioned this to Berto, and he solemnly agreed with me.

"As Paul Williams would say, 'you can get back to the place, but not the time.'"

He looked at me in that *'What? You are crazy'* look that he was known to throw at me at least once a day.

I caught it, and threw it right back at him. "An American songwriter from the 1970s, but *you* wouldn't be familiar...." I grinned at him. He grinned back. We grinned... together.

Andreas had that vacant look of *I don't get it and don't care to...* Nevertheless, he let us play our word game with extraordinary patience. After the prerequisite five minutes, he politely coughed into his fist. We looked at him as if we were seeing him for the first time. He turned to me.

"*Mucho gusto mi amigo!* It's very good to see you again." Andreas pumped my hand like an old well-head.

Although some might find it odd that there would be a number of guides for a burial ground, when you see the complex, you are amazed at its sheer enormity. On top of that, with the interment of 100s of 1000s over the years, and given the number of famed Cubans who sought the Colon as their final resting place, it 'takes a scorecard' to find your way. But that's only the tip of the iceberg as they say. The half-truths, lies and, yes, eventual truths, are all legendary in this hallowed ground. The stories are compelling, moving, and, to a degree, even frightening in their scope. I for one get chills, even on a hot and steamy Caribbean day, when listening to some of the tales of the deceased.

He ushered us into the small office, and poured us small demitasses of thick Cuban coffee. In spite of the heat, the aroma beckoned. We found it refreshing. Berto outlined our reason for the visit, and asked about whatever information Andreas could give us about the mythology of Columbus' return and interment on the island.

"You know all the published stories surrounding Colon. I am more than happy to show you where he *isn't*," he said with a smile. "When the great man was returned to the island after the fall of Hispaniola, he was to be located here, in this great burial. So why is he not here?"

We looked at each other. I was the first to speak. "As far as I know, it's because the cemetery *didn't exist* at that time. The first necropolis, *Espada*, isn't far from here. But it too wasn't founded until 1804- a decade late. When that location became 'overbooked'..." I quipped. Both Berto and Andreas groaned at that one, but soon the smiles appeared on their faces. "Anyway, as I was saying, a new cemetery was laid out, *Cementerio de Cristóbal Colón,* in the late

1860s and inaugurated in 1871. It was never meant for his remains- only as his namesake."

"*Exactamente!* You have learned pretty well." Berto was pleased that I really did pay attention to him sometimes. We walked down one of the main roads toward the chapel. As we passed the Firefighter's Memorial, the three of us paused for a moment. Berto spoke up.

"*Oye*! But did you know that, little known to the vast majority, even Cubans, that Colon *was* to be buried near the chapel at the center of the equal-sided arms of the complex that form a sort of Maltese cross? And why do you think that it never occurred?" Berto gave me a 'gotcha' look.

Then it hit me. "Because the island was lost to Spain when Cuba declared its independence in 1895!" Wow, the plot was really thickening now.

Just as we were getting ready to visit the sanctuary, a motorcade passed very close to us and, in a sweeping arc, drove around the chapel once and a hearse stopped right in front of the door. A dozen cars of various vintages parked immediately behind and a funeral procession quickly formed. Andreas whispered that this wasn't the best time, so we headed back to the small office where a few file cabinets of indeterminate age held all the secrets of the dead.

After rummaging through four drawers, Andreas drew out a folder with a flourish. Unfortunately, his flourish came with a cloud of mildew dust that choked all of us for a moment or two. He hurriedly apologized and got us bottles of water so that we could clear our throats.

"*Lo siento mucho amigos!* I'm really sorry," Andreas blew his nose. "I forget sometimes how long many of these files have sat unattended- and you know what the climate does without the aircondition." The anemic fan eventually blew the must out of the air. He showed us a yellowed, parchment journal. It apparently was a ledger from the archdiocese of Havana that dated to the first year of *Espada*, 1804. The value was not as it related to the cemetery complex when it opened, but for the pages that outlined the clergy responsible for interments. Even though it was a decade after Columbus was brought back to Cuba, the meticulous records indicated after each priest's name the date when each entered into service for the dead. Only three names and years of service extended back to 1795- Father Manuelo, Father Grigorio, and Father Santiago.

"You see, perhaps some answers can be found within the biographies of these holy men." Andreas was pleased that he could help… a bit.

"Where…" I was cut off in mid-sentence.

"You need to go back to *La Catedral* for the church records. In spite of all of Castro's blustering regarding communism and religion, he didn't *dare* destroy any Catholic documents- the Vatican scared the shit out of him!"

We all laughed at the thought of Fidel being scared by anything- even the Catholic Church. But we could see it. After all, when the western world had turned its back on Cuba for a while, there were certain things that not even the Soviets could supply. One of these was the deeply rooted hope of salvation found within the centuries-old faith for the islanders.

Having accomplished all we could here, Andreas led us out of the office and into the lanes of the cemetery.

I never tired of hearing the stories of the cemetery complex; 'a city' in its own right, complete with loves and hates, aspirations and doubts, triumphs and tragedies. It could have been a Cuban soap opera on daytime TV, had the government and its regulation been a bit more lax under Fidel.

The *Cementerio de Cristóbal Colón* was founded in 1876 in the *Vedado* neighborhood of Havana, on top of *Espada* Cemetery. Named for Christopher Columbus, it covers 140 acres. With well over 500 mausoleums and vaults, and over 800,000 'residents', it is an impressive journey into Cuba's recent past. The central chapel was apparently modeled after *Il Duomo*, in Florence, Italy. The architect was Calixto Arellano de Loira y Cardoso, a graduate of Madrid's Royal Academy of Arts. He tragically became this city's first resident, dying before the cemetery's completion. He would design the complex to reflect late 19th century city life, with areas specifically designated for various social statuses, with the rich and famous buried in the most magnificent of tomb plots along the main streets of the axis, leading to the chapel.

Andreas led us down one main corridor, past some of the most beautiful sepulchral art in the world. He knew exactly what I wanted- to make my 'pilgrimage' of sorts. We left the roadway about half-way back, and turned left into the second tier of tombs. There was a simple marble monument with a slightly fading photo in a marble-carved house shrine frame. The legendary Ibrahim Ferrer gazed back at us, with a confident, friendly half-smile of satisfaction. He's saying to us:

> *I am who I am, and I did what I did, and I was good at it. I hope that you think so also.*

One of the world's great *bolero* singers, in 1953 Ferrer began performing with Pacho Alonso out of Santiago, Cuba; the far eastern end of the island. In 1959 they relocated to Havana and renamed themselves *Los Bocucos*, after a drum that was widely used by musicians in Santiago. With Alonso, Ferrer primarily performed many up-tempo songs. However, his heart wished him to sing *boleros*. It was not until almost 40 years later, with the release of the Grammy Award winning *Buena Vista Social Club* album in 1997, that Ferrer's talent as a *bolero* singer would become widely known.

The Cuban *bolero* tradition originated in *Santiago de Cuba* in the last quarter of the 19th century. A group of itinerant musicians moved around earning their living by singing and playing the guitar. It is slow tempo music. Some mistakenly call the dance associated with it 'Rumba.'

In 2004 Ferrer won a Grammy, but was denied permission by the U.S. government to enter the U.S. to receive his award under a vague U.S. law that was designed to prohibit entry by "terrorists, drug dealers and dangerous criminals." Ferrer, who had been granted entry to the U.S. previously so that he could perform in concert, was astounded by the decision. He would say, "I don't understand because I don't feel I'm a terrorist. I am not, I can't be." He would die the following year.

On the right side, next to his photo, is the inscription:

Siempre la recordaremos las esposa hijos nietos y damias familiares
(Always remember your wife, children, grandchildren and other relatives)

Some of the most incredible music to come out of the island in the later 20th century was made by the Buena Vista Social Club. As we proceeded down the lane, and grew near to a particular grave, the haunting beat of *Chan Chan* swirled around my brain. It seemed so loud that I thought everyone heard it. Although originally an old song of the *campesinos* in Holguin Province, the new rendition became the signature piece of the Social Club from their first album. *Chan Chan* was written in 1987 by Cuban bandleader Compay Segundo. The best explanation for the lyrics is that the song relates the story of a man and a woman (Chan Chan and Juanica) who are building a house and go to the beach to get some sand. Chan Chan collects the sand and puts it on a screen to remove impurities. Juanica shakes it, shaking herself; that leads from one thing to another......

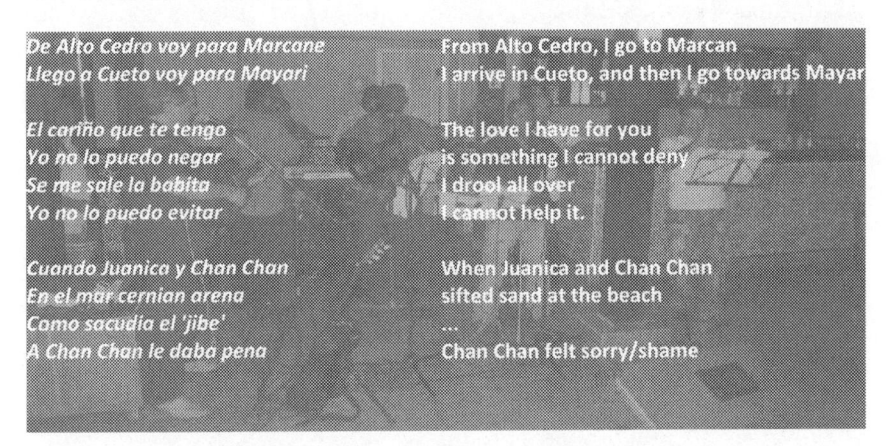

De Alto Cedro voy para Marcane	From Alto Cedro, I go to Marcan
Llego a Cueto voy para Mayari	I arrive in Cueto, and then I go towards Mayar
El cariño que te tengo	The love I have for you
Yo no lo puedo negar	is something I cannot deny
Se me sale la babita	I drool all over
Yo no lo puedo evitar	I cannot help it.
Cuando Juanica y Chan Chan	When Juanica and Chan Chan
En el mar cernian arena	sifted sand at the beach
Como sacudia el 'jibe'	...
A Chan Chan le daba pena	Chan Chan felt sorry/shame

I paused for a few moments, to let the song finish 'playing out' in my head, and according to Jewish custom (although he wasn't), I left a small stone on the grave.

From there, we passed the amazing Firefighter's Memorial. It is the largest, most elaborate, and certainly the tallest, monument in the necropolis. Designed by architects Agustin Querol and Julio Zapata, the Firemen's Monument (*Mausoleo de los Bomberos*) is dedicated to victims of a commercial store fire on May 17, 1890. Inverted torches, branches of laurel and winged hourglasses reflect the temporal nature of life.

Andreas pulled out a folder, and showed us a laminated newspaper article from The Arizona Republican, dated May 19, 1890. News traveled faster than we ever could have imagined over a hundred years ago; if it was sensational news.

Havana, Cuba Hardware Store Fire & Explosion,

AN UNFORTUNATE CONSUL.

Killed By An Explosion of Powder at Havana.

Venesuela's Representative Comes to an Untimely End – Four Fire Chiefs Also Killed

Havana. May 18. – During a fire in a hardware store here last night a barrel of powder exploded. The whole structure was blown to pieces and twenty-two persons were killed. Among the dead are four fire chiefs. The Venezuelan Consul, Don Franciso Silva, who happened to be in front of the building at the time of the explosion was thrown twenty feet into the air and his head literally blown from his body. In addition to those killed, one hundred persons were injured. The explosion caused the wildest excitement throughout the city, and thousands flocked to the scene of the disaster, while the municipal authorities were promptly on the ground and did everything in their power to aid the injured. Several houses adjacent to the burned building were damaged by the explosion.

The search in the ruins has gone on without ceasing ever since the explosion and up to this evening thirty-four bodies had been recovered. Gangs of men are constantly at work in the debris, and many human limbs belonging to no bodies, so far as found, have been taken out.

The relatives of the missing persons are gathered on the spot in great numbers, and as the bodies are brought out some distressing sights are witnessed.

The proprietor of the wrecked hardware store had been arrested.

It is feared that there are several more bodies of victims in the ruins.

Needless to say, this sobered us all considerably. And the feeling grew even more pensive, as we all reflected on our own mortality, and reconsidered the notion that there may be other 'places' out there.

We continued our meandering down alleys and avenues, until we came to one of the more haunting of burials. Over the years, it has gained the nickname of *La Milagrosa- the Miraculous*. Although a relatively modest grave, its notoriety as one of the more 'possessed' grave sites in Colon has given it worldwide attention. It is located just at the intersection of Calles 3 and F. Señora Amelia Goyri died in childbirth in May 1901. In today's scientific world, the diagnosis might have been pre-eclampsia. Her baby was buried at her feet. People claimed to hear crying and whimpering in the tomb. When the grave was exhumed many years later, the baby was found in her arms. This horrific tale grew into a major attraction in the cemetery. The grave attracts thousands of visitors every year, most of them Cubans. *La Milagrosa* always has fresh flowers from the many and varied guests. They come to mourn, and to hope; with reverence, with dreams. The women tap on the grave, hoping to let Amelia know that they are here and obtain her blessing. Plaques of remembrance and prayer have become so numerous that they line the pathway around the gravesite, and spill over to rest against many of the adjacent tombs. Many women pray to her in hopes of becoming pregnant. Tradition also says that, when circumnavigating the grave, you always leave the tomb by backing away, you *never* turn your back on her!

We decided to stay back a bit, because the area was full of young Cuban women, just sitting on adjacent tombs, in silent reverie. Tradition and superstition die hard on this island. After a few moments of this, Andreas hand-signaled us to keep moving down the aisle toward the chapel, lying at the heart of the complex. Just opposite is a small, grassy park-like plot. Andreas told us that it was supposedly here that the bones of Colon were interred briefly, before being relocated, and sent back to Spain.

"But of course, my friends, that is all speculation. There has never been anything to verify any of that," he explained as he conjured up the image of a sorely distressed individual, mourning the loss of a national treasure. No matter where you go in the world, tour guides are the same- *"Always showmen and women, giving the crowd what it wants"* I thought.

We turned and walked away. A quick dusting of the car, and we headed back, the song embedded in my mind the entire journey back to *Habana Vieja*... *'Cuando Juanica y Chan Chan...'*

VIII

Santa Clara, 1957

OSMEL GARCIA SANCHEZ wiped the sweat from his brow. Even though they were far from the coasts of Cuba, almost in the center of the island north/south, and about 120 m. above sea level, the air was still thick with heat and humidity. *How could this be*, he idly thought, *its nearly Diciembre!* He sat down wearily on a rock and drank deeply from his water-soaked canvas canteen. At least it was merely lukewarm, not hot, and somewhat thirst-quenching. The handful of others, taking his lead, also sat down and rested a bit.

Whatever possessed the city planners and developers to take time and conduct this minor survey would forever elude him. He was merely a technician; that was all. Word had gotten out from the city historian's office that the excavation site for the building of a new casino next to the recently opened Santa Clara Hotel had stumbled upon what appeared to be an ancient cemetery. While clearing the land and digging footings for the building, a couple of stone ossuaries had been inconveniently cut in half by a bulldozer. Nothing would have happened, and work might have continued on unabated, had not a couple of the workmen gone into *Bar La Marquesina* and had one too many *cervezas*.

They began shooting off at the mouth, telling of their exploits while working at the job site. The beer both emboldened them and made them afraid at the same time. Being poor *campesinos* from a small village nearby, and adherents to Catholicism, fear of God was deeply embedded in their psyche. On one hand they bragged about the distinct possibility of finding treasure; while on the other their fear of desecrating the dead and eternal damnation was also foremost in their minds. It was just their bad luck that one of the other patrons in the bar that evening was Father Gonzalo, of the *Catedral de Santa Clara de Asis,* The Cathedral of St. Clair of Assisi.

Although the current church was built in 1940 after they pulled down the original one, built in 1725, the Catholic community dated back to the founding of the villa in 1689. It was as old and revered as Spanish Cuba could be; serving as one of the first 7 villas to be populated. Facing the *Plaza Mayor,* it was an imposing edifice in the heart of the town. As Santa Clara grew, much of the open space began to be filled in with homes and businesses, erasing the rural past of the area one hectare at a time.

As the town grew, a small number of Jews originally from the Dutch Antilles opened a trade emporium in the community. Although their numbers were small, the community prospered in Santa Clara and was fairly well accepted. But, as a religious community distinct from its Catholic neighbors, it had its own very small storefront chapel and equally small plot of land for a cemetery. As the city expanded, the Jewish community was forced to relocate its cemetery to just beyond the city limits. Although it was deemed to be sacred, holy, ground, according to biblical proscriptions it was also hygienically unclean; hence its move.

However, apparently not all of the burials had been plotted correctly. In fact, many of the ledgers had also been destroyed over the centuries as a result of mishaps such as fires. So no one in either the city planner's office or the construction company knew for certain what to expect when the first shovels hit the ground. That was the basis for the survey. In reality, the city wanted to only create a paper trail that said there was due diligence carried out and nothing of importance was noted.

All of this was at the behest of *El Presidente,* Fulgencio Batista. He wanted to create a tourist mecca in the heart of the country. The gambling arm of organized crime in the U.S., lead by Meyer Lansky and Lucky Luciano, wished to expand their monopoly on the island- and Batista wished to expand his personal wealth. He felt that both sides could mutually benefit. Part of his delusional vision of Cuba made him believe that the peasantry of Cuba would also benefit through his largesse. He was a firm adherent to the 'trickle down' theory, although nothing actually 'trickled down' to the people.

In fact, for years, his often brutal and violent dictatorship was crumbling, and insurgents led by Fidel Castro, Camillo Cienfuegos and Ernesto 'Che'

Guevara had already fomented a violent response to his ways. Things were coming rapidly to a boil.

The 'Charcoal Vendor,' as Batista was referred to by the peasants, and his indifference to the people, would soon end. But in the meantime, his wishes needed to be fulfilled unless prison (or worse) was your goal in life. So Sanchez slowly got up, clapped his hands to summon his fellow workmen, and they got back to clearing the area around the broken coffins. At the start of the project being overseen by the city historian of Santa Clara and an archaeologist from the relatively new campus of *Universidad Central "Marta Abreu" de Las Villas*, The University 'Marta Abreu' of Las Villas, founded in 1952, local workers who had some experience in digging had been sought. Sanchez, having worked in landscaping previously also knew design and excavation methods, and thus was chosen as liaison to the faculty member.

He had begun to truly hate this role. The wet-behind-the-ears, snot-faced, *nino* who called himself 'professor' was barely out of university himself. A bachelor's degree was all that he had, but that was all that the government required, on this particular job. At just a little less than twice Prof. Ernesto Soto Juarez's age, the landscaper-cum-archaeological-technician despised answering to this youngster. But that was his job and he needed the paycheck dearly. So Sanchez sucked it up and directed the men to lay out the strings of a grid and dig crisp squares, going down 10 cm at a time in as level a fashion as possible. All the while, the archaeologist oversaw the work; preferring *not* to get dirty himself.

Off in the distance, on a low rise a couple of hundred meters from the dig site, a man in a black cassock sat on the grass eating a picnic lunch spread out on a blanket. What was unusual was that every so often he would sneak a pair of binoculars from under wraps and pretend that he was bird watching. In reality, he would gaze across the sky before settling the lenses on the excavation; lingering for a brief moment longer than would have seemed necessary. He would then return the binoculars to their hiding place and resume his lunch.

* * *

In the immediate area of the two broken coffins, there was a good deal of bone dust and a few sharp fragments. The young archaeologist insisted that a screen be used to sift through the dirt there. However, nothing more had revealed itself in the screened material. There were no other signs of human occupation in that particular square. With a small sigh, Juarez directed the crew to move to an adjacent square and begin to gently dig and remove the soil.

Sanchez was moved here, along with 3 other *campesinos*. As they dug down to approximately the same level as the stone fragments that had been unearthed by the heavy equipment, a well worked corner of stone protruded from the earth. Although five meters or so from the other stone fragments, the workmanship appeared to be the same. Sanchez called *el professor* over to the square, all the while telling the workmen to take a short break. *Funny,* he thought, *the boy doesn't realize that what I call him is a sarcastic and mocking name. He actually thinks that I respect him!* The young man slowly eased his way down the 60 or so centimeters into the pit, careful not to soil his chinos (that simply wouldn't do!) to examine the fragment of block.

This flurry of activity caught the eye of the man on the hill. He hurriedly grabbed the binocs, and swung them quickly around to the dig. This time there was no pretense for stealth- the air of excitement down below warranted the blatant peek.

He saw the men gathered around the perimeter of one of the squares, some looking intently, while others appeared to simply be grateful for time off of their manual labor. But he noticed the archaeologist and his foreman in the square, brushing dirt away from a piece of stone. Even with the 10x power of the lens, he couldn't make out what they were looking at. He watched closely as one of them pointed to the small canopied area at the edge of the excavation and mimed as if he was taking a picture. A small, compact crewman went over and rummaged about in a camo green footlocker and pulled out a leather bag and meter stick.

Upon his return, he tossed the stick down and the foreman deftly caught it. The archaeologist took the bag and set it down on the square's edge and unzipped it. He removed a German Hasselblad camera, and fiddled with the settings. Meanwhile, a final light brushing of the area around the stone removed lingering footprints and the measuring stick was gently placed in front of the piece. Suddenly there was unexpected movement from the men all around the perimeter. The young university man gestured as if he was a conductor at the symphony, and all the men lined up tightly shoulder-to-shoulder on one side of the square- precisely the side that faced the man on the hillside.

Santa Madre de Dios! The man on the hill silently cursed aloud. *But why are they blocking my view? Do they know that I'm here?* Realizing what he had done, he quickly crossed himself. Father Gonzalo knew that he would be forgiven for his sin of cursing should he discover what was going on a couple of hundred yards away and below him.

Then suddenly it came to him. The sun was behind him, casting a long shadow by this time of day. He had chosen this spot precisely for that; for in the hazy glare he was all but invisible to the men below as they looked into the sun. But it also meant that the squares of excavation were half in-half out of the sunlight as well. This would create terrible photographs. He had to hand it to the archaeologist. Although he might be quite young, he had been schooled very well. He had ordered the workmen to stand tightly packed next to each other to create an impromptu screen that would cast the entire square in shade- thus allowing for a very even photographic venue. *Bueno mi amigo*, he thought.

But his line of sight was all but gone. Ten minutes of photography and the men were dismissed. Apparently something funny was said by the foreman, as the men all began to laugh and walk back to their squares. The order to call it a day must have been handed down, as they started to pack up their tools and carry them to the storage shed. Meanwhile, the foreman and archaeologist had removed the stone, placed it in a wooden box, hammered the lid shut, and carried it out of the pit.

Por favor, please, I beg of you in the name of God, put it in the shed where I can easily get to it! Father Gonzalo nervously fingered his Rosary Beads in this silent prayer. It was to no avail. Once out of the hole, the two men lugged it to the jeep and placed it in the back storage box. By this time, all of the equipment was packed away, the shed locked, and the men began to scatter toward their homes. Osmel Garcia Sanchez drove the archaeologist and the find back to the university campus.

The padre now packed his picnic stuff as well, and, while walking down the opposite side of the hill, plotted a way to get into the offices to see what was in the crate.

* * *

Osmel glanced over at the younger man, sizing him up in a bit of a new light. He was impressed with the way that the archaeologist had handled the situation with the stone ossuary fragment. He was intrigued, yet not overly excited. He prevented the men from jumping in and removing the stone from the earth before it was photographed and measured. Even Osmel understood the importance of recording things exactly as they were discovered. He still thought the *niño* was a little shit at times, and definitely wet behind the ears- but maybe, he thought, just a bit 'damp!" He smiled and started humming a tune.

"*¿Cuál es ése?* What's that tune?"

"Eh?" Osmel asked his passenger. "Sorry?"

"What's the tune you're humming? I'm not familiar with it." Ernesto Juarez inquired of him. He seemed truly interested.

"*Que?* You're not familiar with Benny Moré, Senor Juarez? Why, he's just the greatest Cuban popular singer of all time, that's all. He has a way with many styles that originated in the eastern part of the island. There are many types of *son* music, but *son montuno* is one. The '*montuno*' came from the mountains where *mi familia* came from. This one is *Bonito y Sabroso,* 'Nice and Tasty'."

"Okay, but me, I prefer Elvis and rock and roll- and please, Osmel, call me Netto!" The young man laughed and sang. "Don' step on my blue suede shoes!" He proved that he knew modern rock and roll. After all, Blue Suede Shoes was only 2 years old. But he also proved that he couldn't sing a lick. Osmel took both hands off the wheel and covered his ears, laughing all the time. *The kid isn't so bad a companero after all, even if he can't hold a tune,* he thought.

Just around the corner was the small campus of *Marta Abreu* University. Because of some student unrest, aimed at Batista's regime, campus security had been augmented by the national police, so twice they were stopped and had to show identification papers. Finally, they were able to find a parking spot only a few paces from the loading dock door of the building that held the faculty of the social sciences- of which anthropology and archaeology shared a small suite of rooms and storage/lab facility in the basement. While Osmel unloaded the smaller buckets that contained other finds from the dig site, Netto took out a key ring that held no fewer than a dozen massive keys. He ran his fingers over each on the ring, searching for the proper mate to the lock on the door. After trying a couple, the right one turned to the side and a familiar 'click' meant that the door was now unlocked. He smiled and shouldered his way into the building. As the door was on a pneumatic hinge, designed to prevent anyone accidentally leaving it open, he stood by and with his body held it open for Osmel- who carried in 2 small buckets. He set them just inside, and went back for the remaining finds. Once they all were in the building dock area, the archaeologist wedged a small piece of wood under the door, propping it open. Then the two of them returned to the jeep to get the larger, heavier crate.

Just as they were unlashing the box from the jeep's rear bed, a figure turned into the alley and headed toward them. Father Gonzalo approached with his head down, face hidden by the broad flat-brimmed hat that he wore, apparently deep in thought. He stopped and looked up, and suddenly smiled at the two excavators.

"Pardon me, *senors,*" he said, a bit embarrassed. "I was just out for a walk, 'talking to God,' as it were, and actually lost track of where I was going." He laughed easily and stuck out his hand. "Father Gonzalo, from the Cathedral."

Both Netto and Osmel shook his hand in turn, muttering return greetings and introductions as well.

"As you can see, *Padre*, you're in the heart of the university campus. We've just returned from working on a salvage dig near *Plaza Mayor*, which is soon to be the site of the new Santa Clara Hotel. When digging the footings for the building, a bulldozer uncovered a couple of stone fragments of sarcophagi. Apparently the old cemetery that was located here wasn't fully disinterred when it was moved to the new site last century or so. The city historian wanted someone from the university to oversee digging up any other objects so that they could be respectfully buried in the cemetery. Then the hotel project, which I have heard Batista has taken a special interest in, can be completed with no further delays." Netto had taken the lead in telling their story.

But Osmel had to chime in- "But *Padre*, it is also my understanding that a major casino will be built in the hotel as well, and Batista's *amigos de la Mafia* from the U.S. will split the profits- leaving Santa Clara high and dry!"

"*Callarse!* Be quiet Sanchez!" The archaeologist was truly alarmed. "Don't speak ill of *el Presidente*! Who knows who may be listening." He was referring to the priest also. No one knew which side of someone's bread the butter was on these days.

"It's okay my friends. I too know of these rumors, and believe me, the church has no friend in our president either. Your thoughts are safe with me. But what's in the crate? It looks to be something unusual."- the priest seemingly asked as an innocent question.

With a touch of pride in his voice, Netto Juarez explained that it was a fragment of the lid of a stone sarcophagus. There were definitely symbols and fragmented remains of words carved on the lid. But what they said at this point in time was anybody's guess. The stone would be thoroughly cleaned in the laboratory and, if not clearly readable, experts would be brought in to decipher what was inscribed. Then, barring anything earth-shattering, the remains would be re-interred in the cemetery on the edge of town, and the building could proceed.

Father Gonzalo thanked them for their patient explanation, offered his thanks and a quick blessing for the deceased who once resided in the sarcophagus, blessed the two men, and turned to leave.

"By the way," he said, "I would like to hear the outcome of this intriguing story, and perhaps be the one who could conduct the service of re-interment at the cemetery."

Not an unreasonable request, Netto agreed, shook the priest's hand, and kicked the wedge out from under the door- watching it swing shut. The two then began to lug the crate down the flight of stairs to the basement lab.

IX

Havana, the present

THE RIDE BACK was uneventful and we were both lost in our own thoughts. Me, still with Buena Vista Social Club; Berto with how he was to juggle his next trip with the enticing exploration that was just on the horizon. A thought crossed his mind as we were just a few minutes out from the cemetery.

"We're gonna swing by an office on the way- I'll just phone Yoli to see if she's there." He was referring to our friend and colleague, Yolanda. "She's at the Research Centre for Cuban Culture, *El Centro de investigaciones de la Cultura Cubano*, on *Avenida Salvador Allende*. She's looking up some information for a group that she's guiding next month. A bunch of big shots from Nicaragua and she's looking to soften them up with parallels to their systems so that they feel honored. Truth is, she's also angling for better tips!" We both laughed at that. Due to the economic system, well educated people in the travel industry still made the same meager income as managers in other industries that had no outside world contact. The key came in securing CUC tips that could quadruple the core, official salary that the government paid. In fact, anyone working in the tourist industry could make quite a good living based on this 'second income.'

He determined that she was indeed still there, and that she would be happy to meet us. Rather than take up too much time, we agreed to converge on a small coffee bar on *Avenida Universidad*, just around the corner. Plus, parking was much easier in that locale. I glanced at him and saw that complacent smile on his face and knew for certain the real reason. To Berto, 'easier parking' meant finding a large space that could ensure shade, no dings or dents on his baby.

As we rounded the corner to the café, we saw her sitting at one of the shaded outside tables. When she saw us, the 1000 watt smile lit up the block, she jumped up and embraced Berto with open arms and pecked him on both cheeks. The warmth of the greeting simply confirmed to me the close friendship of the two.

"*Hola amigo*!" she turned to me and gave me a hug as well. "What's new in the detective business?" We filled her in over a thick cup or two. When she heard all this, she was hooked. Based on her connections within the Catholic Church in Havana, we all decided that Yoli should make first inquiries there about Columbus' after-life journeys across the Caribbean and the Atlantic. That would give Berto and me the luxury of taking time to work within other archives in the city historian's office- in essence doubling up on leads.

Half an hour later, we got into the '57 and headed to the old city. Once a parking space had been acquired, we split up, promising to link up for dinner and see what we learned in the intervening couple of hours. Yoli went to the Cathedral, while the two of us headed back to Eusebio Leal's office.

Leal was nowhere in sight, but his secretary assured us that his records were ours for the asking. Since we weren't exactly sure where to look, and precisely what to look for, we simply asked permission to browse. She left us in the archival storage room and merely requested that we announce when we were through so that she could lock up.

I sighed as the massive mahogany door swung shut. Where to start? The first place we considered had to do with the construction of the massive complex of *Colon* Cemetery. These records would have dated to the early part of the 19th Century. Fortunately, the filing system used here was based on chronology, not a random subject matter. This would have made it an extraordinary needle-in-the-haystack search. We would have had to consider all the name changes, which government office had jurisdiction (or *how many* government offices had jurisdiction), church relations, etc.

I suggested that we first look at the records for the *Espada* Cemetery, that lay under the *Colon*. Berto thought a moment and readily agreed. So the first files we sought out were for 1804, the year that plans were laid. Since it took two years to be inaugurated, we also got the files for '05-'06 as well. These were more like ledgers than files, enormous folio-sized folders with papers of all shapes and sizes. *No scanning of these puppies and standardizing of paperwork*, I thought to myself. *What a task!*

As we sifted through the material, we found dozens of correspondences between José Díaz de Espada y Landa, the seated Bishop at the time, and Don Salvador de Muro y Salazar, the governor.

Berto was amazed at all of the private letters that were found here. In fact, the amount of corruption, the level of greed, the improper relations, *and that was referring to the Bishop,* overwhelmed him!

Some of the material that he translated actually made me blush! I hoped that he took it upon himself to give the material he read some editorial license and I told him that. But, no.

"My friend, it truly appears that things haven't changed much when it comes to human nature; regardless of the garb that it is clothed in!" was all that he could say. He was very clear, and apparently sadly so, that this was a direct translation of some of the documents before him.

"Wow," was all that I had. "It seems that Bishop Diaz was in the same league as the Borgias of the 15th and 16th Centuries back in Rome."

"*Que?* I don't follow." Now I was amazed. I had found a 'chapter missing' in the life of the 'Encyclopedia.' I was going to milk it for all that it was worth. It was my turn to wax encyclopedic to my colleague.

"Well, the Borgias were a family originally from Valencia, in the Kingdom of Aragon in Spain. Although unsubstantiated, there were rumors that they were descended from *Marranos,* Jews who were forcibly converted to Catholicism. Their greed and lust for absolute power became apparent when two of the house of Borgia actually became Popes- Alfonse de Borgia was known as Pope Callixtus II and Rodrigo Lonzol Borgia was Pope Alexander VI. They ruled in the 15th Century. The rule of Alexander was perhaps the most frightening of the two. His laundry list of transgressions included adultery, theft, bribery and, last but not least, murder by arsenic poisoning!"

"*Now I'm amazed*! You, my dear friend, are both the Crazy One and The American Encyclopedia!" Berto looked at me in awe.

"Aw, gee, you're embarrassing me! Anyway, you may have heard of a non-papal criminal in the family, Lucrezia. She was a notorious poisoner who was also involved in political intrigue at the highest level. Apparently she went through three husbands who all died terminal cases of death!" I couldn't help but laugh out loud.

"*Madre de Dios* but you're a callous one!" But he was laughing as well.

After a couple of hours of searching through scores of folios, Berto and I decided to call it quits for the day. Regrettably, it appeared that there was nothing that could shed light on Columbus' post-life stay on the island; at least, nothing here.

* * *

About two miles away, Yoli was sitting down with one of the Prelates of the Cathedral. Father Alejandro was an octogenarian with the spring in his step of a 45 year old. Life had clearly been good to him both physically and mentally. He was as sharp as they came, and a delight to enter into conversation with on any given day. He was able to recall events half a century or more ago as if they were just last week. Yoli was heartened by this, as she hoped that his memory could lead her in the proper direction.

He led her to his small office and offered her coffee. She politely declined but opted instead for a bottle of *Ciego Montero* water instead. She had had enough caffeine for the day. She sat back on the spartan, yet comfortable, chair that he offered, as he walked around the desk and sat behind it. In spite of his 'modern' take on the world in general, the staid, traditional approach of the long-established Church still dictated his demeanor in his office.

"Senorita Yolanda, for what do I have this distinct pleasure?" he asked formally.

"*Padre, por favor*, please call me Yoli. I have some questions about the revered Spaniard Cristobal Colon." She smiled that patented gleam.

He too smiled back, but the yellowed, chipped teeth didn't radiate the same feeling. It seemed cool, somewhat forced. It was almost as if he anticipated that going to the dentist would have been more fun than sitting down for a discussion with this woman.

After she left, he quickly walked back to his small office and closed and locked the door. Unlocking the bottom drawer of his desk, he rummaged and withdrew a worn leather address book. He flipped through the dog-eared pages until he found the number that he needed.

Father Alejandro dialed the international code for the Vatican, then punched in the private direct line to Archbishop Dominique Mamberti, the Vatican's foreign minister.

* * *

After being dropped off at the *Nacional*, I went upstairs and took a quick shower, because Berto and I were meeting up for dinner a little later. I hoped that Yoli could make it too; since we hadn't heard from her yet about what she discovered at the Cathedral. As I entered room 235, I thought, *Mr. Flynn, I'm home and going to freshen up!* Then I laughed at myself for still entertaining the notion that he was in residence. After all, I hadn't heard from him, or seen any sign of him, since that first time a little over a year and a half ago. But then, on the other hand, it never hurt to announce oneself.... *just in case!* I turned on the flat screen TV and found a Law and Order rerun dubbed in Spanish. With the volume lowered, I ran the razor lightly over my face, showered and quickly toweled off. A quick change of clothing with plenty of time to spare would allow me to go to the business center for a quick email check; then out to the veranda to wait.

I discovered that no earth-shattering emails of any importance were waiting for me, so I walked back down to the lobby and headed out the massive double doors to the terrace. A fairly good breeze blew away residual humidity from the day, and it was quite pleasant out there. I stepped across the stone marker that was embedded in the pavement- *Hotel Nacional, 1930,* the year of inauguration- and walked about 20 meters down the path, exiting the courtyard that was protected on two sides by the wings of the hotel. At the very edge of the property was a row of cocktail tables and chairs, overlooking the precipitous drop down to the *Malecon* below. The breeze came from about 220 degrees on the compass- in essence from nearly three directions. It reminded me of the Northern Palace of King Herod at Masada, in Israel. In the middle of the Judean Desert, with shade, water and a breeze, that location was a serene one as well in spite of its foreboding setting.

With the sun fairly low on the horizon by now, it was utterly delightful. I ordered a *mojito sin alcool,* a 'virgin mojito' (I wanted to wait til dinner), and sat back and reflected on the sun reflecting off the Florida Straits. A three-piece band strolled around the terrace, playing traditional Cuban music.

Yes, Cuba is thoroughly communist, with 90% of everything today owned by the government. But one of the up-sides of this form of government is the high regard for anything that had to do with Cuban culture. The result was that schools catered to the arts of all types. And then, once finished with school, you never had to worry if you were a musician. You always had a government job. Every restaurant, every public venue, had live music supplied by the government. It was an absolute pleasure. And, on top of that, if you liked the musicians, their CDs were always available for purchase- at a fixed government rate of 10 CUC. No haggling here.

As I sat there, sort of day-dreaming my way through the late afternoon, a wedding procession tooled down the *Malecon.* With horns blaring, the wedding couple sat on the rear deck of a '59 Buick Electra, laughing and waving. Passing cars beeped in return, people waved, and for a moment, it seemed that there were no cares in the world at all.

A tap on the shoulder, followed by a gentle screech of the metal chair as it was pulled away from the table, broke my reverie as Berto sat down.

"I know what I'm having, how about you?" he signaled to the waiter. *"Dos Cristals por favor!"* And soon, a couple of cold beers found their way to our table. We sat back, and watched the sun finish its descent into the sea. At times, quiet was the way to go. As soon as it hit the deck, and sank out of sight, Berto broke the silence.

"Got hold of Yoli, and she'll meet us at the *paladar.*" He was referring to one of my favorite restaurants in Havana, Café Laurent. Although it's only a couple of years old, Café Laurent had already made quite a name for itself in the gastronomic world. Situated just a seven minute walk from the *Nacional*, this private restaurant did little to announce itself. Located just a half block off of *Calle* 21, on *Calle M*, it was the entire top floor of a small five-storey apartment building. The small lift, which holds only a handful of people, gives one a sense of retro things to come. You swing the outer door shut, pull the grate across the entry and push #5. I have walked up the flights faster than this lift.

When it finally comes to a halt, and the doors open up, the atmosphere is a definite throwback to late 50s pre-Revolutionary days. A well-stocked bar, its rear wall lined with 1950s newspaper, enhances the feel. But, in some ways, it seems so un-Cuban! Don't worry, though, the food is flavorful, authentic Cuban fare. As Guy Fieri would say, 'its Flavortown in the heart of the Carib.'

Senor Enciclopedia was considered to be a regular here, and when we got off the lift, both Lorenzo Enrique Nieto and Jose Figueroa, the co-owners, came out to greet him. But I guess that Berto got a wee bit of comeuppance, as Nieto looked at me, and said that he remembered seeing me there a couple of times in the last few months as well. I beamed, and shook his hand. Then, with a certain amount of *proteccione*, we were led out to the rooftop patio that was open on three sides, letting in a pleasant breeze that came off the *Malecon*. A small paddle fan ensured a continuous flow of air-making for an extraordinarily wonderful experience. We sat back, enjoying the view, when, apparently just on the next lift up after us, Yoli came into the restaurant. As she swung around the corner, there was a rush of movement, and head chef Dayron Aviles Alfonso grabbed the girl, swung her around, and planted a big kiss on her!

"I guess they know each other," I said with a straight face. Berto laughed and we both got up. Yoli was impeccably dressed, as flawless as any young woman going out on an informal night on the town in any big city anywhere in the world. No wonder Chef Dayron came out to admire her. Several other heads turned as well. I sensed a certain pride in Berto, seeing his protégé away from work like that.

"*Hola senores y senorita! Bienvenido a Café Laurent,*" Dayron said. "It's with great pleasure that I welcome you all once again." He pulled up the fourth chair and had a quick drink with us. In the process, he recommended *The Cordero Lechal a la Tabaca*, slow-roasted lamb with cream/mint reduction. He said that the lamb that came in earlier in the day was the finest cut that he had seen in a month. My mouth was watering as soon as the word 'lamb' came out of his mouth. Yoli and I opted for that, while Berto went for seafood; the grilled lobster en brochette.

We didn't want to disturb the tranquility of the evening, so we steered away from any business discussions until after the meal. Courtesy of the owners, chocolate cake and mango ice cream were a perfect mate to the thick, rich Cuban coffee that came after. We sat back, enjoyed the air, and then began to plot our next course.

As it turned out, both of our first leads simply didn't pan out. We told Yoli that, although there were fascinating bits of lurid history in the City Historian's Office archives, nothing pointed us in any direction regarding Columbus.

In response, Yoli said that her visit to the archdiocese was less than satisfying as well. She felt like she was back in high school, for her journalism class, when she had gone to the principal's office to request an interview for the school newspaper, and was greeted with an icy, frozen smile that hid any true answers about school issues. However, although no answers were given, the prelate Father Alejandro said that he needed to get permission from higher ups. She was to be invited back for a real interview should that permission be granted.

Berto remarked that he'd only seen her that nervous once; when she turned in her exam for licensed tour guide. "You know, even though you were scared out of your mind, you had nothing to worry about. I knew the quality of your studies and was prepared to give you your license on the spot. But you know the government…." He smiled at that. "Anyway, my assumption was confirmed the following week. Your scores were the highest of any applicant in many years."

She smiled back at that memory, but darkened when drawn back to the present. "There's something that Father Alejandro is hiding, or is hiding for the church. He scares me a bit, and I haven't felt that kind of discomfort for a long time. He was all smiles at first; then I mentioned Colon and the uncertainties about his upbringing and his final burial place. The room temperature dropped about 30 degrees I think. His face still smiled, but his eyes, well…" she couldn't quite put it into words.

"Let me try," I said. "His face smiled but his eyes were dead."

"YES! That's a wonderfully horrible way to put it, but yes. It is a precise definition." She was both happy but frightened as well. At least now she knew that others could understand exactly what her emotions were back at the church offices.

"Perhaps Berto or I could join you if you are invited back, if the approval from on high comes through. At least then you'll have support and the Father will not be so free to intimidate you." They both thought it a good plan if needed. But on my side, I wasn't so sure that the follow-up call would ever be made to her.

We decided to call it a night, agreeing to meet in the morning to plot the next day's plan of attack. All of us walked back to the *Nacional*, because that was where Berto had parked. We crossed *Avenida O* and onto the well-manicured parkway that ran two blocks to the hotel itself. Faint music wafted out the open door to La Parisien Night Club off of the west wing. Cars of all ages mingled with tour buses as they maneuvered to gain access to the *porte cochere* of the entry. Liveried doormen worked their charm on guests and hoped for a good tip.

About 30 feet from the entry we parted ways. Berto and Yoli turned right and up a short drive to the carpark. He was giving her a lift home. I continued into the lobby and then to my room. With no Errol in sight, ghostly or otherwise, I kicked off my shoes, grabbed the remote and got ready for an early evening. I fell asleep watching the *Habana Industriales* deliver a good drubbing to my 'boys,' the *Cienfuegos Elefantes.*

So why are they 'my boys'? It all went back to my first visit to the island. It was the 'fam' trip that the travel agency sent me on, to learn some of the ropes regarding Cuban travel. It occurred just after the Arab Spring, and in particular, the Egyptian Spring which was when I had taken a group to Egypt and we left the country the day before the revolution.

A few days after that, in speaking with the travel agency, the president and I commiserated over the fact that recently, it seemed, everywhere I went some sort of revolution took place! Of course, this led to further discussions about international study and travel. For me and my students, it was a disheartening blow. After all, I had been instrumental at the university in pushing forward the notion that, within the decade, the school would mandate that a full 33% of its student body would take part in some sort of international experience; and at the 15-year mark up the ante to 50%. My rationale was that the world was growing ever so small, and the next generation of leaders needed to acclimate itself to this changing paradigm. The Atlantic and Pacific no longer served as great protective barriers, and we couldn't afford to isolate ourselves.

But the unease in the Middle East and North Africa also made the university administration nervous, to say the least. I could be left out in the cold from the policy that I helped initiate, unless my own horizons were broadened. As we continued our discussion, the agency head began to put feelers out in my direction. She knew of my expertise in the Middle East and North Africa, archaeologically, culturally, historically. But she also was aware of the deep background that I had in Jewish studies, culture and spirituality. So how about this, she inquired. With first the Bush Administration, followed by Obama, the U.S. was beginning to ease some of the travel restrictions to

Cuba- maybe in preparation for normalization. Humanitarian and educational licenses were being granted by our government for direct travel and 'people to people' study. The agency put my name on the license application as a consultant for them, and off I went.

It was during this first trip to the island that I became an *Elephantes* fan. The group arrived in Cienfuegos in early afternoon, much too early for check-in at the Hotel Jagua. The guide, Norberto Suarez (yes, the same Berto! That's how we first met) suggested to the group that we take the bus over to the stadium, and take in a few innings of an afternoon ball game. It was not big deal, because from the second floor up in the hotel, you could see the stadium just off to the north. The roar of delight still rings in my ears.

A quick phone call and Berto found out that the team was playing the Sancti Spiritus *Gallos*, 'the Roosters.' It promised to be a good game, for the home team, as the Roosters had nothing to crow about that season (oohhhhhhhhh, how bad is that!). We pulled into the grassy parking area and went to the ticket booth. The price was one CUC, or about a dollar U.S. As we approached the ticket taker, it was as if we were back in the States, during Spring Training. The stadium held about 6,000 people- kind of like McEchnie Field in Bradenton, home of the Pittsburgh Pirates. It was jam-packed with fans. The sights, the sounds, the smells of popcorn and roasted corn, made my mouth water. The serious fans in the stands watched intently at the action, and, just like in an American ballpark, razzed the umpires and opposing team members relentlessly. Remember, it's a small stadium, and sound carries easily to the field. Just as we were getting seated, one particular *Elefantes* fan apparently went too far for the Roosters' first baseman. He threw down his glove and charged past the first base coach and hurdled the low retaining wall that separated fan from field. The police immediately began to pull fan and player apart, while everyone surrounding them jeered and cheered to their heart's content.

We stayed for 2 hotdogs, 3 innings, and 2 *Cristal* beers (by my personal count) before returning to the bus and going back to the hotel to register. By the way, the home team won 11-2 and peace would reign in Cienfuegos- at least until the next night's game. And that is how the team became my favorite on the island. The game allowed me to see Berto in a new light on that first visit, and secured our friendship in a way that usually doesn't occur between program directors and local guides. And for that, I have been eternally thankful. In addition, it gave me a perspective on baseball that would reshape the way that I watched the game back in the States. And I now also had another 'hated' rival team to add to my list alongside the Detroit *Tigres*, New York Yankees (the Evil Empire) and the Chicago White Sox- The Havana *Industriales*. They were considered the 'Yankees of the Island' because of their outrageous (for Cuba) salaries, condescending attitudes, and 'Capital City Complex.' Come to think of it, it was *exactly* the way New Yorkers think positively of their team while hating the rest of Major League Baseball collectively. Go *Elefantes!*

I woke up just long enough to turn off the TV around midnight, rolled over, and didn't rouse myself til 6.30 the next morning.

X

La Habana, 1795

*H*IS BACK WAS *stiff and sore in so many places. Bending over the kneeler for 5 hours, arms clasped in prayer, draped over the pew in front of him, the Jesuit priest was in physical agony. But it was all worth it as his mind was cleared of all doubt and confusion. His prayers to God had been answered, or so he thought. A path of righteous action lay before him. All was revealed now. Father Manuelo simply needed to put the thought into movement for the sake of the Church.*

But, in addition, the soul of a great man would be put to rest in its proper venue, with his own people.

Manuelo struggled to get up; his knees were screaming at him along with every other muscle, or so it seemed. As he straightened, his eye caught a beam of mote-filled light as it pierced the stained glass. He followed it down and it flooded the apse with glorious color. And then, as if a sign from God Himself, the beam struck the plain wood crucifix behind the altar- setting it ablaze with light....

The priest recalled a tract about church buildings in the Middle Ages, and one of the Catholic Church's greatest architects, Abbot Suger. It was Suger himself who, perhaps single-handedly, altered early floorplans by incorporating the use of flying buttresses. These engineering marvels allowed for the exterior walls of a church to be thinner, and allowed the buildings to rise higher and higher- because the weight of the stone was disseminated, spread, outward onto pillars outside the church. The weight then was divided up as it sank into the ground. With this weight problem resolved, the great Gothic Cathedral of St. Denis became the prototype for the use of stained glass windows. How did Abbot Suger put it? The father asked himself. Ah yes, he said that the light that radiated in from the heavens above was actually 'God's Light.' What a glorious way to state it. And here was 'God's Light' filtering into the great Cathedral in Havana, showing him that God's Grace was with him in what he was about to do.

The pain suddenly diminished, Manuelo smiled, and after a couple of wavering steps, found renewed energy and went back into the private chambers of the church. He went into the archive room, and pulled the dusty cemetery ledger down from the shelf. After scanning the pages for half an hour, he found the entry that he was looking for- the section for unnamed paupers and unmarked graves. He was looking for something particular. And there it was, an unknown male, buried approximately two centuries earlier. Perfect. Now, I need to find someone that I can trust, someone that will believe in what I do for the sake of the church with all his heart.

It came to him quite easily actually. As if God was guiding his every action. One of the caretakers in the church was a deaf mute, whose entire life was spent first in the church orphanage, then as a ward of the church since he would have a terrible time fending for himself. He won't question me, and of course he would remain silent. The Jesuit chuckled to himself. Maybe that's cruel, he thought. But it's all in the name of God.

Just the day earlier, the ship from Hispaniola arrived with the last of the Spaniards who desperately tried to save the island from the French cerdos, those pigs. The plan would need to be carried out perhaps during the transfer to the Cathedral crypt, scheduled sometime in the following days.

* * *

The next morning, the stone sarcophagus arrived. Soon, the sound of a caravan of cavalry and wagons penetrated the massive stone walls of the Cathedral. Father Manuelo, a couple of other priests, and all the employees of the archdiocese hurried out the main entry and stood on the terrace a few steps above the plaza. It was a special sight indeed. A catafalque covered in purple sat on a wagon, bedecked with the flag of Spain. As the soldiers dismounted, everyone crossed themselves and briefly kneeled. They felt that they were in the presence of an extraordinary individual. The commanding officer also crossed himself, apparently muttering a short prayer, as he strode up the stairs.

Manuelo hastened to greet him. It was of the essence that he be the first on the scene in order for his plan to work. The soldier saluted and shook his hand. The Jesuit blessed him, his soldiers, and their cargo, and explained that it would be best if the wagon was moved to the side entry in order to facilitate things. In addition, it was felt that people would be too curious to see a sarcophagus moved into the Cathedral via the front door.

On the island, although Catholicism was as strong as in any place in the New World, native island religious elements still crept into the mix, and native superstition was an integral part. As a matter of fact, the strains of Santeria music at that very moment wafted across the Plaza from a small house shrine opposite on the square. The priest knew of the house, dedicated to the Goddess of the Sea, Yemaya, and the high priest who ran it. And many times he had visited with the hope of conversion in mind. But to no avail, and there was an uneasy truce between the two religious men.

As the coffin was transferred inside, Manuelo thanked the soldiers and blessed them with the sign of the cross as they knelt. He then informed everyone that, until final interment in the crypt, he would lock the doors and stand vigil with the remains of the great explorer until the following morning. No one was to disturb the vestry until then.

As he sat with the stone sarcophagus, he examined it carefully for any signs as to its origin. The only thing that he noted was the inscription with the name of C. Colon. Flanking the name were what appeared to be slanted crosses- but these were heavily chipped and damaged. The plan quickly came together.

At daybreak, the Father said his morning prayers and sought out the Archbishop Alexandro. He knocked on the prelate's door.

"Your Holiness, it is I, God's humble servant, Manuelo, seeking an audience." He was greeted with a deep, rumbling, hacking cough from within. A raspy voice penetrated the thick oaken door.

"Come in, come in Father! Don't stand on ceremony. We are all equal in the brotherhood of God." Another fit of coughing followed this. Manuelo cautiously opened the door and entered into the study of the Archbishop. He strode over to the chair where the man was and kneeled at his feet. In spite of the earlier statement professing equality, the old man in front of him offered up his hand with the enormous signet ring. The Jesuit grasped the wizened, age-spotted hand with both of his, and kissed the ring. He then stood and backed up two steps.

The Archbishop wiped his mouth of some spittle with his silk handkerchief and asked, "For what do I hold this honor of speaking with you Father?"

This was the moment that would make, or break, the entire plan.

"As you are aware, your holiness, I spent the entire night on the vigil with the great man's sarcophagus. And I was somewhat appalled at the state of its preservation." He felt as if he were sweating buckets in the presence of the leader of Havana's Catholic community. "I feel that it is almost a blasphemy to re-inter a man of such stature in so heavily chipped and worn a sarcophagus."

For the first time in the meeting, the Archbishop looked up, intrigued.

"What are you getting at, Padre?" The older man's eyes grew sharper.

"Well, your Holiness, since we are talking about centuries-old remains, with no need for haste… I was thinking that a new sarcophagus, inlaid with semi-precious gems and guilded in just the right spots, might be more befitting the great Colon. And of course your name would be forever attached to this glorious tribute as the one who arranged a 'proper reburial.'" The priest bowed slightly and took yet another step back.

After a couple of moments, the Archbishop stroked his chin, slowly got up and went to the sideboard. He poured himself a goblet of an amber liquid, and then poured another. He gestured to Manuelo to come over, and handed him one of the chalices. "My son, that sounds like a splendid idea! I want to hear more, but you know that time is short."

Father Manuelo then hastened to outline his plan, relating that he knew a couple of stonemasons who could work around the clock to ensure completion with 48 hours. In addition, one of their cousins was a goldsmith and jeweler who would also be more than happy to assist as well. Of course, whatever compensation the Archbishop chose would be fine with them. The priest assumed that the intangible of a direct blessing and 'guarantee' for the next life would be considered to be of unimaginable value as well.

The final piece to fall into place was a touchy one. In order for his master plan to succeed, this last item needed to be given the go-ahead as well. The father then said that he would take it upon himself to get rid of the old sarcophagus. After all, should it fall into the wrong hands, some might get the idea that it too was a 'holy relic' and exploit if for all the improper reasons. This hadn't occurred to the leader of the church in Havana, but he saw the wisdom in the final analysis. He gave his permission for the priest to get rid of the old stone coffin- but respectfully, in dignity, without a trace.

"Get to it young man!" Archbishop Alexandro's excitement was tempered by another round of coughing. He brought the silk square to his mouth, waving the priest away with his other hand. Manuelo backed out of the room, stepped through the door, and nearly fainted with relief. Now, to the craftsmen.

* * *

As dawn broke the next day, Father Manuelo hurriedly said morning prayers, and then sought after the targeted 'partner-in-crime.' The mute was mucking out the stall of the two horses allocated to the Jesuits at the Cathedral. The priest grabbed the young man by his shoulders and spun him around. The startled look gave way to one of recognition, and he kissed the priest's hand. In a very badly broken type of sign language, Manuelo indicated that the servant should hitch the horses to the wagon and come with him. There was no question that he would comply.

Once done, the priest grabbed the reins and the two of them headed out to the small pauper's cemetery out of town just to the west. Since Habana had yet to grow westward, the ride was less than half an hour in length. As they approached, the mute started to fidget. He was clearly afraid of entering the cemetery. Father Manuelo stroked his hand, traced the sign of the cross on the youth's forehead and indicated that what they were doing was a Godly act.

Reassured by the padre, he followed him toward one of the crypts that housed a number of unknowns in a mass-grave environment. They opened the weathered wooden door. Although it was not airtight, badly warped and pitted with rot over the decades, they still were assaulted with a musty stench of decay. The other man's eyes were wide with fear, but the gentle demeanor of the Jesuit seemed to calm him a bit. They stepped inside and Manuelo pointed to a plain coffin with a simple paper tag slid between the lid and sidewall, which the two of them then loaded onto the back of the wagon and threw a blanket over it. They then crossed themselves and set out to return to La Catedral de la Virgen María de la Concepción Inmaculada. Small side streets ensured that they would be little noticed.

They worked their way back to La Plaza de la Catedral, and pulled the wagon alongside the church, next to a small door. It led directly to a rear vestry, adjacent to the stairs that led down to the crypt. The wooden coffin was unloaded, taken inside; and placed on one of two tables in the center of the room. The two men then only had to wait for another day.

And as promised, the stonemason and his jeweler cousin finished the work in record time. The massive sarcophagus brought to the Cathedral was as splendid as the original must have been at the beginning of the 16th Century. The stone inscription was crisp and clean. The name, Cristobal Colon, was precisely etched- flanked by two elegant raised-relief Maltese crosses. Faint traceries of gold highlighted the letters. And above and below were semi-precious gem studs. All in all, it was magnificent.

When the head of the cathedral saw the workmanship, tears filled his eyes. He was grateful to God for allowing him to carry out this task. But, in a small sense, also mindful that he, Archbishop Alexandro of Havana, would be remembered for initiating the action on behalf of Spain. He knew that Manuelo would understand.

* * *

Later that night, when all of the other Jesuits and staff had finally gone to bed, a blanket of silence descended on the church. Manuelo had dozed fitfully for half an hour at a time, but had at last fully awakened by around 3 am. He rubbed his eyes, making sure that he wasn't dreaming. The flag-draped stone coffin was still there, as was the much less pretentious wooden one on the next table. It wasn't a dream, and he was about to create what some might consider a blasphemy; while others would think it to be a righteous religious act.

He put his ear to the door and heard only the sound of silence. He sat in the darkness, his old friend. The handful of candles that flickered in the air currents cast eerie and bizarre shadows that danced to and fro. It was a sobering moment. Cautiously, quietly, he pried the lid off of the wooden box. A distinct odor of dry-rot filled his nostrils, and he gagged a bit. After the coughing spell died down, he took a stole off of a hook and wrapped it around his nose and mouth to filter the air. He carefully brought a candle over and peered inside. He took great pains to hold the brass candle holder upright, so that no hot wax might fall in and ignite the tinder dry remains. Fragments of cloth and a few small fragmented lengths of bone sat in a bed of bone dust. "This was man's fate after death," he mused.

Two short steps took him to the other table and the stone ossuary. Thank goodness the lid was designed in a split format- there being two deliberate halves. It was fairly easy to slide one portion aside. After doing this, and looking down, it became fairly obvious that there was literally nothing to distinguish one skeleton from the other. The state of remains was as decomposed as the other skeleton. He sighed with relief. It would be easier than he thought.

He needed to steel himself for the final task at hand, and returned to his seat for a few moments to meditate and offer a silent prayer. He asked God for guidance, and then tacked on a couple of phrases that beseeched God to forgive him; just in case things went wrong. He must have dozed off, because the next thing he knew, he heard the Cathedral bell tolling four o'clock. He needed to move with the utmost haste now. Morning prayers were only a short time away, and the clergy would begin to rise at any time.

It took only a few minutes, he carefully exchanged all of the extant bone material that there was. The accumulated bone dust he left lying on the bottom; after all, as it stated in the holy book of Genesis, Chapter 3, verse 19, "By the sweat of your face you shall eat bread until you return to the ground, for out of it you were taken; you are dust, and to dust you shall return." Certainly no one would be the wiser.

He then slid the stone lid in place, re-set the wooden cover on the other and lightly tapped the nails down, crossed himself and wiped his hands and face. He hastily ran a rag over the stone floor and removed whatever trace of residue might have fallen, and then returned to his seat as he awaited the knock on the door that would summon him to prayer.

"God rest the soul of the departed, God save the Spanish Empire," and finally, "God please save me as well."

XI

Santa Clara, 1957

CONDITIONS WERE NOT ideal down in the basement of the university building. There was never a place that escaped the humidity on the island. However, flat trays of a desiccating agent were positioned on tabletops and file cabinets all over the laboratory with the goal to absorb as much moisture in the air as reasonably possible. It appeared to be working a bit, as the environment was acceptable. Ernesto Soto Juarez lamented the fact that there wasn't more money accessible to fund proper air handlers for the facility. But the government had other priorities for its money- like quelling the growing rebellion in the eastern provinces. It was moving quite rapidly toward the highlands and Santa Clara. Student groups were increasing their leafleting of the campus, and political gatherings were on the upswing as well. Military convoys were passing through the town much more frequently than ever before. The young archaeologist was concerned that the university might be occupied by police forces or worse- have it entirely shut down.

As the two men prepared their tools for work, he told his foreman, Osmel Garcia, Sanchez as much. However, his concerns fell on deaf ears. Sanchez was a typical *campesino* in that he was as apolitical as they came. In the peasant's eye, life was simply about earning enough of a wage to support his family, while staying below any governmental radar. Live your life and don't make waves was his basic philosophy.

Once everything was in place, they hauled the crate to the photography alcove. This nook was lined with black felt and had a couple of high-wattage lamps mounted on floor stands. Along the back wall was a table that was also covered with the black material. Lying against the floor was a black-and-white meter stick, divided by color into 10 centimeter segments. The stone fragments of the broken sarcophagus were removed and set on the floor.

Juarez explained the procedure to Sanchez, hoping that it might motivate him and his men on the excavation if he understood the importance of the work. With a slightly bemused look on his face, the foreman nodded with understanding. *I'm not an idiota, you child,* he thought. *I fully comprehend all that we are doing, I just don't care all that much. But I'll humor you just for the paycheck.*

The excavation camera was taken from the leather satchel and screwed onto the tripod. Then each stone piece was placed on the covered table behind the meter stick and photographed. The shots were all bracketed above and below the precise reading of the light meter, so that all of the nuances of light, dark and shadow might be captured. Then the best image would be chosen and used. In between the photographing of each stone, the table had to be brushed off from dirt and debris.

"*Senor Profesor,*" Sanchez asked. "Why haven't we cleaned the stones before taking their picture? It would save time and effort."

"A very good question Osmel." The archaeologist got a sense that he was actually getting through to the man. "There is a phrase that we use in archaeology, its Latin- *In Situ*. It simply means 'in place.' That's why we took pictures of the stones before moving them. If they turn out to be really important, then we have a recording that is indisputable. If we move the stones before measuring and imaging, then it's our word against someone else's who doesn't want to believe what we've found. Pictures don't lie. But we take this another step in the laboratory- where we are now. We photograph everything as it came from the ground- dirty and unclean. Then, *amigo,* we go back into the lab and clean everything as thoroughly as possible and re-shoot the objects. That might give us an idea of how they looked when they were first used. Does that make sense?"

The worker looked at the young man with a slightly renewed appraisal. *Perhaps he's not so wet behind the ears,* he thought. "I truly see, *senor,* and I appreciate the chance to be told about the methods that you use. It makes a lot of sense. It is like my neighbor trying to sell his car. He takes a picture of it just off the street, dusty and dirty. Then he cleans and polishes it until it shines, like from the dealer. It will sell better, without a doubt." Sanchez smiled, finished putting the stones back in the crate, and lugged it to the lab tables on the other side of the area.

"Now we clean." Juarez readied a liquid that was in a beaker. But it was no exotic chemical elixir for cleaning. "So here's what we are going to do. The stone is coated in spots with a calcium carbonate encrustation..."

"Wait, what does a lobster have to do with stone?" Sanchez was clearly confused.

The archaeologist laughed until tears flowed from his eyes. "No my friend, *not* a crustacean! An *encrustation* means that something has covered, stuck to the outside, of something. In this case, it is a mix of dust and salt that has become part of the surface of the stone, but is rock-hard as well. However, we're lucky. This type of material is easily dissolved by using an acid solution."

Sanchez' eyes grew as large as grapefruits and he quickly took two steps backward. "Don't worry, relax. We don't need to use dangerous acids that can harm us. We don't need to use rubber gloves and aprons to keep from accidentally splashing on us. We can use an everyday, mild acid wash found in citrus fruits. This liquid is nothing more than lemon juice. This will soften up the stuff."

"Then what?" he was clearly afraid.

"All we need to do after it has soaked in is to wait a few minutes, then use these wire brushes to scrub it all away. Because the underlying material is stone, the wire brush won't harm it. Then with a damp rag we wipe it down and see the stone as if it was just carved the day before."

Although still a bit leery, the foreman clearly was becoming more and more impressed with the younger man. Maybe schooling wasn't such a bad thing after all.

Outside the university building, Father Gonzalo strolled around in a leisurely fashion. He bought an ice from a street vendor, and walked to a bench under a large banyan. He sat down, apparently relishing his cold treat, seemingly without a care in the world. He acknowledged a couple of people who tipped their hats in deference to the priest. He grabbed up a copy of *Revista Carteles,* a weekly news magazine, and scanned through it. What he read disturbed him, although it didn't surprise him. It reported that 20 members of the Batista government owned numbered Swiss bank accounts; each with deposits of more than $1 million. No wonder the rebels under this lawyer fellow Castro and the Argentine Ernesto Guevara were gaining followers by the trainload.

The priest felt that it was no longer 'if' but 'when' a full-blown revolution would break out. And it seemed that America was doing everything in its power to continue to prop up the dictator Batista. It all came down to money. American companies had all but raped Cuba and Cubans in their greedy quest for more. Why, according to Batista's government itself, American firms made profits of $77 million from their Cuban investments, while employing little more than 1 percent of the country's population; and that was just in 1957 alone!

The priest was sickened at a new term just coming into fashion- 'corporate greed.' The capitalistic system had never trickled down to the island's citizens, only those in the employ of American firms. The magazine went on to report that, as the decade of the 1950's was nearing an end, American businesses owned 90% of Cuban mines, 80% of her public utilities, 50% of her railways, 40% of her sugar production and 25% of the banks. In other words, the U.S. owned Cuba- lock, stock and barrel of rum.

Just as he was about to put down the magazine, his eye caught one article that he found incredibly amusing. Just the previous week, one of the new gems of the hotel/entertainment industry had opened up in Havana. The stunning Hotel Riviera had cost $14 million to build. But everyday Cubans needn't worry about Batista's piggybank. It was almost completely paid for by the gangster Meyer Lansky and his organized crime syndicate. The story continued with the entertainment that was brought down from the States for the opening week. The main headliner in the *Copa* Room was a famous actress, Ginger Rogers. However, the article pointed out, Meyer Lansky was less than thrilled with her performance. According to 'unimpeachable sources' close to the crime boss, Rogers could 'wiggle her ass, but couldn't sing a goddamn note!'

Upon reading that, Father Gonzalo quickly crossed himself for reading a blasphemy, but smiled at the imagery it conjured up.

* * *

The wait was a bit longer than expected. Apparently the encrustation was more concentrated than thought at the outset. Juarez intensified the citric acid solution by adding more pure lemon juice with no water to dilute it. It still was harmless to the skin, but, if drunk, would be extremely tart, perhaps overly so for the taste buds. He ran the wire brush gently over the stone's surface and was rewarded with the start of flaking. He was sure that it was only a matter of time.

He told this to his foreman, and suggested that, should he have other things to do, perhaps now would be a good time to take off and attend to them. He also hinted that, should he desire, Sanchez could take the rest of the afternoon off with pay and simply return to the university the next morning. There would be no digging the following day- as the lab procedure took precedence for the short term.

Juarez went back to the stone fragment. What was becoming apparent was that carved imagery of crosses was in raised relief. However, the inscription portions were incised- cut into the flat stone surface. As a result, it would be a slower, more tedious process to remove the encrustation from the grooves. It had found its way in the cut lines, and literally filled every nook and crevice. So, in addition to the bubbling acidic action, once the carbonate had softened a bit, the archaeologist needed to go into each line with a dental pick, to try to 'pop out' the bits and pieces of material.

As he would discover the difficulty in this, his patience began to wear thin. *Santa Madre de Dios!,* he thought. *This is on the verge of being impossible!* But he kept at it. By the time that three quarters of an hour had elapsed, he was so frustrated that he threw his rag down in disgust, with his hands pressing against his lower back- trying to ease the stiffness that he felt there. In addition, while attempting to flake the bits out of the carving, all of the points on his three dental picks snapped off. There was only one alternative.

With mixed feelings, reluctance at leaving but a weary happiness at getting a break, he put on his light jacket and went out in the relative coolness of late afternoon. He would have a coffee, stroll around the campus, and then head over to his dentist's office. For it was during a teeth-cleaning that he got the idea of using old dental picks on excavations and in the labs. Their fine points made short work of clearing around artifacts on-site as well as gently cleaning difficult coverings of material on objects in the lab; such as the work he was involved in now.

As he exited the university building, Father Gonzalo caught sight of him as he began to cross the plaza. He quickly tossed the weekly magazine into the rubbish bin and started to follow the man. It was clear that he was in no hurry as he took a seat at a table outside the coffee bar situated on the perimeter of the small square. As he sat down, the Jesuit slowly strolled over. As luck would have it, all of the other few tables outdoors were taken. It was the perfect opportunity.

"*Hola senor, con su permiso,* with your permission, may I join you at the table. It's such a lovely day and I would hate to spoil it by drinking my coffee indoors. I believe that we met each other the day outside the university."

Juarez quickly got up. Although he wasn't a religious man, he had been taught from an early age that one paid respect to members of the clergy. "Of course, Padre, I remember. I would be happy to share the table and perhaps a bit of conversation as well."

Gonzalo smiled and took a seat. Things couldn't have happened any better. He could now gather all the information that he needed to find out what was so significant in the salvage excavation being carried out adjacent to the old cemetery. After all, when the archdiocese told him of the unexpected findings when the hotel foundation was being excavated, he felt it incumbent upon himself to ensure that no graves were desecrated, and all were treated with the utmost respect. Then, when he saw for himself from the hilltop, he knew that he had to have more information. And here, right in front of him, was that wealth of knowledge. With the proper prompting, he could get it out of him. After all, who better to trust with inadvertent secrets than a member of the Catholic clergy?

The two men both ordered from the waiter, and sat back in a slightly uncomfortable silence. It was as if neither knew how to start a conversation. Finally, the silence was broken with the arrival of the drinks.

"You know," the priest opened up, "my father used to always tell me that it took a hot drink to cool you off on a hot day. I laughed at him for saying this more than once. Until one day I finally tried it. And you know, it's true!" He started chuckling, then burst out into full laughter. The young man joined in.

"My name is Ernesto, Ernesto Soto Juarez. I work at the university as a lecturer and archaeologist." The ice was broken and the two men entered into an amiable conversation.

They discussed life in Santa Clara, the role of the church in everyday Cubans' lives, the role of the church in Santa Clara in particular. Then, the padre deftly morphed into a conversation about the expansion of the new university, and the budding archaeology program. Juarez shifted into his 'lecturing mode' and talked with a great deal of passion about the program in general. He saw it as an opportunity to get in the good graces of the Church, and maybe cultivate a substantial donor as well. After all, the history of the church on the island was integral to the history of the island itself. Who knows, as the American actor Humphrey Bogart would say in his movie, 'this could be the start of a beautiful friendship.'

"*Lo siento Padre,* I'm really sorry to bend your ear like this. Sometimes I get carried away in my love for the past." Ernesto gave a rueful smile. Father Gonzalo patted his arm and assured him that he was not bored in the least. In fact, he urged the young man to explain what his current project was all about. Just as he supposed, the archaeologist almost leaped out of his chair, he became so animated about his current research. He went on to describe in tremendous detail the casino project adjacent to the Santa Clara Hotel.

As the priest listened intently, he couldn't believe his luck. He took it as a grand sign from God Himself, silently giving thanks. He would find out exactly what was going on without having to resort to any kind of illicit activity. This young scholar was handing it to him on a platter- voluntarily. But he would have to carefully word his questions in order to get entirely within the good graces of the university employee. He certainly didn't want to 'spook' him and have him shut down.

So, as was well taught in his courses on pastoral care, Gonzalo gently probed, offered understanding, professed interest in the way that good clergy nurture their flocks. Without knowing it, Juarez was lulled by this approach and gave out all the details that he knew up until now. And as the conversation was directed by the priest, the clergyman guided 'his sheep' as he wished- and that was to get him to offer an invitation. It came, as if out of nowhere.

"You know *Padre*, the Church may be interested in what I may be on the verge of discovering. Apparently the plat map of the Santa Clara Cemetery wasn't accurately detailed and drawn up. And when it was moved nearly a century ago, a burial section that wasn't recorded at all is what I'm examining. And if it wasn't for that casino, well, it really is a mixed blessing isn't it. Although the sin of gambling is the motivation for the construction, we'd never have discovered these burials. And isn't it the Christian thing to do, once we've examined the burials, to have them re-buried with the grace of God in sanctified ground- like the newer cemetery of the Church?"

"I am in full accord with your interpretation my son. If it isn't outside of protocol, could I see what you have unearthed and what procedures you are carrying out to further try to identify the material?" The priest showed a mild interest although internally he was jumping for joy. What better way to discover what was going on than be invited!

The two men finished their coffees, with the Father insisting that he pay the bill. They then walked around the square back to the university building and descended into the lab facility. The faculty member proudly showed the cleric around the facility, remarking with some pride that much of the equipment was state-of-the-art gear. Without bragging, he stated that it was mostly due to grant-writing on his part. The priest congratulated him, and, although he was very anxious to see what was going on with the material from the site, didn't push. He certainly didn't want to give away the extreme curiosity of his higher-ups in Havana. The funny thing was, he had no real idea why they were so interested as well. *Ah well, at least I'm just a few moments from finding out*, he thought.

"And what do we have on this table here?" Gonzalo asked. "It looks like some sort of tombstone."

"You're close," replied the archaeologist. "It's actually a fragment of a lid from a stone sarcophagus. Here, if you look closely, you can see that there is a definite edge carved along one side, with the opposing side gently rounded- that would be the top of the cover. In addition, along the 'rim' if you will, there seems to be some sort of carving that is heavily masked by the calcium carbonate encrustations…."

"Hold on, I'm not a scientist." The priest interrupted Juarez. "Can you explain to me in simple, plain language that a mere servant of God could easily understand." He laughed in a self-deprecating way.

With that thought in mind, the young scholar explained thoroughly, patiently, about the nature of how things got deposited on surfaces, and how they just as easily bonded to the stone. In other words, some materials simply couldn't be washed off with plain water, but needed to be dissolved. The Father took it all in, and readily understood the lay-person's explanation of it all, and smiled with his new knowledge.

"But here's where things get really complicated for me now. I have tried to remove the deposit with a mild acid, in this case, lemon juice. But it's proven to be as stubborn as a mule. I have increased the acidity, using straight lemon juice this last round. But some of it, deep in the incised grooves, fails to be budged. I would try to use physical force, trying to flake it out with these dental picks I have, but run the risk of damaging the stone as well. It is really important, because along this edge here, as you can see, there is evidence of an inscription- not just symbols."

This caught Father Gonzalo's attention and he bent over to look at the edge in question more closely. It was difficult, as it was still in the lemon juice bath in a metal tub. The lemon juice was cloudy and one could barely make out the stone surface. But clearly there were carved lines. As he peered intently, he thought that he could make out a line or two that looked like an upright and tilted cross-piece of a cross. Then there were some letters. But maybe his eyes were playing tricks.

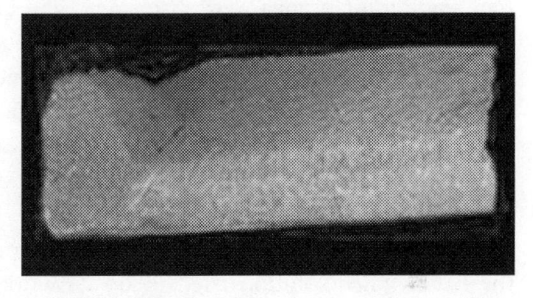

"I will let it soak in the solution for a few hours; it won't harm the stone in the least. Then maybe the sediment will more readily dissolve off the surface. I then can gently use a wire brush to clean and, if necessary, use the picks cautiously. I'm excited about what may be the result."

"I see your excitement and must confess, it is contagious. Please keep me informed."

"I will Padre, rest assured."

With that, the priest looked at his watch and remarked at how fast time went when something of tremendous interest was in front of you. He begged his leave and the archaeologist walked him upstairs and out into the late afternoon in sleepy Santa Clara. The two shook hands and promised to be in touch.

* * *

Father Gonzalo walked back to the *Catedral de Santa Clara de Asis*, went to his room and pondered his next move. He had been told by the Archdiocese in Havana to report what he discovered, and they would be the ones to initiate action should it be warranted. *Should he inform them now, at this point, or wait until the lab cleaning was done,* he wondered. He poured himself a glass of water and sat down in his armchair. It had been a long day, and he dozed a bit. When he awoke, he saw that the sun had nearly completed its downward journey. Although torn between the lure of scientific discovery and his vows to the Church, the Jesuit felt that this ultimate test came down to his faith.

The end result was that he hurriedly composed a short telegram, walked over to the post office, and had it sent out to the *Archdiocese of San Cristobal de la Habana*. In it, he outlined the finds that were made during the course of excavating the footings for the casino next to the hotel. In addition, he noted that some tomb stones were discovered and badly broken. They apparently had come from a previously unmarked extension of the old cemetery; because what had been known was transferred to the new location on the outskirts of town prior to construction. He requested guidance, and hoped that he would hear from the archbishop as soon as possible, with the grace of God.

With nothing left to do, he returned to the Cathedral to have his supper and celebrate evening mass.

Meanwhile, Ernesto went out for a bite and a beer, biding his time while the lemon juice solution tried to do its work. He walked a few blocks to *Avenida San Miguel* and the *El Castillo*. He opted for the pork and *congri*, the traditional black beans and rice. Outside, a couple of street musicians played traditional tunes, and he thoroughly enjoyed the respite. Any rational person would have waited until the next morning to check on the progress of the stone bath, but Juarez was impatient. So after the meal, he went back to the lab before heading home.

Once in the basement, he drained the lemon juice solution from the tub and, with a rubber hose, washed down the stone fragment. Having done that, he gently took his wire brush and ran it over the surface. Nothing. He then took one of the dental picks and tried to flake off some of the encrustation. Nothing. His frustration mounting, the archaeologist walked back upstairs to his small office. He pulled a volume down off the bookshelf and flipped through the pages. It was a treatise on removal of debris from archaeological artifacts. None of the suggested remedies seemed to be viable. They were either too drastic of measures, and he ran the risk of damaging the stone; or they were as conservative as the method that he had chosen- which proved ineffective.

He supposed that the only solution was to contact the University of Havana and see what the 'bigshots' at the main land grant educational institution might suggest. Although he was afraid that he would be seen as a failure, and diminish in stature with the main university, he felt that if he thoroughly documented his work they would see that he had diligently tried everything possible. Perhaps they would even respect his attempt and applaud him for his efforts. He then sat down and composed a report outlining his work and requesting assistance.

This took him the better part of the evening, and he eventually fell onto his bed around 11 that night. At first light, he would make sure that the report with the photographs was on the university vehicle that was making the three-times-a-week trip to Havana.

* * *

The following morning, Father Gonzalo prepared himself to hear confessions, as it was his day in the rotation. But his mind was elsewhere. He couldn't stop thinking about the stone sarcophagus and the encrusted inscription. Even with it uncleaned, he distinctly thought that he saw not a cross but a Star of David. He had gone over it again and again, coming up with the same conclusion. But could his eyes have played tricks on him? This he would need to reconfirm by going back to the university. As soon as the hour was up, he would head over there and visit with Prof. Juarez.

Across town, Ernesto had spent a fitful night as well. He wasn't used to coming home so late, and then 'bringing' his work home with him. He had an uneasy sleep, riddled with dreams about the dead, disturbing the dead, re-burying the dead. He was not superstitious, nor was he 'super'-religious. Nevertheless, he was troubled by the discoveries. On top of that, he was troubled that he was having so much trouble with the cleaning of the inscribed stone fragment. *Who did it belong to? Why can't I get the deposit to loosen and flake off? Am I doing things correctly?* And finally, he thought, *Am I cut out for this job?* As soon as he thought it, he dismissed the idea out of hand. His training had been solid, and so had the salvage excavation that he was called upon to carry out. In addition, he had done absolutely everything by the book to dissolve the material on the stone. It was just bad luck that it was so difficult. He would succeed in the long run, given time.

With his envelope safely placed on the university vehicle, he watched it head to the Havana. Perhaps he would get some answers in the next few days. Juarez turned and went back inside the building and down to the lab. He hoped that the strengthened, overnight bath had been a success. However, when he rinsed the stone, not a single flake of debris washed down into the sink. And there was no further luck with the dental tool or wire brush. He sighed, sat back, and opened his thermos. While drinking his coffee he pondered the next step. The only conclusion that he could draw was to wait patiently for a reply from the main university. There was one thing that he could do, though. He could go 'old school' in terms of recording and documenting, and do a rubbing of the stone surface. Just maybe he could see something on a transfer that couldn't been seen in the photos that he took. At least it would give him something to do.

The archaeologist finished his drink, and, feeling a bit more optimistic, set out for the stationery store a couple of blocks away. There he would pick up some tracing paper and charcoal, in preparation to make a rubbing. It was funny, he thought, that this exercise was exactly the same that he had done as a high school student years earlier. The social studies teacher took the class on a field trip to the local cemetery. There, the students made rubbings of tombstones, as part of their Cuban history class. Each student picked a tombstone, made a rubbing, and was to research the person in the city or church archives. They then would report their discoveries at a school assembly; hoping to re-create a part of their town's local history. At the time it was somewhat interesting, but, more importantly, it got them out of school for a couple of days!

Just as he was crossing the *Plaza Mayor* he encountered Father Gonzalo. He waved and altered course to greet him.

"*Hola Padre, Com'esta?*" The two shook hands. "It's great coincidence to see you this fine day."

The priest smiled warmly, offering his greeting as well. He inquired as to where the younger man was heading. When told of the lack of progress with the lemon juice bath, he looked dejected. However, the rubbing attempt perked him up. Since he had some free time he inquired as to whether he might be of some assistance. The archaeologist was delighted at this turn of events. He enjoyed the Father's company, and truly didn't want to spend more time alone in the basement. The two of them went over to the shop, purchased the needed materials, and returned to the lab.

Once there, Ernesto showed the Jesuit that the stone was still in the same state. Father Gonzalo examined it closely. He clearly saw that the condition was unchanged. He also saw that his supposition might have been correct. The faintest of lines at the start of the inscription were not necessarily those of a tilted cross; but rather were closer to the image of a completely straight six-pointed star- the Star of David used by the Jewish community. To him, this meant that the annex to the cemetery may not have been an annex of the Catholic Cemetery of Santa Clara in use centuries ago, but it *may* have been the Jewish Cemetery for the small community, *next to,* abutting, the other cemetery. If that was the case, then the remains should be moved to the new Jewish Cemetery on the other side of town.

He kept his interpretation to himself. He simply didn't know how to proceed. At this moment in time, with no clear definitions, the best action seemed to be no action. Both men were awaiting communication from their superiors. So for the time being....

Gonzalo bid farewell to the archeologist and returned to the cathedral. Ernesto, got on with the rubbing, and all was on hold. The priest took the long way back. He wanted to enjoy the feel of the sun on his face, he wanted to drive the thoughts about death as far as possible from his mind. The coffee shop beckoned, and he complied. He sat down at the same table that he had shared with Ernesto Soto Juarez just the other day, and watched the school children as they went home for lunch. The joyful, carefree lives of the young lifted his spirits as he sat back and drank. He would take his time.

* * *

Back at the cathedral, the Father passed by the office on his way to his room. The part-time secretary called out to him as he went by, requesting that he stop in. There was a telegram from none other than Manuel Arteaga y Betancourt, the Archbishop in Havana. It was short and to the point. The instructions were as clear as they could be.

FROM: His Holiness Manuel Arteaga y Betancourt, Archdiocese of Havana

TO: Father Gonzalo, S.J.- Santa Clara

God's blessings upon you. With regard to the situation in Santa Clara, consider this telex to be authorization from the Archdiocese, with the validation of the Cuban Government, to take possession of any human remains from the hotel building site and, with dignity and respect, relocate them to the new Catholic Cemetery. Do this with all due haste for the eternal rest of the deceased.

Yours in Christ,
Most Reverend Manuel Arteaga, Vuestra Senoria

The priest was taken aback by the speed with which the Church was acting on this. He thought that at least it would take a few days of bureaucratic paperwork to put things in motion. Apparently not. He was afraid that the archaeologist, with the backing of the university, might push back on this- to gain a bit of time in order to complete their research and testing. Maybe a visit to the Santa Clara mayor's office would help smooth the way. He certainly hoped so, for he didn't enjoy any type of confrontation. It just wasn't in his nature.

And then, what to do about the nagging suspicion that centered on the so far illegible stone inscription? *Was it really a Jewish sarcophagus? And, if so, how do I carry out the Archbishop's wishes?* The thoughts kept swirling around as he carefully folded the telegram and put it in the folds of his hassock. He smiled at the secretary as he turned and left; careful to thank her with a calmness that he certainly didn't feel.

XII

Havana, the present

DAWN BROKE OVER the Havana Harbor to the east of the *Nacional*, and I watched from the room that I shared with Errol Flynn as the sun peeked through the rapidly dissipating clouds. It had been a restless night; I couldn't help but think of all the dead ends that Berto and I were encountering in our quest to find out more about the intrepid explorer. Today, we were to go to the *Patronato* to see if they had any further information that could shed light on Columbus' true identity. I quickly dressed, headed down for breakfast. Even though I ate a leisurely meal, with the prerequisite three cups of coffee now, I was still afraid that I would be way early. I knew that the guide's hours were, oh, just a couple off from my routine. I mean that, when he's not guiding, he begins the day two hours later than me; but on the other end he stays up and can drink coffee (or other libations) with his friends to a much later time in the evening.

I opted to take a short stroll out the back of the hotel. I bounded up the stairs from the basement restaurant and into the lobby. The concierge was just changing out the display placard that announced the evening's entertainment lineup in *La Parisien*. It said, '*Su major noche en la Habana!*'- 'Your best night in Havana!' I had seen the cabaret show once, and I don't think that the advertisement was overstated. The music, the dance, the showgirls, all hearkened back to a by-gone day and age. It was a real throwback to 'the open Cuba' of the late 1950s when the island was a wide-eyed playground for the rich and famous.

From there, I swung to my left and through the double doors toward the patio. I stepped across the stone inset that read 'Hotel Nacional, 1930' and into the well protected patio and lawn. The architects had done a great job in their design, as the H-shaped hotel wings to the rear protected the guests from wind on three sides. The air was cool, crisp and, at this early hour, lacking the build-up of humidity. I sauntered over to the northern edge and the low retaining wall, and peered down at the *Malecon*. In spite of the hour, cars and buses were already zipping along in both directions. Fishermen stood or sat on the seawall and cast their lines into the breaking surf at the base of the cliff. I thought that it was such a shame that Americans had been denied this spot of beauty for over half a century. But, according to my sources, that was all about to change. I walked a bit to the east and west, watching the rising sun across the Straits of Florida, breathing in the clean air. I glanced at my watch and saw that I still had a couple of more minutes. However, the calm was suddenly replaced by the start-up putt-putt-putt of a lawnmower, as the groundskeepers began their daily ritual of keeping the grass perfectly manicured, the shrubs ideally trimmed. It felt that you were walking on exclusive country club fairways. So, reverie shattered, I retraced my steps and headed through the lobby to the main entry. The bell captain snapped to attention and crisply greeted me, while holding the door. Down the steps I went, and then out to the drive to wait for my friend. I stepped from the curb as it rounded the corner and headed down the entry road.

With a fist bump we greeted each other and I sat back in the 'plush vinyl' as we headed out.

"But where's Yoli?" I asked.

"She's got to check in to see her father. He's had a couple of physical problems, and she promised to visit on the way to meet us. I suggested to her that she come to the *Patronato* straightaway from her father's place. It's actually very close to the family house. It only is a matter of timing. I gave her an approximate time." Berto was always one step ahead of the rest of the world.

We maneuvered to *Calle I* in the *Vedado* District. Our destination was just a couple of blocks off of *Avenida de los Presidentes*. The president of the congregation, Adela Dworkin, was to meet with us. Also waiting in the lobby behind a pair of exquisite doors with raised bronze reliefs of the 12 tribes of ancient Israel was the diminutive Yoli. Looking at the two women as they stood side by side, I got a sense that, between them, *anything* could be accomplished. The air that they projected was one of formidability and resolve. Yoli whispered something in Adela's ear, and both pointed at us and laughed.

"*Que?*" Berto asked. "What's so bloody funny?" Neither woman answered, but both just kept on laughing. "So maybe someday *we'll* know," he said to me pointedly. With all of the ice broken, we got down to matters at hand.

Although we were both familiar with the Bet Shalom Synagogue, Ms. Dworkin felt it incumbent on her role as president to fill us in with background. Berto and I looked at each other with bemused smiles and allowed her to continue.

"Our temple is the largest in Havana, built in 1957 just prior to the revolution. At that time, there were 15,000 Cuban Jews --- ten times the present Jewish population. By the 1990s, our synagogue had deteriorated due to a lack of funds. Windows were broken. Birds were nesting above the pulpit. Today, this 300-seat synagogue that you witness has been restored with the help of friends in the United States, Canada and other countries. It reopened in May of 2000." She clearly loved the congregation and discussing her Jewish heritage.

I asked her to go on. Before she did, she asked if we would like a coffee. Both of us nodded our appreciation for the gesture. When it came, she continued.

"Connected to the Beth Shalom is the *Patronato*, which functions as our Havana Jewish community center. The Patronato features a full library, with an impressive collection of Jewish books, including many texts in Yiddish. After all, many of our ancestors were of a European background. And you know, for a long period of time in the early part of the 20th Century, we were all called *Polackos*, Poles- the natives thought that the only European Jews were Polish Jews. And, no matter how hard we tried to educate them, the nickname stuck with us until after the 2nd World War. *Lo Siento*, I'm really sorry to digress like that."

She continued on. "The library is a popular source of reference and education for Jews throughout the island. Adjacent we have a computer classroom with the highly prized internet access. The religious school has scores of students, from pre-school through Confirmation Class. Since there is no rabbi present in Cuba, it is up to the young adults to conduct Shabbat services; which are vibrant and well attended."

I inquired about the pharmacy, between bites of a delicious almond cookie. Adela beamed with pride. "The *Patronato* complex also boasts a pharmacy, where the B'nai B'rith Cuban Jewish Relief Project and other supporters try to keep the shelves well stocked with antibiotics, vitamins, prescription and over-the-counter medications, as well as medical supplies. It is mainly through the contributions brought here by foreigners that we are able to maintain a supply that keeps our heads just above water, as you say. As you know, the Government pharmacies are usually sparse. Dr. Rosa Behar administers the pharmacy and distributes these important supplies to the Jewish communities throughout the island when we have a surplus. As you are also aware, Cuba is color and religion-blind. At least, on paper." She smiled, this time a bit ruefully.

"We are all too familiar with best intentions," I said. "However, this I do know. I see young people walking the streets wearing a *kippah*, a skullcap, and no Cubans think anything of it. Cuban Jews are treated equally alongside all other Cubans. A reflection of this is how you all run your pharmacy. From my understanding, it is open to everyone in the neighborhood, not just Jews."

"It truly is a pharmacy for the people. And for this, the local population is grateful." The president was gracious and humble. "But please, have another almond cookie." A Jewish mother is a Jewish mother is a Jewish mother.... But that didn't stop me, Yoli or Berto.

* * *

After our delightful visit and refreshments, we offered our thanks and 'good-byes' and left the synagogue. Unfortunately, we came away with no added information about Columbus or his whereabouts. The only things that might help would be to go to the Orthodox synagogue of Adath Israel in *Habana Vieja* and then the *Guanabacoa* Cemetery on the east edge of Havana, and see what records might remain there.

"So why are we stopping at the synagogue?" Yoli asked as we got to the car.

"The records for the cemeteries, no matter how incomplete, were divided between the congregational archives and the cemetery office itself. Why? I have no idea." It was another Cuban mystery to all of us.

We hit the *Malecon* and then headed along the west edge of the harbor, going past much of the old city to the southern end. Berto found a 'valet' for his car, and we then walked the few blocks to the corner of *Picota* and *Acosta* streets. It was a quick visit. The solitary gentleman sitting there in one of the pews was old beyond years. Apparently he whiled away his days, contemplating God and his remaining time here. He knew of no records, nor did he know of anyone who knew of the records as well. The small nondescript office was locked and there was no sign that it had been opened for days. For us, it was back to the car and the tunnel that would take us under the harbor and to the east side.

The tunnel begins at the *Paseo de Prado* in Old Havana. It was built between 1957 and 1958 by the French company, *Societé de Grand Travaux de Marseille*. It is 733m long and 12m below the harbor level. As we approached, we entered the tunnel under the watchful eye of the Cuban patriot, Máximo Gómez, whose bronze statue guards the entry. Once through the tunnel, we were in the area of the *Morro* Castle. What would have been an hour-long trip before the tunnel had been reduced to minutes. From here, we got onto the relatively new *Via Monumental*, a freeway of sorts. Berto breezed through an abandoned toll booth arcade, and headed to the area along the coast adjacent to the village and stadium facility that Cuba built for the Pan American Games in 1991.

Fidel Castro said, *"The Pan American Games are an international commitment our country undertook. It is a sacred promise we must honor. We are a country of honor."* However, given the state of affairs in the early 90s, with the collapse of the Soviet Union and, with it, the subsequent collapse of Cuba's economy, the achievement was far from being the success Fidel envisioned. Mud became the dominant landscape element in the East Havana sports complex, which included the stadium, pools, velodrome and tennis center. And it still is. Poor craftsmanship, augmented with poor building materials, led to the disaster. Water from numerous leaks slopped across the basement levels of the stadium. There were no toilet seats in bathrooms at the athletes' village or locker rooms in the arenas. The metal roof of the pool complex already had been patched by the time the first event was held. Concrete work in the stadium was rough. The whole project has an air of planned obsolescence, with the decay that began August 19, the day the Games came to an end. But in the end, 679 U.S. athletes broke the ice and participated.

As we drove past, Yoli mentioned that her father had been one of the workers on the complex.

"You know, everyone in the older generation was still optimistic about the nature of the communist dream. Fidel asked *everyone* to chip in and volunteer their time after their regular workday in order to see this vision of the Pan American games become a reality. He also knew that it would be somewhat of a slap in the face to George Bush's America- a kind of Communist success story. My father came here at five every evening and worked for 4 more hours a day; with no pay, only a small meal offered. This went on for several months." Tears filled her eyes.

She went on. "I still think that his emphysema originated with the constant breathing in of concrete dust and asbestos fibers on the construction site."

Berto and I offered our sympathy, but also he tried to reassure her that the illness could be a result of a wide variety of things, including genetics- and not to dwell on it. I glared at Berto. My glance said to him, '*That was definitely the wrong thing to say!*' She sat back in the rear seat and was quiet for the remainder of the ride, until we reached the junction that would lead us to the *Via Blanca*, and *Guanabacoa*.

As we entered the outskirts of the town, we passed through the *La Jata* neighborhood. Yoli perked up a bit.

"This is where my father's family came from! Back then, as he told me, it was all farmland waaaayyyyy outside the city." She perked up as she explained.

"But we're only six miles from the eastern edge of Havana," I said.

"But in the 1950s, this was waaaaayyyyyy outside," she reiterated. We all laughed at this.

Berto made his way through the area, and, on its fringe, was the Jewish Cemetery. It was built on land that previously was the *Finca el Aguacate*, the Avocado Farm.

The land was then bought by the Jewish community of Havana in 1906. They laid it out in typical Jewish tradition. Enclosed by a privacy wall, just inside the gate was the small office and adjoining room for washing the deceased. On the outside wall of the building, there was a working faucet to allow visitors to wash their hands upon leaving. Space was available for over 1600 graves, and today most of them had been used.

I remarked to Berto and Yoli that it was a sad state of affairs when the life of a community is all too often reflected in its cemeteries. This was the case for the Jewish community in many places throughout the world. Cuba was no exception. With a vibrant population of 15,000 in the late 1950s, it had now dwindled to under 1500 today. This was mostly due to the revolution, and voluntary exile of the Jewish community which was an integral part of the upper class elite of Cuba. They stood to lose it all with the coming of communism, and therefore sought to take as much with them as they could while they could.

The *Guanabacoa* had tombstones engraved in Yiddish, Ladino, Hebrew and Spanish; all bearing testimony to a way of life long past that included immigrants, rabbis, businessmen and war veterans. These veterans came from World War II and the Korean War most recently. However, there was even a Jewish veteran who came to Cuba to fight in the country's 1895 war of independence as well.

According to Jewish tradition, from this location in the world, the stone were all aligned on an east/west orientation; in other words, towards Jerusalem. In addition to the Jewish nature of the inscriptions, many also had the letters 'EPD' inscribed as well. I was unfamiliar with this and asked the two Cubans.

"That is an abbreviation for *en paz desonse*," Yoli answered. "It simply means 'Rest in Peace.'"

Berto and I put on *kippot*, skullcaps, as we entered. Yoli found a handkerchief and bobby-pinned it in place.

Inside and to the left, on one of the main avenues just by the enclosure, could be seen the earliest Latin American memorial to the Holocaust- erected in March, 1947. We walked over to it as our first stop.

Yoli translated the inscription- *"Honoring their memory in this place are buried several bars of soap made from Hebrew human fat, part of the six million victims of Nazi barbarism that occurred in the twentieth century. Peace to their remains."*

"That's quite a sobering statement," she said.

As we stared silently, the caretaker of the cemetery came toward us down the path. He had been alerted to our presence by one of the street urchins who saw us drive up. We quickly explained that we would like to view the registry, because we were seeking information for the Office of the City Historian in Havana. It was a stretch of the truth, but serviceable. Out here, in *Guanabacoa*, the mere mention of an important official was enough to get total cooperation. The wizened gentleman, who looked as if he could have been employed here at the time of Columbus, was gracious enough to let us into the office, show us the leather-cracked, heavy, dusty volumes, and then discretely withdraw to let us work unfettered. He merely asked for us to give a shout once done and outside of the cemetery grounds. He felt that we shouldn't disrupt 'his guests', as he put it.

Before we got to the books, we took a brief walk around the wall-enclosed compound. What struck us immediately was the level of what appeared to be recent vandalism. It was somewhat surprising, and definitely disturbing. Berto quickly walked back to the gate and called out to the caretaker, who, in his slow, deliberate pace, hadn't gotten more than a dozen or yards from the entry. Yoli and I caught up to the two of them within a few moments. As the old man got his breath back, Berto asked about the desecrations.

"*Senor*, it is a tragedy, but what can an old man do? I live a couple of miles away, down this road. And even if I lived here in a cottage right next door, what can I do as an old man?"

"But who is responsible? We have respect for our own, regardless of their faith!" My Cuban friend was beginning to get angry. I grasped his upper arm from behind and gave a warning squeeze. It wouldn't do to alienate this old man and, by extension, his community. Plus, he was right- what could he do anyway. Berto relented a bit, his harsh tone giving way to a saddened timbre. He asked again in a gentler tone. The caretaker responded.

"*Senor*, I do not know who did these things, but I do know the circumstances. These tomb defilers were definitely not purely Catholic in spirit. It has to do with the blending of religion with some of our African ancestors. We do have in *Guanabacoa* a large population of these *hibridos*. These people mix a blend of Catholicism and African religious rituals. They are called *Regla de Palo Monte*. It is an extraordinarily secret religion, *si*?" He turned toward Berto for verification. He nodded imperceptibly for the man to go on.

"They believe in two things over all- The veneration of the spirits of the ancestors, and the belief in natural and earth powers. They fill vessels with sacred earth, sticks (*palos*), human remains, bones and other items and believe that it will appease the gods. Because this cemetery is relatively distant, and that Jews were part of the first covenant with our God, their bones should be holier than others. They feel that keeping them in their house shrines means that they can ward off the 'evil eye' of the Devil." The warder hurriedly crossed himself at mentioning that 'name.'

He went on. "Many of our police are members of this religion and so they 'support' this activity by responding to the vandalism very slowly- if at all. I am truly sorry for this, but I can do nothing. If I push, they will punish me." He bowed his head and turned back toward home. A few steps later, he paused and glanced back over his shoulder.

"God will take revenge for the souls of the *Judios*, He will make sure of that."

We watched him go for a couple of more minutes, and then re-entered the complex.

After nearly an hour, we were exhausted. Berto and Yoli had scanned through two volumes each, dating back to the first creation of the cemetery. Although it was a start-of-the-20th Century complex, there were a few graves that were transferred here from other places. Yoli noted that there were several re-interred graves that came from Santa Clara. A couple were very old. This gave her an idea.

"You know, the Santa Clara Jewish Community's origins can be documented as being much older than the 'modern' Havana Jewish Community. We know of the island's Jews during Spanish rule, and that there was a gap for quite a while. But in the central highlands, the lineage seems to be less broken. I think that we should head there, to Santa Clara."

Berto chimed in. "We all know the president of the current Jewish Community there, David Tacher, and I think that he'd be more than happy to see us, and explore the possibilities out there. We needn't inform him of our quest precisely, but see as we progress how much is warranted to tell. And, if we get somewhere, I for one would be happy to fill him in."

We agreed to this plan. As we exited *Guanabacoa*, we used the faucet to wash our hands as was the custom. As we walked out of the cemetery, I lagged a bit behind, offering up a prayer for those and hoping that the spate of desecrations might come to an end.

By the time I was done, the caretaker had been summoned, and locked the wrought-iron gate behind us. With a nod, he slowly began his journey home. I looked back at the tired, but proud-looking portal that led to the next stop on the journey for Jewish souls. We piled into the car and headed back to Havana. I've rarely been in Berto's car when it was so quiet.

XIII

Havana to Santa Clara and back, 1795

*F*ATHER MANUELO SUDDENLY realized that he had just passed the point of no return. The newly created sarcophagus of the great explorer, Cristobal Colon, now contained the remains of an unknown peasant from the island, a couple of hundred years old. A thought crossed his mind, and he started to laugh- but then caught himself. "He's not a couple of hundred years old, but he sure looks like it!" This irreverent thought eased the pent-up tension that flowed throughout his body. Soon, it will all be over.

Dawn was breaking in a short while, and the old sarcophagus and the second, wooden coffin needed to be gone by first light when morning prayers were to be said over the hero of Spain before transfer to the crypt beneath the cathedral. Manuelo silently drew back the bolt that shuttered the small side door and went outside. Sleeping in the bed of the cart was the mute, covered by a horse blanket. The Jesuit Priest gently roused the man without startling him. He crudely signed for him to follow back inside the church.

Once inside, he indicated that together they were to move the plain casket to the wagon. It took just a few minutes, since the scant remains that were left were so fragmentary the box was actually quite light. They slid it onto the wagon bed and covered it with the blanket. The more difficult task was bringing Colon's old stone coffin out to the wagon as well.

A wooden dolly that was used to bring in wine casks was leaning up against the wall. The men brought it in with them, and rolled it to just under the table with the coffin. Then, with great exertion, were able to slide the stone onto the bed of the trolley. Both men wiped themselves with a towel and took some deep breaths. They then, as quietly as possible, took it outside and to the cart. From there, they heaved and pushed and slid it up a couple of planks that they used to create a ramp. Finally, it was up onto the wagon bed.

In the wagon was a cask of wine. With that also placed beneath a tarpaulin, the lumpy items could not be recognized for what they were- as long as no one flipped the blanket back and away.

The mute was told to remain with the cart and not let anyone near it. Father Manuelo would come back as soon as the new sarcophagus had been blessed, and moved into the crypt. He rightly assumed that the main pomp and circumstance would be the following Sunday after Mass, when the crypt would be officially blessed and sealed.

Only an hour had passed by the time all was accomplished. The burial was completed and the Cathedral was getting back into its regular rhythms. Archbishop Alexandro would preside over the official interment, and Manuelo decided that he would ask for a few days leave of absence 'to visit relatives' in Santa Clara. He was certain that his request would be granted.

As the crypt was temporarily sealed, the priest confronted the Archbishop.

"Begging your Holiness' pardon…" he started.

"Yes, Father, what, pray, can I be of assistance with?" Archbishop Alexandro turned to look at the cleric. He seemed to be lost in thought, and Manuelo decided to be bold and come right out with it.

"I have just received word from my family in Santa Clara that one of my cousins, who I was very close to, has taken seriously ill. They're not sure of the outcome, and are sufficiently worried to request that I come visit. No, no- don't take it wrong your Holiness. They didn't come to ask me to prepare to perform Last Rites or anything that drastic. Just that my presence might aid in hastening his recovery. You know. I have worked diligently on the nobleman Colon's transfer, may he rest in eternal peace. And now, since he is interred, and you will be presiding over the official ceremony this coming Sabbath day… well…. I thought that…"

The Archbishop smiled warmly, if not a bit distractedly. He placed his hand on the Jesuit priest's shoulder.

"Yes, yes, Father, by all means. Give comfort to your family, enjoy your time together. I will pray for the speedy recovery of your relative. Take your time and return when you feel that it is appropriate. Vaya con Dios, Padre."

And with that, he turned and walked away. Manuelo dared to breathe in deeply for the first time in what seemed like an eternity. He hastened to his room and packed a small valise, including his stole and vial of Holy Water. In the kitchen he grabbed a large wedge of cheese, length of sausage and a couple of loaves of bread. He filled his flask with wine, and then filled a second one with water. Then he went out to the waiting wagon and the mute attendant. The order given, the two of them set off down the cobbled street and headed south and east, around the harbor. Once on the other side of the harbor, they would head almost due southeast to the province of Santa Clara, and its capital city. It would be a long, two day journey.

* * *

They spent the first evening on the road at a small community called Cuatro Esquinas. It meant 'Four Corners.' However, the only corners that Manuelo saw were at the intersection of the road to Santa Clara and a crossing that led north to the village of Banos de Elguea and the Atlantic Ocean's Strait of Florida. Even though there were maybe two dozen residents, the priest and servant chose to camp out about a kilometer away- away from prying eyes. After all, a fully loaded wagon from Havana was not an everyday occurrence in the highlands.

Rising at first light, the men re-kindled the previous evening's banked fire, and brewed some coffee. They ate some bread and cheese, kicked some dirt and extinguished the fire, and rode into the sunrise. By the time most of the field hands had begun their work, the two had put the hamlet several kilometers behind them.

As the sun rose higher and the temperature climbed, the Jesuit was really happy that there was nothing more than bone fragments and dust in the coffin. Had there been any human remains, the stench in this heat would have been horrific. He silently crossed himself and closed his eyes. With the servant at the reins, he could afford to shut out the world around them, secure that the other man would, without question, follow the orders entrusted to him- for the Church's sake. At least this is what the priest had signed to him at the very beginning.

By dusk, in the near distance, they could just faintly make out the few twinkling oil lamps that marked the first houses of the Santa Clara community. But again, as was the case the previous evening, they opted to pull the wagon off the road and into a copse of trees; all but hidden from view should any late evening travelers pass by. The Father signed the other man that this evening they would not build a fire. He indicated that it was because, so near the town, there might be highwaymen and robbers. It wasn't safe, so they would make do with the remaining cheese, sausage and bread. Washing it down with wine or water would suffice. As always, the mute went about his tasks with no complaint. And for this, just prior to bedding down, Manuelo went over to the fellow, placed his hands on the servant's head, and offered up a prayer on his behalf. The mute looked up and smiled, took the priest's hands, and kissed them. He then returned to his bedroll and fell into a deep sleep.

* * *

When the two awoke, they knew that the goal of the journey was at hand. This time, Father Manuelo manned the reins to drive into Santa Clara. Being somewhat unfamiliar with the community, he paused for a moment just inside the city limits and inquired as to the location of the house of the leader of the small Jewish community. The laborer that he stopped to ask looked at him as if he was an idiot. He shook his head and merely pointed in the direction of the town square; and then indicated to go beyond that. As they approached the square, he stopped once more. This time, handed a shopkeeper the paper with the name of the stonemason written on it. This time, the response was much friendlier. With a smile, the man explained that the quarryman could be found just a mere two blocks away. That would be their first stop.

Once there, he asked after the cousin of the Havana mason, and was directed to the dust-choked back room. A smallish man covered in stone-dust was busy appraising a block of granite. He turned and saw the priest and the servant. He quickly wiped his hands on his apron and extended one of them in greeting. After introductions were made, the Jesuit drew forth the note from the fold of his cassock, and offered it to the mason. The man took it, and held it up to the light coming from one of the windows. But he grasped a hold of it upside down. Then, after a moment, he confessed to being unable to read and handed it back.

Father Manuelo smiled benignly and gently took it. It wasn't a surprise that the man couldn't read. However, this in no way diminished his talent as a mason. While the note was read, a smile creased the face of the artisan. He interrupted and said that he had the greatest respect for his cousin, and that the two of them had learned their trade together as apprentices. The Father remarked that if the man was taught the same as his cousin, then he would be held in high esteem anywhere in Cuba. This appeased him greatly, and he no longer was as wary as when the two from Havana entered his shop. He bade them to sit, and called out to his boy to bring in some refreshment.

While waiting, the reading of the note was completed, and the mason was quick to agree to what was asked of him by his big-city relative. He also agreed to box up the major fragments and give them back to the father, for he understood the significance of what had been asked of him. The priest was to return the next day.

Having concluded their business, Manuelo and the servant then went to seek out the elders of the small Jewish community. About a mile away from the square, they drew up to a nondescript building that was unadorned save for a small six-pointed star that sat unobtrusively on a window ledge. Sitting on the broad covered porch that ran the full width of the structure were two old men. As the wagon came to a halt, they stood silently.

The mute servant sat in on the driver's bench while the priest got down and walked up the steps of the building. He greeted the two, and politely asked if he could speak with the leader of the community. Both smiled and pointed at each other, then they started to laugh. When asked what was so funny, they replied that everything in the Jewish community was done via 'committee,' and that they were the committee because no one else wanted to be a part of it. They roared with delight, and Father Manuelo couldn't help but join them. As the laughter died down, they asked what they could do for the man of God.

He explained the dilemma, that someone of the Jewish community of Havana had died, and, according to other members, the man had relatives in Santa Clara. But no one knew who it might be. The Havana community didn't have the means to bring the deceased all the way to the town. The good Father said that, as children of Abraham also, it was incumbent upon him to do a good deed for the Jews.

The old men asked some pertinent questions, and came to the conclusion that there were no Santa Clarans with recently deceased family members from Havana. However, even though the mystery deepened, they did agree to provide a burial plot and bury the remains in the Jewish cemetery adjacent to the Catholic Cemetery just outside of town. The Jesuit conveyed this via his simple signing to the servant, who nodded in understanding. The burial would be the following day.

That evening, they went round to the stone mason's. He had done as promised, and had broken up the stone sarcophagus with no further question. Manuelo and the mute took the largest fragments, and reverently placed them in the wood coffin on the back of the cart. The Father then nailed the lid shut and said a small prayer.

The next day came and went. The coffin was buried according to Jewish custom with little fanfare. A small plaque identified it simply as "Ben Adam," a son of Adam, since he was not known.

Father Manuelo and his companion returned to Havana and the Cathedral. Neither spoke a word of their journey to anyone- taking the secret to their graves years down the road.

XIV

Santa Clara, 1957

AFTER SPENDING A couple of hours in meditation, Father Gonzalo came to the conclusion that there was no way to get around the edict from His Holiness in Havana. But since no one knew of his suspicions about the old stone sarcophagus, he could do what he wished. He decided that, erring on the side of conservative action, he would figure a way to get the stones into the Jewish cemetery of Santa Clara. If it was a Jewish inscription, then the fragments would have a proper home. If it was a Jewish inscription, then they would be a sacrilege if buried in the Catholic cemetery. To him, this would be a win/win and no one would be the wiser.

The following morning, he walked down to the university in order to find the archaeologist Juarez. On the way, he stopped at his favorite coffee shop off the plaza to get 'fortified.' To him, this meant significantly more than just coffee. He sat down outside and the waiter approached.

"*Buen dia Padre, Com'esta?*" he asked.

"*Muy bueno camarero, y usted?* You know, today is a filled day and I need a lot of energy. I think that I'll have a *pastelito* - the one with guava filling." He smiled.

"It's a great choice; they just came out of the oven not a handful of minutes ago. They are puffed to be as light as clouds, filled to almost bursting with the sweet filling! But you know, the cream cheese ones are just as good. How about if I bring you one of those as well- on the house?" he winked at the priest and hurried off to the kitchen.

Gonzalo sat back and savored the day, satisfied that he had made the right decision. The coffee and pastry came, simply heightening his pleasure. He would enjoy every moment and every crumb. When done, he stood and brushed a few flakes from his cassock, left a couple of pesos on the table, with a good tip, and proceeded to the campus.

As he approached the building from the side, he saw the university jeep and the man that he assumed was a dig crewman loading it up with equipment.

"*Por favor*, are you Osmel Garcia Sanchez? With the salvage excavation at the new construction site?" he asked. "I think that we met before, forgive me, my memory is not what it used to be."

"Yes, I am *El Profesor* recently made me the foreman for the site." It was clear that he was proud of his title. "I do remember you. For what can I be of assistance, Padre?"

He told him that the professor was in the lab, not in his office. The Jesuit priest thanked him and went inside and downstairs. He found Ernesto Soto Juarez finishing up on his checklist for things to take out to the dig site. He only had a couple of more days work before the city officials wished to turn the site back to the construction company. He felt harried, and clearly looked it. He turned just as the Father entered the facility.

"*Buen dia Padre,*" he wiped his hands on his shirttail and held it out. Father Gonzalo grasped it with both of his and smiled warmly. He had come to like this young man and his dedication to his work. He would try to make this as painless as possible.

"I'm afraid that I have some unfortunate news, Netto. I got this telegram from Havana yesterday, and wanted to share it with you as soon as possible. But in thinking it over, I feel that you'll agree that it's the best for the soul of whoever the departed might be." He handed the flimsy over to the archaeologist- who took it with a bit of apprehension.

> FROM: His Holiness Manuel Arteaga y Betancourt, Archdiocese of Havana
>
> TO: Father Gonzalo, S.J.- Santa Clara
>
> God's blessings upon you. With regard to the situation in Santa Clara, consider this telex to be authorization from the Archdiocese, with the validation of the Cuban Government, to take possession of any human remains from the hotel building site and, with dignity and respect, relocate them to the new Catholic Cemetery. Do this with all due haste for the eternal rest of the deceased.
>
> Yours in Christ,
> *Most Reverend Manuel Arteaga,* Vuestra Senoria

He read it through once, then again. Although the news was disappointing, it said nothing about entirely shutting down the project. Granted, he couldn't work directly on the material, but he did have photographs. In addition, there were still the other artifacts to catalog and analyze- the pottery sherds, a couple of metal fragments, even a coin or two. And after all, it was a salvage project to begin with, and nothing was *in situ*, still in place as interred decades, or a century or so ago. He breathed out a bit heavily and, with a sigh, handed the paper back to Father Gonzalo. The look on his face said it all.

"*Padre*, I am disappointed. But, you know, as a secondary excavation, who knows what the construction men destroyed. We were lucky to find what we did. The only thing that I'm saddened about is not being able to fully clean and identify the stone sarcophagus fragments. I'll just work off the pictures. I will still get to publish a short article. And that is as important for my career. I'm glad that I was called upon to carry this out."

Gonzalo put a hand on the man's shoulder and gave it a brief squeeze. "I know that you'll go far in your field. Your tenacity is a tribute to the academic world. Your scholarship techniques are advanced, and will put you at the head of your department in a few years- I'm sure of it." The words meant a great deal to Juarez, and, emotionally, he stumbled over his words of thanks.

"I guess that you'll be taking the material to the cemetery soon?" he asked.

"Yes, but first I need to secure transportation after speaking with the caretaker there. You know, we need to locate a plot, etc, etc, etc...." he held out his hands and mimicked the gabbing of city officials. Netto laughed at this. He offered his jeep for the day after next, since now he assumed that, once given official word based on this telegram, he would just need a couple of days to shut the site down. The priest accepted with thanks. He too would need the time to finalize arrangements on his end.

They parted ways, promising to meet up two days hence. The priest headed off to the Cathedral's office for the cemetery, Juarez to meet his foreman, Osmel, and give him the unfortunate news. The only good thing was that now, he could continue on with the other dig at an old hacienda outside of town that he had put on hold for this salvage work. He could then offer up 'the silver lining' to Osmel by inviting him to become foreman of that project instead.

* * *

Father Gonzalo walked swiftly to the *Catedral de Santa Clara de Asis,* and entered the Diocesan offices, where one of the attendants was in charge of caretaking the cemetery. By that, it was meant to be a 'paper' caretaking. There were laborers on the grounds themselves whose sole task was tending the plots, digging the graves and overseeing the physical aspect of funerals.

"*Hola,* Alfredo." He extended his hand and the secretary shook it. He even attempted to kiss it, but Gonzalo gently lifted the man who had hastily knelt before him.

"My friend, that's only reserved for the Archbishop, you know that." He smiled warmly.

"*Si Padre,* but I'm just practicing for the day that you become the spiritual leader of Santa Clara." Alfredo replied with a wink and a smile. The two men understood that this was a private running joke between the two of them. But secretly, both hoped that it would someday come to be the truth.

"I have a job for us, but it is a very important one that needs a certain degree of, shall we say, discretion." The priest went on to explain what needed to be done. After he finished, the office employee pulled out his handkerchief and wiped his brow.

"*Oye padre,* I hear you. It is a bit unusual. However, I fully understand what you're talking about. The *peces grandes,* those big fish, in Havana haven't seen what you saw- or thought you saw, or saw what you thought..." he started to laugh.

Gonzalo joined in, the tension of the moment had dissolved. So now the next step was to speak with the Jews of Santa Clara- numbering only about

20 now. Jose Tzarfati was the elder, and since there was no synagogue nor community center any longer, the 'congregants' would meet in the salon of his house for prayer and meeting. Because they had dealings before on a spiritual level, he was familiar with the house on *Calle Buen Viaje*. But in order not to alarm the man by simply showing up on his doorstep, he sent Alfredo over there with a note asking if it wasn't a problem if he could stop over the following day to discuss a 'spiritual matter.' The priest hastily scribbled on a piece of paper, wrote Tzarfati's name on the envelope, and sealed it. He gave it to Alfredo, and told him that after he delivered it he could just take the rest of the day off and go home. The man smiled at this, wished the Father a good blessed rest of the day, and left the Cathedral with a smile on his face, humming a tune. Perhaps he could be home before the children got out of school, and he and his wife could have a coffee with some peace and quiet.

* * *

The following morning, after prayers and concluding his turn at the Confessional, Father Gonzalo went to the administrative office. There was no one present, but stuffed in his mail cubby was a hand lettered envelope. He tore it open and discovered a note from Jose Tzarfati. The man would be happy to meet with the priest, whenever he would like. Tzarfati went on to extend his hospitality by offering coffee and refreshment at his home whenever the meeting would occur.

Gonzalo smiled at this. The more he found out about the Jews, the more he respected them and their spiritual identity. He had long felt that the near-universal condemnation by the Catholic Church for killing Jesus was a 19 century-old overreaction to events that had spiraled out of control in the 1st Century. Even in seminary school he had his doubts about some Church doctrine. For example, he questioned the trumped up, over expanded role that the Jews had ascribed to them in the imprisonment and death of Jesus.

When the young seminarian had returned home on school holidays, he increasingly expressed his frustrations and doubts with his father. Although his father never went past the 5th year of school, never went even to high school, Gonzalo believed that he was wiser than any other man he knew. It was 'life-learning' as the older man had said time and again. That was more important than a piece of paper. He recalled the conversation with him about Jesus, and the Jews. His father reminded him that Jesus was Jewish also, and lamented the fact that the Church forgot that whenever it was convenient for the Christians. But he explained it in such a way that Gonzalo never forgot it, and tried to instill that sense of all being children of Abraham.

Son, this is how an uneducated man sees things. What I say may not be exactly what the Church teaches, but, to me, it is what God believes. Just as all our main roads lead to the Plaza Mayor, any road that a person takes to God is the right road. As long as you get to God is what matters. I have long felt that we are all brothers in believing, but on different paths.

Do you remember your first years at university, before the seminary? You went away to Havana, the big city. Small village life was stifling and so, well, simple, that you wanted to try everything. I saw that you experienced so much, and I saw that for a while you turned your back on us 'peasants.' Your mother and I were hurt terribly but we let you explore the world.

Then, you discovered your path. No, not necessarily going to Seminary, but your path in life as a human. I remember that it took you three years to return home and ask me to go to the taberna for a beer. I smile every time I have that memory. We talked as men openly for the first time and I realized something so very important. One of the most difficult things that we do is make the change from parent-child relationship to adult-adult relationship. When we are all children, as we explore the world, we sometimes lash out at our parents for their old, dated ways of doing things, and living their lives. Here's an example: I grew up with the wonderful music of Ernesto Lecuona that became standards for us, like Malaguena. You, on the other hand, liked this crazy Norte Americano, Elvis... What I'm trying to say is that we all have our own paths, but finally you accepted that the path that your mother and I took was right for us; and we finally accepted the path that you took...for you. It takes wise people to accept the idea that, as long as we respect each other and don't harm each other, we can get along together.

I guess, son, is that I don't think that the Church and the Jews have begun the process of acting like adults with each other. The Church is still lashing out at its 'parent' after almost two thousand years. Its time we grew up and looked at Jews as cousins, not someone to be hated.

A warmth washed over the Jesuit as he fondly recalled his father. Tears welled up in his eyes, and he longed to visit with both parents again. Unfortunately they were called to God a couple of years earlier. He wiped away the tears and sat back. As he composed himself, he smiled at another thought. When that comparison of all being children of Abraham came to him, he was reminded that it was precisely what Jose Tzarfati had said in his note. Abraham and Sara opened their tent to anyone passing by in the desert. They knew that the offer of hospitality was essential in the wilderness, for anyone unfamiliar could easily die there. Offering food and shelter was one of the blessings that God conferred on the righteous- helping those in need. Tzarfati the Jew was making the same offering to Gonzalo the Catholic, and it was not lost on the priest.

By this time, the workers at the Cathedral had begun to filter in and pick up their assignments for the day. Gonzalo stopped the groundskeeper for a moment.

"*Hola* Alfredo!" He smiled and shook the laborer's hand. He explained that he had gotten a reply from Jose Tzarfati, and wanted the church employee to take a follow-up note to the other man. He hastily scribbled a reply, then, as an afterthought, signed it *Shalom* with his name and sealed the envelope. The priest handed it to the man and told him to wait for a reply and return with it immediately. He walked outside the Cathedral, sat on a bench in the plaza, soaked up some sun and looked forward to meeting the head of the Jewish community.

* * *

Jose Tzarfati was waiting on the steps to his house, and smiled as Father Gonzalo approached. It had taken half the day, but finally the message-exchanges were successful in setting up a meeting. He grasped the Father by both shoulders and gave him a hug, welcoming him to his house. The two entered and walked through the hall, flanked by rooms, to another doorway that led to an interior atrium. Typical of all houses in warm climates, and also typical of security concerns, there were no windows on the front wall of the row house, nor the back wall as well. The fewer the breaches in the exterior walls, the less chance of break-in. So, you may ask, how does the owner get light and air inside? Simple, the house would be designed like the ancient Roman atrium- with an open courtyard in the center, surrounded by the rooms that opened onto it. All the light and air came from 'within.' In addition, a cistern or fountain would bubble up as well. This supplied the house with an internal water supply.

Tzarfati's courtyard was decorated in a traditional style, ceramic tiles lined both the floors and the walls. The quiet burbling of water in the center fountain enhanced the serene setting. At this time of afternoon, the shade was a welcome necessity. A small wrought-iron table surrounded by chairs already had a pitcher of lemonade and, surprisingly, the padre's favorite *pastilitos*. Apparently someone had done a bit of interrogation of Alfredo in the earlier memo exchange! Gonzalo smiled at this and took one of the pastries and waved it at Jose.

"You've been spying on me! You've seen me at the coffee shop on the Plaza Mayor!" He laughed as he said that. The head of the Jewish community simply gave a half-bow and smiled. "But first, we need to bless this bounty." Fully aware of the delicacy involved, the priest simply said, "Our Father, we are thankful for your bounty and grace, bringing your half-brothers in faith together." A nod of thanks by Tzarfati indicated his thanks for the ray of hope between faiths. The two chatted a bit about Santa Clara, the weather, and other issues of mutual concern within the community before getting down to the nature of the meeting.

Gonzalo explained what had occurred on the building site of the new casino, and the role of Ernesto Soto Juarez, the archaeologist at the university. He outlined the nature of the salvage dig and the finds. In addition, the priest was transparent about his suspicions regarding the fragmented stone ossuary; and that it indeed may have been one of a couple of Jewish burials in the grounds adjacent to, but not part of, the old Catholic Cemetery that was decommissioned when the hotel was built years earlier. He also explained that the Church had thought that it had removed all the graves and transferred them to the new cemetery location. Of course, the records they had only pertained to the Catholic grounds and not the Jewish cemetery immediately 'next door' so to speak.

"As you know, *Padre*, our existing cemetery is only a couple of decades old. It was founded only in 1932, with the first burial coming in July that year. Although now it is right on the fringe of town, in the small community *El Barrios Los Syrians*, just back then it was far outside the city. It never even had an actual street name associated with it- merely an extension of *Calle San Miguel*. The locals called it the Syrian Cemetery because of the community. That's kind of funny, they got it wrong like that. I guess we all look alike!" He smiled, then chuckled, then roared with laughter. It was infectious.

"And so now, the real name is *Cemetario Israeli De La Communidad Hebrea De Santa Clara*, the Israelite Cemetery of the Hebrew Community of Santa Clara. So what is it exactly that you are proposing? Yes, we had an old one as well, and we felt that we, too, had moved all of the graves in accordance to our tradition. But, as you so clearly indicate, it is possible, no, *probable*, that we might have missed a couple just as you did. After all, we're just human, eh?" Another chuckle.

The Catholic Priest felt that it was only proper to move the remains to a place within the Jewish cemetery. And, in a gesture of good will, offered the services of the stone mason he was familiar with (at the Church's expense) to build a small mausoleum for the remains.

With a look of surprise, and gratitude, Jose Tzarfati grasped both of the Jesuit's hands and pumped them up and down; then embraced him in an enormous bear-hug. As the two broke, tears welled up in the older Jew's eyes, he was unaccustomed to such compassion from the Catholic community.

In the meantime, while it would take almost a week for the task to be completed, the Father suggested that the stone fragments be brought to the small cemetery office and stored under a prayer shawl until they could be interred. Since, according to the Father, there were no human remains, this would be considered entirely legitimate within Jewish law. Then, with the small structure's completion, the sarcophagus stones could be placed inside, and whatever prayers were deemed correct could be read over them with the re-interment.

* * *

After the successful meeting, Father Gonzalo returned to the Cathedral and summoned the casket maker who had a contract with the Catholic Diocese in Santa Clara. He told the man that he would need a couple of plain wooden coffins. The explanation that he gave was that there were some remains discovered on the grounds of the new casino building site and, according to the Archdiocese in Havana, they were to be re-buried in the Catholic Cemetery. He showed the man the telegram from the Most Reverend Manuel Arteaga, the *Vuestra Senoria*, confirming the order.

With the promise of having the two caskets the following morning, Gonzalo hastily scribbled another note to Senor Tzarfati and had Alfredo deliver it by the end of the day. Within the week, as promised, a small, simple stone shrine, measuring a mere two x four meters, only a meter and a half high, was waiting in the empty far corner of the walled cemetery enclosure. Inscribed just under the pyramid-shaped pediment over the low entry, in Hebrew and Spanish, was the message- "To our unknown ancestors- *A nuestros padres desconosidos.*"

* * *

And before anyone knew it, the deed was done. A plain pine casket containing stone fragments that *might* have been part of an ancient Jewish sarcophagus now rested in the far corner of Santa Clara's Jewish cemetery. Another plain coffin with the simple inscription burned onto the lid, "unknown servant of God," was lowered into the ground in the Catholic cemetery, and no one was the wiser. Father Gonzalo felt at ease. He had done the bidding of the Archdiocese of Havana without alarm. The members of the Jewish community felt that 'one of theirs' had returned home. And finally, the archaeology department of the university concluded its salvage contract work with the city and excavations could continue on other projects in the Santa Clara province.

The priest smiled, crossed himself, and walked out of the church into the sunlight- his favorite coffee shop awaited.

XV

Guanabacoa to Havana to Santa Clara, the present

I WAS CLEARLY dejected, and apparently it showed. Both Berto and Yoli tried to cheer me up with light banter and dark chocolate. But neither was working, and for dark chocolate *not* to have an effect on me was an indication for Berto how serious the depression was. He decided that a slight diversion was necessary.

When we approached the junction to the tunnel highway, Berto continued past and headed north. I hadn't even noticed. I didn't even pay attention as he took *Avenida Jose Marti* across the *Cojimar* River. It was only when the small village of *Cojimar* was in our sights that I sat up in the back seat.

"*Que pasa amigo?* What are we doing here in *Cojimar?*" I was now fully alert. "Is there something here that I'm missing?"

"No, not at all. I just felt that the time was ripe for just a weeeeee bit of RnR!" He grinned that infectious grin of his, while Yoli turned in her seat, smiling as well, and grabbed my hand and gave it a squeeze.

"Its tea time somewhere in the world where the flag of the British Empire doesn't exist." He clearly was mixing his metaphors but who was I to question. As we got to within three blocks of the harbor area, the small shacks gave way to a little park with a gazebo in the middle of it. It stood just across the street from the compact 16th century fortress, *El Torreon*.

This very small fortress protecting the *Cojimar* harbor had a history that belied it miniscule size. I saw an opening with Berto, and I walked right in!

"What's that about the British Empire? Are you really forgetting this fortress? Don't you remember the command of *Luis Vicente de Velasco e Isla*? The British expedition against Cuba under Lord Albemarle landed here and attacked the fortress from its landward side. The fort fell when the British successfully mined one of its defensive walls."

"Aha, one of my favorite places among many favorite places," he said a bit sheepishly. And now I was smiling. We parked behind a '56 Chevy Bel Aire convertible, baby-blue with a cream ragtop that was down. Yoli waved at the driver. Apparently, every tour guide in Havana knew this man. His job in *Cojimar* was to drive to the fortress parking area every day, park and get tourists to snap some pictures with his 'baby.' The CUC tips were better than any regular salary. All he had to do was maintain the car in pristine condition- at least on the exterior.

Inside the gazebo of limestone was a life-sized bronze bust of The Old Man himself. The bronze bust has quite a story. He was so well respected, well-loved, by the small village of *Cojimar*, that the fishermen, as a tribute to the man, in 1962, donated the bronze for it from their boats —using propellers, cleats and other fixture pieces to be melted down.

The small harbor here was Hemingway's usual anchorage for the *Pilar*, and this was also the village where his fishing captain/friend, Gregorio Fuentes, lived. Together, the two of them would go out into the Florida Straits for a fun and booze-filled day, or that rare occasion when they would 'hunt' Nazi subs; then return to the small fishing port to continue with the fun and booze-filled day… on land. They would dock and walk over to *La Terraza de Cojimar* and, most of the time, drink themselves into oblivion (and then back). It was also here that, seated at what would become their enshrined private corner table overlooking the water, the stories that became the *Old Man and the Sea* had their origins. But there was one other matter of note as well; the birth of a beverage. Of course, it is named after the fabled sea captain- The Don Gregorio. It's Blue Curacao, maraschino cherry liqueur and rum. As I rule, I usually don't drink anything of a color that's not part of any alcoholic beverage color wheel- but this is an exception. It's absolutely delicious. But you need to beware, it certainly doesn't taste like you're getting a 'buzz' on, so mind your intake.

So after an hour's respite, we headed back to Havana. But Berto wasn't done with us in terms of RnR. We arrived in *Habana Vieja* just in time for dinner. And of course he had the perfect place to cap off a mini-Hemingway tour; the Ambos Mundos Hotel.

* * *

The Ambos Mundos is one of the epicenters of Hemingway's Havana. It was built in 1924 on a site that previously had been occupied by an old family house on the corner of *Calle Obisbo* and *Mercaderes* (Bishop and Merchants Streets). A five-storey structure, it was designed by Luis Wise Hernandez. Five years after it was built, a rooftop dining area and kitchen complex was added. This gave stunning views of the harbor from the top of the building. To enjoy a meal here, under the stars, was a delight for anyone.

After the usual '*proteksia*-parking' of Berto's car, we walked the few blocks from the *Plaza de San Francisco* along *Mercaderes* to the hotel and restaurant. We entered the angled entry, pausing to admire the signage of the hotel, and walked through the bar area and reception to the ancient, caged Otis Elevator.

"It certainly looks like the kind of bar that Papa would visit," I remarked. "But, on the other hand, it's too clean!" I was well aware that, for the tourist industry, the ground floor had been totally restored. In fact, the last time that I was here, an American-Canadian film crew was shooting scenes for a movie on Hemingway's life, appropriately called 'Papa.' It was fascinating to see all sorts of folks dressed to kill in 1940s fashion.

However, that's almost where the restoration ended. The rooftop restaurant/bar/dance floor had also been renovated and restored; again, for tourists. Regrettably, what was in between had never had the luxury-due in part to the many other hotels within a short walking distance from *Habana Vieja*. So how did I know? Unfortunately, I had spent a couple of nights here in the past.

Although my friends did their best to dissuade me at the time, I had wanted another 'Hemingway' experience under my belt. I have since kind of regretted it. The rooms remained identical to the heady days of the 1930s, 40s and 50s. There was no air conditioning, anemic paddle fans tried to stir the thick, humid air. Being right at the corner of two of the busiest streets in *Habana Vieja*, the noise could not be blocked out by the windows overlaid with wood shutters. And finally, anyone with high sensitivity to mold and mildew would have a terrible time- it's just the nature of the environment without modern amenities.

But as they say, on occasion, if Room 511 was good enough for the writer for nearly a decade until he bought *Finca Vigia*, then the hotel could be good enough for the ambience… once. But, with apologies to James Bond, once *was* enough!

We took the caged elevator up to the roof, 'guided' by one of the hotel staff who operated it. Yes, I said operated it. It's just part of the experience. We finally arrived, after two days (ok, I'm joking, but it did seem to take forever) and got ourselves a table. Of course, even before we sat down, the customary, complimentary *mojitos* magically appeared over our left shoulders. In addition, small bowls of olive oil and bread graced the table. Berto, Yoli and I dug in, since we hadn't eaten much all day. There was very little talk at first, as we lessened the hunger pangs within a few short minutes. Then we sat back and relaxed. Once the *mojitos* were gone, I ordered a round of *Cristal*, wanting to savor the slightly malty taste of the beer with the food.

The house band began to set up, as a couple of *San Cristobal* tour groups arrived for the evening. The bandleader came over to us and greeted us warmly. He knew all the guides from the agency, and me from my several visits. I pulled a couple of photos of the band from my previous visit from my shoulder bag and gave them to him. There were enough copies for all, and he thanked me profusely. I told him that it was my pleasure, and I looked forward to some good tunes later in the evening. He got up when the food arrived, to let us enjoy our meal in peace. It was just as expected, *ropas viejas* in a slightly tangy sauce, with *morros y christianos* on the side. Both were staples on the island, traditional and tasty.

As we completed our meal, the band completed its first 'song;' the ancient Chinese melody called 'tun-ing!' When I told that to Berto and Yoli, the groans could be heard all the way back to the *Nacional*, about three miles away. But they were smiling all the while as well. Then the rhythmic music kicked in. A couple of songs by the great artist Polo Montanez, from *Las Terrazas*, led off the first set. Well into the third song, from the room adjacent to the outdoors dining area, two lithe Cubans walked in. Juan Carlos and Jamila were the professional dancers contracted to *San Cristobal* Agency to entertain guests and try to teach them Salsa. Watching them glide across the dance floor was a treat. They moved with such fluidity, such grace. No human being had the right to be so agile- as if they didn't have a bone in their bodies. But watching them endure the agony of teaching two-left-footed tourists to ChaCha... well... priceless!

When you have a couple of *mojitos* inside you, you think that you can dance like Fred and Ginger. The tourists had a great time, and we had a great time watching them. The other guides from the groups came and joined us for coffee as well. The hours passed swiftly until Berto noted the time, and the fact that we were going to go to Santa Clara the following day.

We bade farewell to our friends, waving to the band and the Cuban dancers, and opted to walk down the five flights to ground level rather than wait for the lift. It was probably quicker anyway.

We proceeded down one flight, and paused for a moment. No, we weren't winded…yet! I just wanted to pay homage to Room 511. This rather small, nondescript chamber was home to Hemingway and his wife Martha Gelhorn for nearly a year until she 'went stir crazy' in that small room. Hemingway hosted scores of guests, drinking and smoking incessantly there. Finally, she put her foot down and they found *Finca Vigia;* which they first rented in 1939 and finally purchased in 1940 for $12,500.

Before the Cubans caught on to 'capitalistic notions,' the *Ambos Mundos* simply had a velvet rope across the eternally open door of the room, left exactly as it was when the Hemingways lived there, down to the small desk and portable typewriter. However, once President Obama allowed for 'people to people' missions, and interest swelled in everything 'Hemingway' on the island, the door was firmly shut; until a bell captain came to collect 2 CUC just to open the door for a peek!

I had seen the interior of the room in the 'pre-capitalist days,' so we certainly weren't going pay to do that again. It was just a 'moment of silent respect' thing for me. And besides, the mildew-laden air was oppressive- so down we continued to the final, open last flight of stairs leading to the lobby. The descending view was panoramic to say the least, and quite pleasant. The film crew had packed up and left, leaving the lobby and bar to patrons. If you closed your eyes for a moment, you could almost hear the great man holding forth with a cigar in one hand and *mojito* in the other.

* * *

The following morning, over *café con leche* and *pastilitos* at the *Nacional*, we planned our journey to the east central part of the island- Santa Clara. Berto had picked up Yoli, with their bags in the trunk of his car, and I had already checked out of Room 235. I told the clerk that Mr. Flynn would be staying, and he had a hearty laugh at that. He handed me my 'get out of jail free' card. At the *Nacional*, the only way that you got your luggage upon departure was if you had a 'check-out card' from Reception. This guaranteed that there were no non-paying 'escapees' from the hotel. Actually, it was an effective program. It also meant that no bags were inadvertently left behind from any tour group. I left my rollerbag at the Bell Captain's desk for the departure.

Downstairs, Berto and Yoli were already into it, but sort of ignoring the full-scale buffet. I couldn't figure it for the life of me. It was a sumptuous feast to say the least.

"You know, it might be *days* until we have the opportunity to eat this well again," I said as I headed to the hot food bar. The chef greeted me with a sincere smile and a rapidly whisked three-egg omelet with cheese, onion and mushroom. He started it as soon as he saw me enter the restaurant, knowing what I liked because of the many stays here over the past two years. I thanked him, my mouth already watering from the savory aroma. I grabbed a hard roll and cup of coffee and returned to our table. Just as I started to sit down, the other two got up.

"And *now*, after our 'introduction,' we can get to the heart of things!" Yoli looked very seriously at me. Berto burst out with his hearty laugh. A handful of Canadian tourists (how did I know? Try the multitude of 'Maple leaf' t-shirts) looked over at us as if there was a silent conduct to be followed while eating. We all looked back at them, and Yoli and I joined the laughter as well. One or two of the Canadians grinned, but kept right on eating.

As the pair returned with laden plates, I remarked, "Make nothing of them, they are still pissed because they haven't held on to the Stanley Cup for a decade or so!" Berto laughed at this as well. But Yoli, well, she hadn't a clue.

"Who's Stanley? And why would Canadians have his cup?" Her winter sports innocence was charming. But after all, it is Cuba. And winter sports were a rarity until the 1991 Pan American Games.

* * *

Breakfast finished, I grabbed my bag, turned in my 'escape card,' and we loaded up the car. With plenty of gas and a full complement of ration cards, we were set to head off to the east. Rationing is part of the Cuban notion of communal equality that translates into a system of food and other commodity distribution known as the *Libreta de Abastecimiento*, "the Supplies Booklet." It began in March, 1962 and was seen as a natural extension of the true communal nature of the nation as envisioned by Castro and his followers. The excesses and inequities characteristic of the Batista Regime were to be done away with once and for all. As a result, the universal health care (CastroCare!), education and welfare of the people 'from cradle to grave' became first and foremost the priority of the new government. Everyone was giddy with an optimism not seen on the island for over a decade.

Most items are distributed at the local Ration Store, or *bodega*, or, with meat and fish products, at the local *carnicería*. Other goods could be purchased with coupons in the *libreta*, such as cigarettes, cigars, matches and cooking fuels, and gasoline. The prices in the ration book were set about 20 times lower than the free market. The rationale by Castro's Cuba was that each and every citizen had to have guaranteed a minimum daily allowance of food, regardless of their economic status.

Regarding gas, although heavily subsidized by Chavez's Venezuela in the past, the cost was still exorbitant. The ration book allotted you 10 ½ gallons a month. That's a drop in the gas tank so to speak. It meant that Havanans rarely left the city. People needed to rely on public transportation- spotty at best. However, key jobs in the economy meant a couple of things. One was the perk of getting to drive a government car (and government gas). The other was a special allocation for your own car if you were in one of these positions. As a higher-up in the travel/tourism industry, Berto got an extra allocation should he choose to use his own vehicle. As for restrictions, on paper this was for business use. However, everyone, and I mean everyone, turned a blind eye to this, and all routinely used the allotment for all sorts of purposes. So the bottom line was that we had plenty of fuel and coupons for this journey.

Once again, the sun brilliantly reflected off the Florida Straits as we motored down the *Malecon* around the harbor to the *Autopista*, or National Highway. We picked it up just east of the city proper. The first leg of the run was from Havana to Santa Clara, finished in 1979. It ran about 267 km, and was built with 8 lanes from the capital until km 32; the rest with six lanes to Santa Clara. Beginning in 1990, this monumental work had to stop due to the drastic decline in Cuban trade with the socialist bloc and the USSR mainly because the fuel allotment to Cuba was reduced from thirteen million tons to four, forcing plans to readjust construction. In 2008 Cuba vowed to continue to build the National Highway, implementing a plan to add the three lanes missing in the stretch from Villa Clara, Sancti Spiritus, totaling 60 kilometers.

As we proceeded east, it was a surreal experience. Here you have, in stretches, a pristine superhighway- with 1940s and 50s cars tooling down it. I saw the way that the national highway system envisioned by Eisenhower probably looked in the early 1960s. There was probably as much (or as little) traffic as in those days as well. However, every once in a while, a lane ended, or was impassable, with piles of construction debris laying on it, overgrown with weeds. It was not as if this was modern-day construction. It was a sad sign of that immediate halt to construction in the early 90s.

We would pass old cars, newer cars, bicycles, and ox-drawn carts as well, as we barreled down the highway. There were scores of individuals standing patiently under bridge overpasses, out of the intense sun, looking for rides. In addition, there was something else not seen on freeways elsewhere; local farmers selling their goods to passers-by on the road. In one stretch, I saw a man with strings of onions and garlic. On another, there were cheese sellers. It was a veritable farmer's market out there. On occasion we saw people stop to purchase goods, but it was a hard sell when someone was driving by at a *blazing* 55 mph!

About two hours into our ride, Berto slowed down to make a rest stop. There was a small 'zoo' of sorts that took advantage of the prime location just off the highway. There were gift shops, food kiosks, penned 'critters' and, of course, con-men. The first thing that tourists saw as they exited the bus and entered through a trellised approach was a traditional 'carny-style huckster.' This fellow was the entrepreneur's entrepreneur! On a large table were laid out 10 small 'cottages' with doorways facing inward. In the center was another 'cottage' on a form of 'lazy Susan.' (And who was Susan, and why in the world was she called 'lazy'?) Anyway, this fellow, upon hearing the arrival of a tour bus, would rouse himself from his perpetual nap, and spring into action.

"*Ola senors y senoritas!* Welcome to my humble 'family' of small furry friends! This once is Esmeralda! She seems to be quite lost and wants to find her way back 'home' to her house. But which one is it? Will she go to house #5, or house #2? For only one CUC you can take a guess, and if she enters that house, you can win a prize! Come over and help my sweet Esmeralda to find her home!"

Some people were intrigued, some thought it funny, while a couple of 'do-gooders' from the good ole US of A whispered about animal abuse under their breath. Children, on the other hand, found it delightful! And of course how can a parent deny their sweet *niños?*

CUCs were plunked down on the table, and when the numbers were taken, our 'host' placed Esmeralda the Guinea Pig in the central house, and then spun the round table with a mighty heave! When it stopped, a wobbly Esmeralda exited the house on the disc and began to walk around the perimeter. (*I thought she was a bit tipsy, but of course I would be too if I were spun around at breakneck speed!*) A sniff here, a sniff there, finally she entered into one of the houses.

The 'spinner' clapped his hands with delight. "Well, it seems that Esmeralda found her way home, to *Numero Dos*! We have a winner!" With that, a little girl squealed with delight and jumped up and down. The man handed her a carved mahogany figurine of a dancer, engraved with *"Cuba"* along the hem of its skirt. She was thrilled, the parents smiled, and Esmeralda? Well, she most likely netted 7 CUCs for her owner, and a kibble to munch on.

After the brief respite, we all returned to the car. Yoli dashed ahead. On our way, I punched a number into my Cuban cell phone. Because of the U.S. embargo, no cell phone companies from the states can offer service on the island. As a result, I was given an ETECSA phone. It stands for *Empresa de Telecomunicaciones de Cuba S.A.* (In English, Telecommunications Company of Cuba) In a rare move of accommodation, in exchange for building the network, *Telecom Italia* was given a 27% ownership stake; an incredibly large percentage on the communist island. However, in his wisdom, Raul felt that only an outsider company could provide the infrastructure. He was right. Although expensive, it is a wonderfully reliable network.

"Allo David, *com 'esta?*" I got ahold of the Santa Clara Jewish community president just as he was walking out his door. I let him know that we were well on our way as we were entering Villa Clara Province. He was delighted and looked forward to seeing us. I mentioned the Los Caneyes Resort restaurant as a good place to meet. He agreed to see us in a couple of hours.

* * *

After the brief respite, we all returned to the car. Yoli dashed ahead.

"SHOTGUN!" Yoli screamed and dove into the front seat. I wondered to myself, *Where did she get that from?* But then I remembered about Cuban TV. 'Modern' network programming from the U.S. was banned, but reruns from old Hollywood were a staple of the Cuban diet. 1950s and 60s sitcoms were the rage. Many Cubans were extraordinarily well-versed in school-taught English, but learned their colloquialisms from the small screen.

I smiled and let her get settled up front. It allowed me to fulfill two essentials for the rest of the trip- catching a bit of a nap as I stretched out, and keeping me from continually being scared out of my wits as I watched the way that Berto navigated his beast around potholes and '58 Plymouths.

I cozied up to my jacket tucked under my head and was out like the proverbial light within moments.

It seemed that the subtle rhythms of the car stopped only minutes after departure. But as the engine was shut off, the now familiar 10-second rattle of the timing chain dying down, I heard Berto and Yoli prepare to get out, declaring that we had achieved our Santa Clara destination. I sat up and rubbed my eyes.

"Where are we?" I drowsily asked.

"It's time for lunch." Came Berto's reply. "We're at Los Caneyes." Located on the outskirts of town, this was a resort of sorts for Cubans, and a sometime stopover for tourists on a budget. However, as was the case with all government-owned establishments, it had a more than passable buffet and great ice cream!

The campus consisted of a couple of main buildings that fronted an enormous pool. The residential quarters were smaller buildings that ran around the rest of the perimeter of the public space/ pool complex.

We entered the dining room and were seated. After the customary *mojito* was placed in front of each of us, we made a modest toast to our expected success. Immediately after I had taken the first sip, Berto jumped up and made a beeline for the hot table that awaited. He apparently was hungrier than either I or Yoli imagined. As we sat back and laughed, he called from the buffet table and asked if we were waiting for an invitation. Neither of us had to be asked twice.

As we ate, I reviewed what I thought to be the best plan of attack. Before leaving Havana, I called the Comunidad Tikun Olam and spoke with the president, David Tacher. I had met him several times before, and he had spoken to the various groups that I had previously brought to the island. In addition, he had guided us to the Santa Clara Jewish community's cemetery.

Just as Berto was approaching the ice cream station in the Los Caneyes restaurant, David walked through the door.

With a broad smile on his face, he said, "Great! I'm just in time for the desert! I love ice cream!" He grasped my hands in a quick shake while hurriedly walking toward the stacked bowls. He greeted Berto, a longtime friend as well, and began scooping to his heart's content. A few nuts and whipped cream dollops later, he and Berto came back to the table and began to dig in.

"Nothing like it! Except for maybe Coppelia! *Tuercas de helados de chocolate y pino*, chocolate ice cream and pine nuts! Wow! Pass me that bottle of water please. Hmmmm, better. Sorry, but I missed lunch and you called and......"

"We get it, David. No need to apologize," Yoli smiled, that mile-wide gleam, lighting up the room. "Can I get you another bowl?" she slyly asked.

As David settled down a bit, actually breathing instead inhaling his ice cream, he grinned sheepishly and patted his stomach. "Enough is enough! I must watch myself."

"From your mouth to God's ears," I muttered under my breath- knowing that, in spite of his protests, there very well could be another assault on the dessert buffet table.

As he took his spoon for one more lap around the bowl, David lamented the state of the Santa Clara Jewish community. Called *Or Hadash*, his beloved community has dwindled to around 40 people. However, as he proudly announced, "they have the spirit of 400." With the dawn of the 21st century, his community became the recipient of substantial (for Cuba) funds from Jewish agencies around the world. This allowed the community to move into a new home, a new, although nondescript, center. At its opening, it was sorely lacking in Judaica, not even having an Ark for the sole Torah scroll. But, with the door opening just a crack to humanitarian and educationally oriented and licensed trips from the U.S., more funding was soon on its way. By 2012, enough money had been raised, in conjunction with other in-kind donations, to have a beautiful, elegant Ark shipped courtesy of the Canadian Jewish community. However, it lay boxed up, in pieces, for several months until finally it was built. Leftover money went to the refurbishing of the rooftop patio. One wall would be decorated with an extraordinary mosaic wall depicting Jerusalem and the Western Wall.

David was unapologetic in his fairly mild, but pointed, criticism of the world's Jewish community 'forgetting' about Cuba's Jews for decades until the new century. However, in the same breath he was also effusive in his praise for their efforts in recent years. All he needed to do was to point at the new center and its furnishings.

We all agreed somewhat with his assessment. But I still gently reminded him of all that American Jewry had done over the past decade. And all this in spite of some of the reactive paranoid measures of the government.

"Don't forget what happened to Alan Gross a few years ago. He was an American international development expert who was working in Cuba as a U.S. government contractor for the U.S. Agency for International Development (USAID) when he was arrested as a spy in 2009. He was prosecuted in 2011 after being accused of crimes against the Cuban state. He supposedly was bringing satellite phones and computer equipment to members of Cuba's Jewish community but, as alleged in a documentary by Saul Landau, Alan's objective involved setting up Cuban dissidents with a sophisticated satellite communication systems that would work through satellite phones and laptops that were untrackable and impenetrable. He served nearly five years of a fifteen-year prison sentence in Cuba. Gross's wife, Judy, after fighting to persuade the organized Jewish community to rally behind a humanitarian campaign to free her husband, publicly criticized President Obama and U.S. policy toward Cuba. On Dec 17, 2014, Gross was freed by the Cuban government. Gross departed Cuba on a U.S. government plane. He was released on humanitarian grounds by the Cuban government at the request of the United States.

Earlier in December, Pres. Obama said that 'The Cuban Government's release of Alan on humanitarian grounds would remove an impediment to more constructive relations between the United States and Cuba.' It's truly amazing how things work politically," I lamented.

At this, Berto, Yoli and David burst out laughing. A slightly tense moment had been diffused by… the truth, with lies, as Senator Al Franken of Minnesota put it in his popular 2014 book. I breathed a sigh of relief, I had stuck my foot in it, but successfully pulled it out with no apparent damage.

David stood up, "I want to swing by the cemetery to check up on things, if you can give me a lift."

"Funny that you should mention it," Yoli replied. "That's the main reason for our visit to Villa Clara! Funny how things work, eh?" She winked and we all laughed again as we made our way to the 'Berto-mobile.'

* * *

XVI

Santa Clara, the present

WE SLOWWWWWWLY DROVE through the back alleys of Santa Clara, guided by David Tacher. Even though we had all been to the cemetery before, its rather well hidden location remained a mystery to us even with our guide. But there was another reason for the slowness. The alleys were unpaved, rutted messes. Berto was scared to death of getting a puncture, or worse- having a stone chip jump up and 'bite' his baby; flawing its flawless finish. It took us about twice as long as a normal ride to get to there. And on top of that, once at the cemetery, Berto had to offer one of the local boys a bit of *proteccion* to watch over the car- protecting it from other kids, birds and other 'acts of God' not usually covered in any typical insurance policy (had he an insurance policy, that is!). In addition, he promised another couple of Cuban pesos to the kid if he would wipe it down from all the dust gathering on its once-gleaming finish. The boy gave him a look that hovered somewhere between admiration and disgust; admiring the car and its pedigree, disgusted that he might receive pesos instead of the more highly prized CUC. Nevertheless, a deal sealed with a formal handshake was still a deal.

The site, serving both of the Jewish communities of Santa Clara and Cienfuegos, had sprung up in the district known as *El Barrio Los Syrians*. With no actual street name, the location is an extension of *Calle San Miguel*. Founded

1932 with the first burial on July 10, 1932 and the last in 1986, the cemetery contained less than 100 burials.

We approached, walking the gauntlet of street urchins from the neighborhood. The dirt path led to an adobe *temenos* wall; enclosing this sacred precinct. The term came from ancient Greece, simply referring to a sacred enclosure. Religious communities world-wide had adopted the term. We found the caretaker, and borrowed a couple of *kippot*, skullcaps, from him. He led us inside after unlocking the gate. Immediately to the left, in a small garden-like area, was the Holocaust Memorial.

In 2004, the Memorial was dedicated by the community. There are 10 cobblestones making up the entry path which were brought from the Warsaw Ghetto. The cobblestones were donated by the U.S. Holocaust Museum.

The imagery is extraordinarily compelling. Created by the non-Jewish Cuban artist Waldo Garcia Mederes, etched barbed wire cuts diagonally across the black stone. Parallel lines symbolize the railroad tracks that brought refugees to the internment camps. The lines then lead to actual brass rails embedded in the earth at the base of the monument. It is a sobering monument that forces us to remember the horrors of war and humankind's inhumanity from time to time. But the ultimate feeling is one of eternal optimism and hope; with the Magen David, the Star of David, arcing into Heaven- offering a symbol of unity and oneness with a spiritual conviction that seems alien to Cuban philosophy.

The inscription reads-

> *"Mustios sobrevivientes,*
> *esculpinos en bronce*
> *la tenaz promesa judaica:*
> *recordar siempre*
> *y etonar melodías*
> *que sumen*
> *seis millones."*

"Survivors faded, sculpted in bronze the tenacious Jewish promise. Always remember and sing melodies that add up to six million."

I picked up a pitcher lying on the ground against the wall of the caretaker's hut. I filled it with water from the tap and walked over to a sole tamarisk tree, from the Galilee, fronting the memorial. Tradition dictated that the tree gets watered by visitors. The indelible connection between Cuba's Jews and Israel was strongly felt by all. A few moments of silent meditation ended, I began to explain to David the real purpose of our journey, and what now appeared to be the highly likely re-discovery of the remains of one of the most celebrated explorers that the western world had ever known.

* * *

Outside the gated entry, around the bend, just over 100 m down a narrow dirt road, a nondescript black Lada taxi pulled up. The fare got out and paid the driver. The cab then backed down around the bend and sped off in a cloud of red-brown dust. Immediately, the man was accosted by the street urchins of the neighborhood. He had come well-prepared. A few pens, hard-candy jawbreakers and Cuban baseball cards later, the small crowd dispersed with a wave of the hand and quiet words of *'no mas!'* The soft-spoken, yet forceful presence of the man impressed even the most hardened of these kids, who were trained not to accept 'no' for an answer until perhaps the 5th go-around. Not a single one of them suspected that this person was a man of God, on direct order from the Archdiocese of Havana, acting on direct order from the Vatican itself.

Father Alejandro positioned himself in a small copse of trees, about 50 m from the main road immediately outside the cemetery. He settled in for what might turn out to be a couple of hours, give or take. The priest leaned against the bole of a tree, unslung his backpack and drank greedily from a bottle of water. He certainly didn't need to worry about relieving himself as there were dozens of trees to choose from- secluded from any prying eyes. He then reached back and pulled out a heavily thumbed-through copy of Consuelo Varela's treatise on Colon, *Cristóbal Colón: Retrato de un hombre*. He had been through it at least a dozen times, but never got tired of the description of the man and his Godly mission.

The familiarity of the text meant that he didn't focus as acutely as he would have on a first reading. As a result, the heat and drone of insects in the distance lulled him gently to sleep. He began to nod off, and dreamt of better things in a world to come. The last thought he had was that he sorely wished that he had brought some chocolate to boost his energy and something stronger than water to drink...

* * *

Inside, after our respects had been paid to this stunning Holocaust Memorial, we summoned the caretaker from his small adobe office/tool shed. David thought it best to discuss things with the man, because of the long history that the 2 shared in a professional way. We all agreed and hung back just a few paces, as he delicately broached the subject at hand. For the longest time, the old man kept shaking his head 'no' with every question gently posed by the president of the Santa Clara Jewish community. It was clear that he wasn't making any headway at all. David came over to us, certainly exasperated over the difficult situation. Then I wondered out loud whether a small contribution to both the cemetery fund and generous tip of appreciation for the good work of the caretaker might smooth the way. In a universal, typical shrug of the shoulder gesture that said, 'it couldn't hurt,' I pulled 2 twenty-CUC notes from my pocket.

"Try these," I told David, and he returned and went into the building. A few minutes later, he poked his head out the doorway and motioned us all to come in. The wide-eyed caretaker was stuffing the notes into the pocket of his stained *guayabera* and pulling a dusty, cobwebbed ledger from one of the top shelves bolted into the back wall behind his small desk. He blew on it and a cloud of moldy dust headed out the glassless side window. At least it wasn't aimed toward us.

It must have been at least *folio* in size, but then that is all relative.

"Wow, that's one large book!" Yoli exclaimed. "What would that be called?"

I told her, and related that one of the earliest 'folio' works was the Gutenberg Bible of the mid-15th century. "It looks like the cover is in sheepskin," she went on. "So how did this size come around?" Her curiosity was piqued.

"It seems that it all went back to the sheep, as you correctly stated. Medieval books were the size they were because medieval sheep were the size *they* were. Remember, paper wasn't the original medium for document creation- at least not in Europe. Medieval books were made of parchment, which is a fancy word for sheepskin.

"So take your average sheep: skin it and trim off parts that encased the legs, and you get one gigantic sheet of parchment, way too big for most bookmaking purposes. But that's fine, because you can fold it in half and you'll get a huge but manageable pair of leaves (four pages counting front and back), which you can gather with a lot of other similarly sized leaves and make a *folio*-sized book. From there you can just imagine folding it again for *quarto*, and again for *octavo*, and so on."

"So it is the best, economical and practical use of hide, with little wastage! I totally get it," she said with a smile. "Does that mean that we have a realllllllllly old ledger on our hands here?" We all looked at each other while the caretaker just smiled- not comprehending a word that we had said.

We took a long look at it, and came to the conclusion that it indeed was an old volume. David and Berto both agreed that the script appeared to be written in the Castilian dialect, and could date as early as the 18th century, but they couldn't be certain. The ink was faded with age. The parchment was cracked and very brittle. In other words, no one would swear to it.

But David was doubtful. After all, he told us, the Santa Clara Cemetery was only founded in the 1932, and serviced both Santa Clara and the town of Cienfuegos. If this document was indeed that old, why was it here in a 'modern' Jewish cemetery?

"I have an idea." They looked at me in such a way that said *inquiring minds want to know...* "I *do* come up with an idea now and again!" I said somewhat indignantly.

I laid out my proposal to them. Some of my best connections regarding the Jewish world were in Israel, the Israeli Department of Antiquities and Museums, to be exact. One of the associate directors in the antiquities section was a dear friend, Kati Ben Ya'ir. She had helped me on numerous occasions with regard to other archaeological mysteries surrounding ancient Israel and the Jewish people. Her work regarding the 'rediscovery' of Israel's pharaoh and in bringing back to Israel 'lost' scrolls last seen in Nazi Germany endeared her to me in a wide variety of ways. Of course, her position in the museum system and world of archaeology in Israel was solidified as well. I explained all this to Yoli and Berto in the shadow cast behind the caretaker's hut by the setting sun. There were probably two hours of daylight left by now.

It would be impossible to get Kati over here to Cuba on such short notice. Although relations between the countries was cool, it was not as bad as the U.S. embargo and total lack of relations for decades, until the Obama Administration. Her position in IDAM was not just secured, but elevated to such a degree that she was almost indispensable for the tasks that fell under her purview. But I thought that I had an answer.

"Here's what I figure we can do. First, let's prevail upon the caretaker to 'borrow' the ledger for just one day. I'm certain that another 20 CUC will take care of that. Then, to the best of your combined abilities, you will scan the book and see what might jump out at you."

"I DON'T WANT ANYTHING JUMPING OUT AT ME!" Yoli hissed at me in a theatrical 'aside' voice.

Berto, David and I laughed, only to be cut off by fits of coughing and choking. "Nothing is going to bite you," Berto said to her. "It's just an idiom."

"Don't you dare call me an *idiom*!" She fumed at him.

"It's a figure of speech! Not an insult!" David implored. After all, his role as peacemaker in Santa Clara was well known, and he plied his trade now as best he could.

"Oh," she then said meekly, eyes cast downward. "I guess my English is reallllllly miserable, eh?" Tears started to well up.

I quickly tried to smooth things over. "Your English is great! Tremendous! Even I don't know all the colloquial phrases and expressions. How could anyone ever expect someone who didn't grow up with the language to follow them either?" I gave her a big hug and my kerchief, to wipe away the tears. We all laughed a bit at that and I continued.

"Okay, so if there are certain pages that jump, er, stand out to you, I will take a photo of them and then email them to Kati in Jerusalem. She'll know who to show them to. Then we can Skype with her and forge ahead with the next step. Sound good?"

They both agreed, and we were able to strike a deal with the caretaker as well. My wallet kept getting lighter and lighter as the day progressed. The caretaker gave us the ledger, wrapped in an old, moth-eaten blanket that he had- admonishing us to take good care of that bit of government property; expecting its timely return by midday tomorrow.

Meanwhile, David had called Los Caneyes, and secured rooms for us. We then left the cemetery, not noticing the man leaning against a tree off to the side, 'dead to the world,' sound asleep and gently snoring. We walked the couple of hundred meters to the car, protected by the lad who Berto had paid. It was safe, secure, and polished so well that we needed to put on our sunglasses. We got in with our on-loan treasure and headed to the hotel.

* * *

A half hour later, while the group was checking into the hotel, the man stifled a groan and shifted his body away from the small rock that seemed to embed itself in his lower back. He woke with a start and saw that the sun had nearly completed its journey below the horizon. He cursed inwardly, hurriedly crossing himself in the process, as he scanned his surroundings. Just down the road, a mangy dog trotted toward the *barrio*. Other than that, not a living soul could be seen. Nor could any parked vehicles under the trees.

He sighed, and approached the cemetery gate. However, it was padlocked, the caretaker nowhere in sight either. The long trek back to the parish house was not one that he savored, especially since now, with the sun rapidly setting, the neighborhood dogs would be out and about, looking for meals or just to have a good time with those with enough mettle to walk these alleyways. Perhaps, a mile or so down the road, he might have a chance to hail at best a small pedicab that could negotiate the narrowest of lanes until the paved roads of town could be reached. With a final 'anointing of a tree,' he began a well-paced walk toward Santa Clara's center of town.

About halfway through the *barrio*, a figure loomed in the rapidly approaching darkness. Father Alejandro hurried to catch up to him.

"*Permisso, senor,*" he called from several meters away, not wanting to spook the man. As the man turned, the priest recognized him. "Aren't you the caretaker of the cemetery *senor*?" He politely inquired.

"*Si, padre.*" The answer startled him.

"So how on earth did you know that I'm a priest," he asked the man.

"It's easy. As I am walking home, at night, I am always cautious. At every corner I stop and look around at my surroundings, then proceed. I saw you a couple of blocks back."

"Ok. But how…."

"The way that you deport yourself. Even without vestments, you hold your head high, with a very confident stride. It's entirely different from the way that people walk in this neighborhood, most certainly. I figured out that, one, you were not one of the locals, and two, who else but a holy man, regardless of the faith, would be visiting a cemetery if you had no real business there."

Alejandro was taken aback. "So according to your notion, why would I be at a Jewish burial place?" He clearly was worried about 'blowing his cover' for the time being.

"It is quite clear me, in spite of the fact that the Jews are considered to be 'people of the book' even though they deny our beloved Jesu Christos, they are still holy in the eyes of God and deserve to be saved. Perhaps you have found a way to save them, even after death." The man simply shrugged his shoulders, as if he actually believed what he said. "I respect them, but I too feel that they need be saved. So I work to watch over them as well."

The priest looked at the caretaker with a mixture of amusement and amazement. This unpretentious villager had a profound outlook on religion, with apparently no schooling past the first few grades of grammar school. He admired the man, and, as a result, he crossed himself, placed his hand on the peasant's head, and blessed him. The look of gratitude was unusually satisfying to a priest who felt that he had lost his mission with God. It seemed to return to him at this moment. He felt sure that he could ask the man anything, and get nothing but an honest reply. In addition, he felt that he could now trust him to say nothing further to anyone else about their chance meeting.

After a couple of moments of questioning, the two parted ways with a heartfelt *"Vaya con Dios"* on both of the men's lips. He now knew that the trail had not gone as cold as he originally had feared. All he needed to do was to return to the cemetery the next day to discover the true reason for the others' visit to the Jewish graveyard, finding out what 'old book' they borrowed and why.

* * *

We met on the terrace overlooking the pool area. Sitting under a thatched umbrella, the waiter had deposited the customary *mojitos* in front of us, with a bowl of olives and chips since it wasn't quite dinner. Berto and David had done a cursory scan through the pages of the ledger and were a bit disappointed. The dialect seemed to stump them, even though they were native Spanish speakers. In addition, the handwriting script was badly faded, in a poor state of preservation, with stains that all but obliterated scores of entries.

"I think that it might be best to eat, then retire to our rooms to look a bit more tonight before turning in. Privacy would be best." I left it at that, we all ate from the sumptuous spread sponsored by *'Senor Jimmy Buffet'* (our own private joke), thoroughly enjoying the live music- a staple in every government-owned restaurant.

Later that evening, after looking through the book again, we felt that it was fairly certain that the entries were alphabetical rather than chronological. But what period of time did this list pertain to, and *where* did the list come from? After all, it certainly wasn't from Santa Clara. I began to photograph the folio sheets with my mobile, with the hope of then emailing them to Kati to Jerusalem. After shooting a dozen or so pages I took a break. As Yoli, Berto and I continued to debate the origins, David, for the third or fourth time, continued to carefully page through the book once more.

"Hey guys, come look at this!" he exclaimed excitedly. "I think that I've found something here. Take a look at this page, and then this one following."

"What are we looking at?" Perhaps we were all tired, as no one noticed a thing. That is, until David pointed it out to us.

"Look here, very carefully. See the binding, the seam? If you examine it very closely you'll notice what easily can be missed. I only saw it this time because I inadvertently looked through the bottom half of my bi-focals! A page has been deliberately, almost surgically, removed from this ledger! It has been cut out so that it would still pass inspection except for the most minute of examinations. I would have to say that, due to the sharpness of the slice, it would have had to have been made recently. And by that I mean 19th or 20th century, certainly not hundreds of years ago."

We sat back, stunned at this turn of events. Perhaps there wasn't now as demanding a reason to get in touch with Israel, and Kati. I voiced this concern to the others. However, rightly so, they insisted that I send off the photos that I took. At least we might get a better handle on the age and venue of the book- to verify some details.

David came up with another idea just before he left for his home.

"It seems that my next step would be to contact the *Hevra Kaddisha* of Santa Clara. The presidency of the organization has resided in the same family since the cemetery's inception in 1932. It's the Tzarfati Family. I'm sure that I can prevail upon one of them to talk with us tomorrow, if that's all right with you."

We all heartily agreed to these two avenues of action, and bade each other a good night. As I soon as I got back to my room, I texted Kati in Israel and attached a couple of the photos that I had taken. She most likely wouldn't need any more at this point to verify whatever she could. And I had downloaded over a dozen onto a flash drive should she need more. At that point, I slipped the wrapped volume under my pillow, and didn't think that I'd sleep a wink out of concern for its safety and security. I also wondered if the others would stay awake running things through their heads... just before I nodded off.

* * *

The beep-beep-beep of my alarm on the mobile roused me from sleep at the ungodly hour of five am. I hadn't been awake that early since the last excavation I was directing in Israel a few years earlier. I groaned, and rolled over, and waited for the second set of beeps at the five minute mark. At the four minute mark I knew that it was useless, so I shut off the alarm and got up and splashed some cold water on my face. Why torture myself, you might ask. It was an easy answer, a sign tacked on the back of the bathroom door said it all- *hot water would be available in the hotel starting at 5.30am every day*. So it wasn't by choice.

A quick calculation put Israeli time at 12.30pm and a great time to catch Kati on her mobile, probably still at her office in the Rockefeller Museum in eastern Jerusalem. Built by the British during the Mandate between the great wars, it started life as the Palestine Museum. We have a saying in the Middle East, and especially in Israel- "Blame it on the British!" As a matter of fact, most of the difficulties arising in that part of the world could be laid directly at the doorstep of the Empire. However, in this case, it was a blessing. Wherever the British became an occupying force, they took an interest in the indigenous culture and society, and went to great pains to preserve and protect its history and archaeology. Hence, the creation of the Palestine Exploration Society and its home, the Palestine Museum. Following the 1967 War when Jerusalem was re-unified, the museum was remodeled, refurbished and renamed- to the Rockefeller Museum. This was due to the large sum of money infused into the project by that family. Restoration efforts preserved the wonderful architectural presence of the structure, down to restoring the reflecting pool in the courtyard, surrounding galleries and the several storey octagonal tower that housed offices and the library. In spite of all that, it was relegated to 'second chair' by the Israeli government; due mainly to the fact that, while Jerusalem was divided for 19 years, a magnificent new museum campus, the Israel Museum, was designed and built away on the western side of Israeli Jerusalem. Situated across the valley from the Knesset, or parliament building, it was a masterpiece that was envied around the world. As a tip of the hat to its Rockefeller counterpart, the main headquarters of IDAM, Israeli Department of Antiquities and Museums, was located there. It was a fitting tribute.

I hit my Skype app and listened to the be-beep-beep-----be-beep trill of the Skype ringtone. The sound of Skype 'swallowing' and connecting allowed the lovely Ms. Ben Ya'ir to fill the small screen.

"*Ahlen habibi!* Or should I say *Hola Senor*!" My heart melted a little at the sight and sound. She had that 1000 watt smile that could light up a room, oh, 8000 miles away. And she knew it! I was smitten...

"Ju look mahvelous," I said in my finest Ricardo Montalban imitation. "It's so good to see and hear you. Isn't modern technology a miracle? Did you get my text with attached photos and what do you think? Did you find someone to take a look as well...?"

"*Shwayeh, shwayeh... kol hazeman ata holech yashir l'avodah?* All the time you go right to work? No 'how are you dear Kati? What are you up to Kati? How is work with dear old Amnon, Kati?' How do you say it- 'What am I, chopped liver?'" She started laughing, almost uncontrollably- indicating that she was just playing.

But she had me worried for a bit there. I guess that I was a bit abrupt, champing at the bit to get information. I apologized, and began to explain the entire situation. She could see the stress in my face, and commented on it. I relayed to her what had transpired regarding the ledger, and how nervous I was holding it- with its return just a few hours away.

"Yes, I got the pictures, and yes, I had someone from Hebrew U.'s linguistics department take a look. It does look to be Castilian Spanish, and yes, it is a style used in the 18th and early 19th centuries. The letter formations are the key. It is a bit like your Colonial English and modern English. You know, when the final effs actually look more like small cursive esses. Here's what I mean..." She began to write. *Isn't Skype great*, I thought. What then appeared on the screen was a traditional small letter- f. Then she wrote the late 18th century version- *f*

"Ah... I get it. So stylistic change in an alphabet is a lot like stylistic change in ceramics." It made perfect sense. Just as I was about to comment, she broke in again.

"There is another thing that is really confusing to me, us, over here. We looked at the second page that you sent, and I thought that you said you were in Santa Clara? Some of the small print on the page refers to Havana. *Ma Koray?* What's going on?"

I sat back, dazed. What indeed was a ledger from Havana dated to the late 1700s doing in a cemetery office that is only 75 or so years old? In addition, why was a page *somewhat recently* cut out; and where was it? I told her of this new development and she, too was bewildered. I had work to do, and so did she. We promised to be in touch soon should anything turn up, and then signed off.

I cleaned up a bit, shaved, and headed to the restaurant for breakfast. By now it was pushing 7am and the place was beginning to show a lot of life, as a couple of tour groups were eating just prior to departure. I grabbed a wonderfully 'aromatized' cup of coffee, a couple of croissants and fruit, and found a table. As I headed back to the omelet bar, David walked through the door. He came over.

"Don't you ever sleep?" he asked me. I responded in kind, shaking his hand. "I hoped to catch you all to let you know what I have in store this morning, just in case you missed me." He winked and placed an order before I got a chance. I hurriedly asked for onion, cheese, mushroom and green pepper and together, we walked back to the table. On the way he, too, grabbed a cup of coffee.

"So where are the others?" I assumed that they still were asleep, or on their way, and told him so.

"What's your plan then?" I asked when we returned from the bar with our orders. "Wait, where's the Tabasco? OK, where were we?"

"I wanted to let you know that I was headed out to *Virginia* this morning..."

"Huh?! Where? What *are* you talking about?" I spluttered over my coffee. I was totally lost now.

He saw the confusion in my eyes, and laughed heartily. "Oh, it's a neighborhood in the western side of Santa Clara! *THAT* Virginia! The Tzarfati family lives on *Calle Esparza* in that area. You know, the heads of the burial society. They agreed to have me over for coffee around 10am. And here's the most intriguing thing of all- when I told them about an unusual ledger found in the cemetery office, they said that the family has been waiting for this particular call for decades; yet nobody did."

Just then, Yoli and Berto arrived. David and I saw them walk in the door, but true to a good Cuban's common sense, they made a beeline right to the coffee machine before coming over to us.

"Santa Clara is known for its coffee, because the *Escambrey* Mountains just to the south- have great coffee plantations," Berto slurped. The look on his face said *1) I really needed that drink and 2) I'm now in heaven ready to face the day.*

Yoli was more circumspect. "You shouldn't stay up most of the night talking with your fellow tour guides and bus drivers." She punched him in the arm. (There was a lot of that going on.) David excused himself, needing to get going. The rest of us tucked in to the buffet, fortifying us for the day's activities to come.

* * *

David Tacher headed out through the *porte cochere* of the hotel, and hailed a taxi. In just a few minutes he was at the Tzarfati family home, where the adult great-grandchildren of the original president of the *Hevra Kadisha*, the burial society, were waiting for him. The prerequisite greetings out of the way, the current matriarch of the clan brought out coffee and almond cookies. Everyone was anxious to discuss the matter at hand. It became immediately apparent that this close-knit family had a tremendous sense of loyalty to the dwindling Jewish community, even at the risk of incurring the wrath of the government. The current head of the society, Alfonso Tzarfati, spoke in glowing terms of the great honor that the Santa Clara Jewish Community had bestowed on his great-grandfather all those decades ago, entrusting their dead with his care. He had done such an exemplary job that, upon his death, the community felt obliged to offer the position to his son. And from there, a dynasty of sorts was born. It was not considered to be a burden, but an honor; a matter of respect and dignity. For this small community took great pride in its faith and the maintenance of the graves of their ancestors. It was now clear why the cemetery grounds were immaculately maintained. The caretaker was well 'taken care of' and he carried out his duties without question, even though he himself was not Jewish.

David was aware of all this, and profusely thanked the family for their diligence. His relationship with them was a couple of decades old, ever since he himself had become president.

"So, my friends, why have you been waiting for this visit for years?"

At this, Alfonso went into a back room and returned moments later with another old ledger.

"It's not as old as we had thought, when we first saw it tucked in a shelf in grandfather's house. Apparently the weather had taken a toll more heavily than we all believed," the burial society president said. "Yet, I am not all that surprised. After all, our cemetery only dates to the first part of the 20th century. This one ledger seems to span 1956-1960. It is what was folded and slipped between a couple of pages that interested us."

David's curiosity was aroused.

Tzarfati turned a few pages, and slid out a glassine envelope. "My grandfather felt that, whatever this page was and where it came from must have been of value to the Jews, so he placed it in this sleeve to protect it as best as possible from aging. But as you see, the ink has deteriorated and faded terribly. It is so faint....."

The community president's eyes widened to nearly twice their normal size. Common sense prevailed. "Do you have any cotton gloves, or a lightweight piece of fabric?"

One of the women left the room and came back with pieces of cotton. With a slightly shaking hand, he grasped the page inside the protective covering with the cloth and slowly removed it. The first glance told him that this was a much older page than the ledger it was hidden in. The second glance at the faded lines of text made him feel that it was an accounting of names and dates, nearly illegible, *but written in the same Castilian script* as the ledger in the others' possession back at Los Caneyes.

"Do you mind if I take it with me? I mean both the volume and the sheet? I have colleagues in town who have been led here by other mysteries surrounding Cuba's Jewish community." David was vague in his description. If things got dicey, he wanted plausible deniability for the Tzarfati family- one never knew what kind of reprisals could be in store should things 'head south', as the Americans would say.

So with handshakes all around, and the offer of a lift back to the hotel, David bade farewell to the family in charge of the community's ancestors.

* * *

Once back at the hotel, everyone exchanged news on what had been accomplished over the past hour or so. Berto, Yoli and David were keen to pour over the more recent ledger, as it was in a more modern Spanish hand that was easier and clearer to read for them. While they did that, I busied myself with photographing the mysterious page. I took the same great pains in handling it that Tacher had, because we were all familiar with the way that oils in the skin could easily degrade and damage parchment. Once I had laid it out on a linen bedsheet, I examined the edge of the document. I used the cell phone camera to zoom in on the page- giving me a much closer view than with the eye. I put it side by side with the ledger that we had borrowed from the cemetery caretaker's office and was shocked. It became clear that this page had been cut out of the book and the two were deliberately separated from each other. Was it done by the senior Tzarfati decades ago, or more recently? The cut line told no stories. I finished shooting and was preparing to send the pix off to Jerusalem, when my phone 'pinged.' The text message simply said, "Hey Bedouin man, call me." I had no doubt as to who it was from, even without a name. Kati Ben Ya'ir used that as my nickname when we needed to be circumspect. Who knew who was listening in on (or reading) conversations. However, I did send the pix out via text.

I got everyone together and we reviewed where we were before I called. It seemed that the cemetery ledger for Santa Clara was exactly what its cover page indicated; the activities of the *Hevra Kadisha* for both Santa Clara and Cienfuegos in the last years of the Batista Regime. Of note was the exacting detail of activity. The loss of every soul in the small Jewish communities apparently was felt with great emotion. The communities mourned their losses in a very personal way, and they were recorded for posterity in great depth. This gave us insight into the lives of the Santa Clara Jews through their deaths. Yoli remarked that she felt that she was at every funeral ever recorded. It was sobering.

One entry was a mystery to all, even David. In 1957, it made reference to a small mausoleum that was constructed to house the remains of an individual or of a couple of individuals who were unknown to the community. Made of marble, it was located at the very rear corner of the enclosed cemetery compound. David, as did all associated with any activity in the cemetery, was aware of it, but paid little attention to it. Although the cemetery rarely had local visitors, there being so few survivors today, to his knowledge not a single soul ever inquired about that particular tomb.

It was only about two x four meters in size, and quite low- about one and a half meters at its peak.

"As soon as possible later today, after we return the ledger to the caretaker, we should examine the tomb and see if there is any more detail that we can get from it. It certainly would be worth our while even if it isn't pertinent to our task at hand," Berto articulated his thoughts. We all seconded the notion.

Just then my phone 'pinged' again. "Are you calling, or what!" I laughed at the electronically transmitted impatience of Kati in Jerusalem. When asked about why I was laughing, I told them. They all smiled and agreed that I should call ASAP.

I decided to Skype again, with all present. As soon as the connection was made, I hurriedly told Kati that everyone was there with me so that nothing embarrassing or 'suggestive' might be said. (After all, there *was* a personal history.) She made it clear that she was delighted to meet all of my Cuban friends, profoundly regretting that she couldn't be there in person to share in the adventure. And, as it would turn out, would be *quite* the adventure!

I quickly filled her in with what we had discovered, with all of my companions adding any pertinent data that I might have left out. Berto and Yoli took turns describing their translation of the 18th century ledger from parts unknown. David explained details about his visit with the Tzarfati family and recovery of the 1957 ledger of the Santa Clara cemetery. He also became quite animated about the page that the family had saved- tucked in that ledger.

Here I broke in. "This page is the one I just sent you a bit earlier. We noticed that it was delicately cut out of the 18th century book and hidden, apart from it. However, just as the case with the original pix that I sent, the writing is badly faded and stained, and because of its Castilian script, almost impossible for us to comprehend. That's where we hoped that you and your colleagues could shed further light in some way." The expectant look on all of our faces said it all to Kati.

"I am delighted to help, as are my friends at Hebrew U as well." Everyone saw the smile on her face. "It seems that there are some archaeological recovery 'tricks of the trade' that we took advantage of."

She went on to explain how ancient documents discovered in the Judean Desert in 1946-47 would precipitate scientific advancements in textual preservation, analysis and photography. The Dead Sea Scrolls have been considered to be one of the greatest archaeological discoveries ever made. Initially seven scrolls were found by Bedouin in the northwest quadrant of the Dead Sea Valley. Since that time, hundreds of scrolls and scroll fragments have been unearthed; giving a unique glimpse into the world of Judea roughly two thousand years ago. They shed light on a world turned upside down that saw the brutality of the Roman Empire, coupled with the rise of Rabbinic Judaism and early Christianity.

"However, due to the age of the documents, and some of the circumstances in which they were hidden, many were badly damaged and seemingly unreadable. Scrolls that were 'melted' together due to the presence of tar that was used to seal the store-jars, or whose ink had fused with the parchment, preventing easy unrolling, were thought useless. But it is precisely challenges such as these that oftentimes lead to amazing scientific innovations. IDAM was at the forefront of many of these gains. Some of them had to do with photography, and others computer imaging. This technology is applicable to the documents that you are dealing with in Cuba."

Upon hearing this, the Cubans all applauded, with looks of awe on their faces. Although I was familiar with these technologies, my friends were still somewhat left out in the cold (war) over these new scientific techniques. Only the highest echelons of Cuban academia were privy to these advances, in part due to the embargo.

"So how does this help us out here?" was the question on everyone's lips, but vocalized by David Tacher. "Please, don't hold us in suspense any longer! I implore you!" The others wholeheartedly agreed, their faces showed an eagerness that was indescribable.

"The easiest way is to show you" Kati said. "Check your text messages now," she said, looking directly at me. "Open the images and I can readily explain. As your idiot says, 'a picture is worth a thousand words.'"

"You mean 'idiom,' not 'idiot', don't you?" I feigned mock effrontery.

"Who knows, maybe I did mean 'idiot'," she said with a sly smile. The others laughed at me while I downloaded the pix.

Kati went on, "You know what you can see in the ledger and the page. But look at what you can see with the different light source of infra-red. Voila!" We gathered around my mobile and looked at the photos. Sure enough, under infra-red light the faded and faint letters stood out in greater contrast to the parchment. It was as different as night and day- or maybe night-vision and day-vision. They others were duly impressed, ooh-ing and aah-ing as I scrolled through the images.

"Here's what my language experts have ascertained. The older book that you sent me a few pix from seems to have been written concerning one of the original cemeteries in Havana, *Cementerio Espada*."

"But that was the forerunner of the *Cementerio de Cristóbal Colón*!" exclaimed Berto. "It was constructed almost immediately after the Spaniards were forced to evacuate Hispaniola, making Cuba their main base. This was all around 1795." I could see the wheels turning more and more rapidly in 'Senor Encyclopedia's' brain.

"So now we have a fairly close date for the Castilian ledger," said Yoli. Everyone was quickly getting up to speed on this.

"Since we know what technology to use, and since the photographer's studio is just across the hall, I gave him the digital of the single page that you sent me an hour ago. He understood the urgency of my request. Of course, it didn't hurt that I bribed him with a meal at the Sea Dolphin Restaurant. You remember it *habibi*, the one with the shrimp platter you could die for? And by the way, when you get back here you are paying!" She winked across cyber-space. Berto punched my arm, and the others started ribbing me to no end.

"I told you this was an open line!" I tried to look indignant, but couldn't help laughing. We all started laughing at that point. "So don't hold us in suspense."

"Ok, so what we could see was an amazing entry in the ledger. Remember, this is the page that was torn, er, cut out. I have sent it on to you and you should get it… about now."

The 'ping' announced the arrival at that very moment. "The I-R scan was able to collate the pixels and sharpen the image to a phenomenal resolution. On one line, as you should be able to clearly see now, it says…"

We looked at the new, 'cleaned up' image and were dumfounded.

"…… *Colon Cristoforo*!"

You could hear the proverbial pin drop. Nobody said a word, nobody was even breathing, or so it seemed. After an eternity…

"Holy shit!" "*Madre de Dios*," Yoli crossed herself and David? Tears welled up in his eyes.

Kati was stunned at the ensuing silence on the other end of the Skype connection. "Are you guys alright? Are you guys still breathing?"

I said, "You've done it again, Ben Ya'ir. You've found another way to blow my socks off! Not to mention the others here as well." We all started laughing and hugging each other. I kissed the screen. She was smiling. It seems that the light at the end of the tunnel was now nearer than it ever had been. A mystery *might* be about to be solved.

"I know that its night over there, and you should get home. We've hours of daylight and lots of legwork ahead of us. I'll be in touch when we make all sorts of clarifications. *Ani ohav otach,* Kati. *Layla tov,* good night."

"Me too, Bedouin man! *Yallah*, bye!" and the signal was lost.

As soon as we clicked off, I became the brunt of the cruelest of cruel hazing and verbal abuse, and if it had been from anyone but these three friends, would have merited retaliation. But then what are friends for, if not to give you good-natured grief.

* * *

Across town, at the parish house for the cathedral, Father Alejandro was finishing his third cup of coffee. *At least the staff here know how to brew a good cup,* he thought. The copy of <u>Granma</u> was unfortunately two days old.

Apparently the parish priest here kept the most recent edition to himself for a day or so before turning it over to the staff. There was nothing to note in it, and probably nothing of note in the more recent copy as well. It no longer served as the true 'Voice of the People,' but rather was a self-serving tribute to the rapidly fading Castro Dynasty. Raul had already stated that he would not run again in the next election, a couple of years hence. Others were jockeying for the slot, with the most notable frontrunner the current Vice-President of the Council of State, Miguel Diaz-Canel; an extraordinarily young 52. He would be the first leader-in-waiting to *not* have been a part of the Revolution with the Castro brothers. A hard-working member of the party, he had been working his way up the ladder for over 30 years. Father Alejandro thought that there certainly was going to be an incredible shift in Cuban politics at the next election in three years.

As the sun rose over the steeple, and the streets surrounding the compound teemed with people, the priest began his trek out to *El Barrio de Los Syrios*. As was the case yesterday, he dressed in civilian clothing. This time, however, he attempted to walk slower, and a bit less rigidly- taking the advice of the Jewish cemetery caretaker to heart. Hopefully he would not stand out as noticeably as the previous day- when he was 'made' by the caretaker. The father silently crossed himself with the fortunate luck that seemed to be on his side. It was a bright, sunny morning. The low humidity made the walk pleasant. He took his time, in no rush. Suddenly his head was filled with an old song from his youth.... "*ti-yi-yi-yime, time's on my side, yes it is...*"

* * *

Over the third, or was it fourth, cup of coffee, the group took stock of the situation. The main premise that developed presumed a couple of key points if it was to be proven valid. David ran these points down for us, and Yoli jotted them down on paper.

"First," he said, "the older ledger that has now been re-united with its cut page came from Havana in the late 18th or early 19th century. Second, it seems certain that the remains of Columbus were indeed buried in Havana, transferred from Hispaniola; after the French (this was associated with a '*feh, feh, feh*' as a commentary) occupied the island. It was clear that the Spanish did not want a national hero to lie in occupied soil. Third, at some point in time before the late 1950s, the sarcophagus and remains of the great explorer found their way to Santa Clara and *maybe* the Jewish cemetery. However, no one in Havana wanted word to get out, so the entire ledger for the years covering the move to Cuba accompanied the body. And finally, fourth, when the elder Tzarfati discovered this, he surreptitiously cut out the page with Colon's recorded burial and hid it; while at the same time restoring the original book to its place on a dusty back shelf of the caretaker's shed. Does that sum it all up?"

We all agreed that it was the clearest explanation yet of a murky situation.

"But why is he here, if indeed he *is* here, at all?" I was still troubled by all the circumstances of the move. "We need to find out two things. One, what details can we ascertain about the mausoleum back in the corner of the cemetery. And two, how did the mausoleum come about in 1957. That is, if we accept the newer ledger information."

A few murmurs of consent meant that we all were in accord.

"So, how do we find this out?" I asked the Cuban contingent. David thought a moment and came up with a plan that made the most sense.

"Back to the Tzarfati family," he said. "Perhaps there are other documents that the *Hevra Kadisha* has that relate to the administration and care of the cemetery- not necessarily burial ledgers. You know, stuff dealing with finances, actual caretaking duties, mundane stuff."

Yoli laughed. "You refer to that precise category of activity- 'stuff', that is the catch-all for whatever can't really be defined." Apparently she had picked up on that term that Berto and I both used often, for lack of better 'terms.' At that, we all laughed again.

* * *

I felt that it might be too overwhelming for us all to go back to the Tzarfati residence, since it was clear that they were overextended by the first visit. By that I mean that they felt it was incumbent on them to offer us a great deal of hospitality- it was their expectation, based on a religious imperative; even though it may stretch them financially. Abraham and Sarah had opened their tent to anyone who strayed from the path. In the ancient world, the landscape was oftentimes a greater enemy than 'your enemy.' The biblical world was a dangerous and hostile land for all who traveled through it. So, as humans, we all were to set aside our differences for a while when it came to survival. It was once of the essential *mitzvot*, 'blessings,' given to ancient Israel as part of the 613 in the Hebrew Bible.

David explained this to Yoli, and in the process refreshed Berto's knowledge as well. When she asked about such an overwhelming number of things to remember and do in the name of God, he went on to explain that the Jewish concept of the relationship between God and humans, and humans and humans, was radically different than the one that evolved out of Judaism to shape the newly minted 'Christianity' in the 1st century CE.

He went on, relaying how in Judaism, given that we're all created in the image of God, (at this point Berto rolled his eyes, silently thinking that in some instances God must be 'God-Awful' ugly!) we come into this world good and 'write our own books,' with informed decision making. The episode with the Garden of Eden was simply a way for God to impart human consciousness on Adam and Eve, allowing them to make their own choices.

"It also created the clothing industry!" Yoli giggled.

David smiled and continued his narrative. So to Jews, the Garden episode awakened in humanity the ability to choose right or wrong, good or evil.

I interjected, "So to both the Jewish community and God, it didn't matter if wrongdoing was in the mix. It was expected, because we as humans are, well, *human*, and not perfect. Only God is considered a true perfect entity."

"So if we are prone to screwing up as you Americans say, how do we get forgiveness from God? Isn't that what Jesu Cristo did for us?" Yoli was clearly perplexed, but intrigued.

"Aha, here's the way we deal with it. We know we're going to make errors, or sins, if you will. But there is a built-in 'sin-forgiver' in the Jewish scheme of things. It's called the Ten Days of Awe, *Rosh HaShanah* through *Yom Kippur*."

"I've heard of that. Isn't it a fish that they love in Northern Europe?" Berto had that sly look on his face. Then he broke out in a wide smile. We knew he was joking, but Yoli, hmmmm, maybe, or not. Berto could be a cruel jokester.

I continued. "After prayer and reflection, culminating in a 24- hour period of fasting, we are all given a clean sheet for the coming year; knowing that there will be black marks soon to come."

"Wow!" she was clearly impressed with this. "So we're not born sinful, and need to get baptized and observe Christian laws and believe in the divinity of Jesus, who died for our sins."

I hastened to make it clear that the most important thing was that all of us find a path to get us to 'The Center'- God. And that it didn't make a difference which path to take as long as we got to the same goal, living a godly life while residing on earth. At this, she breathed a small sigh of relief at the reassurance of her faith. Nevertheless, she was still intrigued by all this explanation.

"Maybe I'll look into this more after this 'stuff' is all over. David, will you help me find a contact in Havana?" she asked.

"Of course, with pleasure," was his response. At that, we dropped him off at the Tzarfati residence, and the three of us returned to Los Caneyes for a bit of RnR.

At the Tzarfati's, over tea, David explained what had transpired, and where we were in our quest. He vividly described the work done at the small mausoleum, and the mystery that was still with us. At this point, he asked if there were any of the administrative journals still around from 1957 that might clarify how and why the sarcophagus made its way from Havana to Santa Clara.

"Thank God that *Abuelo* was, as you say, a packrat. He kept everything written about the cemetery. He took his job quite seriously, and I hope to be remembered in the same way."

David thanked him profusely, on both a personal and professional level. A few moments later, the man returned with another ledger, similar to the other that David had seen. However, this one was not simply a list of 'occupants;' it was more like a diary and accounting record. This one was dated 1955-1960.

Over another cup of tea, and the inevitable almond cookie, he skipped through the pages until he reached 1957. At that point, he slowed down considerably and carefully read each entry. He knew that he could flip over the accounting pages- he didn't need to know how much the flowers in their pots cost that particular year. Rather, in between, in chronological order, were entries pertaining to interments, maintenance and upkeep, etc.

It was slow reading. The elder Tzarfati may have been a pious man, with a heartfelt task assigned to him by the community, but his writing skills and handwriting were atrocious. And there seemed to be two handwriting styles as well. When David pressed the current *Hevra Kadisha* head, he told him that his father, as a young lad, would often write the dictation of *his* father for the entries. What should have taken under an hour to read was now stretching out to two, and approaching three.

David massaged the bridge of his nose, rubbing the tender spot where the improperly adjusted reading glasses pinched and chafed a bit. It had never bothered him before; but then he never wore them for two hours straight. A glass of bottled water revived him a bit, and he resumed his reading.

Just as the hour hand of his internal clock passed three, he inadvertently twitched a bit. With a finger to the page, he backed up a line or two and reread the entry.

> *This day, I was approached at the cemetery by a certain Father Gonzalo, from the Cathedral in Santa Clara. He brought with him a letter signed and sealed by the Archbishop of Habana himself. Since my reading is not exactly my strength, I asked my oldest boy to read it for me. However, I told the priest that it was just a reading lesson for the kid- I HAVE MY PRIDE! I would not give the pleasure to this man- especially from the church community. It said that during the course of city development of Santa Clara, an old cemetery came to light. The Archbishop went on.*
>
> *'It seemed that, at the end of the 18th century, because Santa Clara's community was so small, and that only a couple of Jews lived there, the holy cemetery was used by all. A small corner was*

reserved with a couple of plots for Jews. Why? Because you still are People of the Book and deserve a dignified, holy resting place even if a separate burial ground is not practical. If it would please the Jews of Santa Clara, I would be honored if they would accept one of their own discovered in the recent city excavation work. We of the Church have begun the process of relocating our Catholic ancestors in the current cemetery. However, now that there is a Jewish cemetery, it is only fitting that the remains be transferred there. I remain, in the name of God to whom we all answer,

His Holiness Manuel Arteaga y Betancourt, Archdiocese of Havana'

I listened to my son with pleasure, as he read this letter. I was proud of him, and made sure that he knew it. I then addressed Father Gonzalo and told him it would be an honor for us to take in one of our own. The priest then stunned me. He said that since the deceased was unknown in 1795, when he was moved to Santa Clara from Habana, and remained unknown, the Church in its gracious compassion would pay for a small mausoleum to be built for the remains. Although my attitude toward the Church in general remains the same, I have a warm regard for the Santa Claran Priest who probably found a way all his own to make these honorable arrangements.

I look forward to its completion, and interment of the remains. I will tell the stonemason contracted by the Church to engrave this- "To our unknown ancestors." I will make sure that my son writes this epitaph in block letters of Hebrew, so the mason may chisel it. (I thank my son for helping me to write this all down, as well- God bless him.

David hurriedly called to his host. When he related what he had just read, a look of astonishment crossed his face. Apparently the Jewish community had no idea of this burial relationship with the Catholic Church in the 18th and 19th centuries. Nor was the re-internment of 1957 common knowledge either.

Now that this was all clarified as far as it could be, David thanked his hosts and hurried back to the Los Caneyes to tell the others.

* * *

So now we headed back to the cemetery to return the old ledger (still minus its page) and to survey the marble tomb out back.

Off we went in the 'Berto-mobile,' of course with the top down. It was a lovely day in Santa Clara. However, just was we were approaching the 'Syrian' neighborhood, Berto pulled over. "What's up?" Yoli asked.

"I'm just going to put the top up. After all, remember that the path was a dirt one near the cemetery, and I don't want any dust in the car, and hopefully not too much on it!"

I rolled my eyes. "Why don't we just walk from here?" I wasn't serious, but Berto *actually gave it a moment of consideration.*

Common sense won out. "It might be a good thought," he said, "but we need to have the ability for a quick departure just in case." *Phew*, I thought, *he finally came around.*

Top up, car buttoned down, we rolled the remaining half mile or so to the gate. The same street urchin was there, with his trusty *schmatta*, or rag, prepared to defend the honor of Berto's car to the death if necessary. (As long as the tip was good!) Berto 'high-fived' the boy and tore a five Cuban peso note in half, with the promise of the other piece when we came out and the car was taken care of. The dirty face broke into a smile and said, *'no hay problema, señor!'* None of us noticed the *campesino* under the tree across the path.

We walked into the compound, and directly to the small shack. The caretaker looked up from his newspaper and smiled. We returned the volume and thanked the man for allowing us to examine it. David told him that we were going to take a walk around the grounds, and that he was simply going to point out to his guests some of the 'more important' graves relating to the history of the community. We donned *kippot* and began to wander aimlessly around, stopping at various graves, should the man be looking out his window. He wasn't, as every couple of minutes Yoli glanced back at the building. David's running commentary was loud enough to wake the dead, but also in keeping with our 'quest.' It was enough to lull any casual listener to sleep.

Eventually we made our way to the far corner. It was just down a subtle incline, and, as we would discover, actually took us out of the line of sight from the hut adjacent to the entry. This was as perfect as it could get. The small marble mausoleum looked forlorn and abandoned. Apparently the caretaker hadn't got around to trimming the grass and pulling the weeds in this part of the sacred space in a while; say, perhaps years. The water-stained surface was a bit pitted, and the only inscription was badly worn. However, it was clear enough to get a reading. David remarked that this was actually his first visit to this area. Most of his visits, with guests and tourists, were only to the front and the Holocaust Memorial. He teared up and apologized in a soft voice. Whether it was to us, or to the residents of the cemetery, we didn't know.

Yoli traced her finger over the weathered inscription. "I assume that it says the same in the Hebrew text as the Spanish," she said. And then read the following:

"לאבותינו לא המוכרים
A nuestros padres desconosidos."
(To our unknown ancestors)

We stood in silence for a moment, paying our respects to those whose remains might lie in the tomb.

"So now we face the dilemma- do we try to open the door and see what lies within?" I had to ask the pointed, if a bit blasphemous, question.

It was really up to David to respond, as it was his community, his cemetery, his *Hevra Kadisha*, or burial society; that he would need to deal with. "It is in the best interest of the *Communidad* that the cemetery be maintained, with dignity and care. If an area is not well-tended, as is apparently the case, it is incumbent upon us to make it right. After we clean around this mausoleum, perhaps borrowing a brush, rags and bucket of water, we can enter to ensure that all is in order. After that, I will gently reprimand the caretaker for his lack of 'taking care' of the far corner. But he will not lose his job, as we will keep it among ourselves. He won't want to broadcast what has transpired."

It was a perfect plan for us. David and Yoli went back to the hut to get the cleaning supplies and Berto and I sat down and waited, our backs to the adobe enclosure wall.

"What do you think? Could we have found the end of Columbus' last journey? It seems to me that whatever is inside may have become nothing more than dust….." my thoughts trailed off.

Berto turned to look at me, smiled, and nodded his head in agreement. "We'll see soon enough, eh *amigo*?"

Moments later the two returned, and started to restore the perimeter – giving due respect to the occupant or occupants, whoever they may have been.

* * *

In the meantime, the caretaker hurriedly went outside the gate, and over to the copse of trees. The 'farm hand' leaning against the tree stood up and brushed himself off. The older man faced him, bowed ever so slightly and crossed himself.

"What are you doing?" hissed the 'farmer.' "Why do you think that I look this way? Because it is 'All Saints Day' and I'm dressed up in costume?" The anger spilled over. "Stand up straight and face me as if we were man to man! And tell me quickly what you know and return to your duties."

The caretaker related all that he had seen and heard from the group of four. He tried to be circumspect, because he also was aware that, should anything go amiss, he would be out of a very cushy, to him, job. He explained about the ledger that they had borrowed. But they told him nothing about it. He then went on to indicate that they had taken a great interest in the small marble mausoleum, apparently dated to the late 1950s, at the back corner of the graveyard.

"Right now, *padre*, er, *permisso, senor*, the people are simply cleaning around the tomb and giving it a place of honor once more. I swear, I know nothing more! You must believe me!"

The father had no reason not to trust the man's words. He was a peasant, and no more. His simple view of life led the priest to think that he was incapable of inventing anything outside of what he could see and hear. He gave the man five pesos for his time, blessed him, and sent him back to his post to await the group's return of the tools and cleaning material. He felt that he need not caution the man about saying a word to the others about the priest; but merely shook his finger. The caretaker, trembling, with wide eyes, nodded that he fully understood and turned and walked away.

What to do, thought Father Alejandro. *Do I approach them in the cemetery? Do I wait for them outside, then confront them? After all, they too are acting out of faith and their own spiritual beliefs. Children of God- the phrase has more meaning to me now than ever. Or do I do nothing and write it all off as an exercise? I have been sent from Habana on a fool's mission!* No, wait, he hurriedly crossed himself again. *It most certainly was not a foolish mission, or that the Archbishop decided to get me out of the way for a while as a punishment for something I don't consciously know about. IT IS A TEST OF FAITH! A test of unwavering loyalty to God and the Church. And now in order to pass this test, I must come up with the correct answer.* He prayed for a few moments and came up with his course of action. The priest walked down the hill, away from the cemetery, and never looked back. And as befitting a poor servant of the Lord, he went to the Central Bus Station to get the next people's transportation to Havana, and home. He had served the Church in the best capacity that he knew how, and felt sure that he would be rewarded upon his return. A spring returned to his step, and a slight smile on his face as he walked through the sunlit neighborhood.

* * *

"Well, that's it," said David. "The area around the tomb is as if it had just been built and finished. It certainly doesn't look to be over half a century old."

And he was right. The grass was neatly trimmed and edged. The marble enclosure was a gleaming panel of grey-white striations and veining on a pale background. The inscription above the lintel had decades of dirt and debris scraped out the letters, in deep shadow, glared back at us like the eyes of the dead; dark, bottomless holes that knew no depth. It wasn't malevolent or sinister, but rather, a sort of affirmation of what lay beyond.

"So now, do we enter?" Yoli was like a small child on the verge of an incredibly exciting adventure. You could almost see the gleam of anticipation in her eyes. Given a 'thumbs up' by the president of the community, she grasped the bronze handles and pulled with all her might. She blew out a breath of air, sucked in another, and mightily pulled again- to no avail. She wiped her perspiring brow and plopped down in the grass just outside the doors. *"Madre de Dios!"* she said under her breath; and closed her eyes. She then snapped them wide open and clapped her hands. "There's oil on the bench outside the caretaker's hut. I'm going to get it." And with that she was off.

"I know that look," Berto said. "When the *nina* gets it into her head to do something, she damn well does it, no matter how many tries!" He laughed at that and sat down on a low bench a few feet away to await her return.

A few minutes later, with a new water bottle tucked under one arm, and a small oil can wrapped in a rag in the other hand, Yoli came back, smiling.

"I was really worried that the old man might think that something was up if I asked for oil, since all we were doing was 'cleaning.' So I asked for more water since it was so hot and humid out here. I also gave him a couple of pesos," she slyly winked. "He was too distracted by almost a week's salary to notice the oil that I quickly wrapped in the cloth." She was grinning ear-to-ear as if she had pulled off an amazing magic act. She deserved accolades for thinking on her feet like that.

"Bravo! Bravo!" Berto was applauding her sincerely. Yoli beamed. Since he was her mentor, his praise meant everything in the world. "Now, you can do the honors."

Yoli applied a liberal coat of oil to the bronze hinges and the deadbolt. As she put the can down and prepared to pull, I cautioned her to wait a few minutes. The oil needed time to seep into the hinges, and thoroughly coat the bolt in order for it to work. With a small 'hmmph!' she sat down with her back against the cool marble and closed her eyes. *Ah, the impetuousness of youth*, I thought.

"So, *it is time yet?!*" The phrase came out more like a demand than an inquiry. Yoli was clearly excited and anxious. I saw in the faces of the others the same anticipation, but slightly more muted. With a slight nod of the head, the young woman jumped up and practically flew to the mausoleum door. I tossed her a rag, and she hastily wiped down the deadbolt slide. The cloth turned a dull green from the copper oxide that had encrusted all the metalwork over the decades. "Yech!" was her response as she tossed the rag away and applied a bit of pressure to the bronze piece.

Finally, after a great deal of grunting and pulling, with a squeal the bolt began to slide in fits and starts. You could clearly see progress, due to the distinctly different coloration of the metal, from where it had been exposed and where it had sat, nestled and protected within the strike on the opposite door. A few moments later, the deadbolt itself showed only 'bronze,' as it slid entirely out, unlocking the door.

"Wow, this is it," Yoli panted. It was harder than she had ever thought.

"Yes, this is it," David replied.

"Well, thank you both for that. You must work for the Cuban Department of Redundancy Department!" was Berto's response to both. We all laughed a minute.

"- but wait a moment," was David's continuation, with an upraised hand. He closed his eyes. On one hand, what they were doing ran counter to everything spiritual that he had been taught as a Jew. *You don't disturb the dead, you don't desecrate graves.* But on the other hand, he was in fact doing the honorable thing in trying to identify an unknown Jewish grave- a task which was both honorable and holy given the history of Jewish communities and their persecution throughout the world. There was a saying in the Jewish world that referred to the fact that the history of the life of many of the Jewish communities around the planet was reflected in its 'death'- meaning the cemeteries. All too often, the communities ceased to exist; yet their burials remained a mute constant.

Yoli felt that the honor of opening should go to the president of the Santa Clara Jewish Community, not an outsider, and she stepped aside. A gentle nudge from her propelled him to the door, and he slowly pulled it open; a door not used since it was first shut in 1957.

The air that rolled out was damp-smelling, musty and most likely full of mold spores. I gave Yoli an extra handkerchief that I had, and all of us covered our noses and mouths. There was nothing to do about the eyes; yet no one was terribly affected- apparently no one was allergic. But we were cautious nevertheless.

"Sure is dark in there," the young girl said. The tension was broken once again. I smiled, and shined the torch we brought around the interior. In its dim beam, we could make out a solitary, plain-looking stone sarcophagus resting on the dirt floor in the back corner of the crypt. We all approached it with a bit of trepidation. A faint six-pointed star was engraved on the lid- nothing more. Could this in fact be the casket that housed the remains of one of the great explorers that humanity had ever known? Was it the 'final,' final resting place of a hero of the Jewish community?

The decision was made. We would try to slide the stone sarcophagus lid off enough to peer into the block of stone; just enough to get a peek and see if there was anything to see. But that would be easier said than done. The block, carved to look like the roofline of a building, was a solid triangle. Dirt and debris had formed a sort of seal with the base. However, after a few moments of grunting, and pushing, and shoving, and more grunting, that tenuous seal was broken and the lid moved ever so slightly. The metal blade of the small garden shovel that was used to clear weeds around the outside acted as a lever. It gave just enough of an edge so that we, in a concerted effort, were able to maneuver the lid around a pivot point to allow us about a 60 centimeter gap- enough to shine the light inside and get a glimpse.

I took the flashlight and held it just to the rim. Everybody crowded around me, and tried to get a peek in the sarcophagus. All of a sudden I starting laughing and backed out of the gap.

"What's so bloody funny?" exclaimed Berto. I turned my back to the sarcophagus and slid down onto the ground. By now, I was laughing uncontrollably. "What! WHAT?" he demanded of me.

"I'm sorry, couldn't help it." I wiped tears of laughter from my eyes. "It's just that I was reminded of the descriptions of Howard Carter in 1926." The looks of confusion were, as they say in the commercials on TV... 'priceless.'

"OK, here's the thing. Back in 1926, when Howard Carter, Arthur Callendar and Harry Burton excavated King Tut's tomb in Egypt, they came across the only unopened and unrobbed tomb in the King's Valley at that time. Their benefactor was Lord Carnarvon, the 8th Earl of Stanhope. When Carter discovered the sealed door, he had to telegraph London of his find- then *wait* for three weeks til the Earl could get his noble ass to Luxor. As the story goes, after getting the telegram-"

"What's a telegram?" our young guide was perplexed.

"Imagine an *Instagram* on paper." Berto was always patient when it came to 'youth'- except when he wasn't!

I went on. "Anyway, it took Carnarvon a while to get to Southampton and his yacht. From there he had to sail through the Straits of Gibraltar to Alexandria, Egypt. Carnarvon and entourage had to get their 'land legs' back and stayed in Alex for a couple of days. Then they took a train to Cairo, only to board a two-masted *Dhahabiya* in order to sail upstream to Luxor. All told, it was slightly over three weeks until Carnarvon showed. Carter must have been pulling his hair out by then. This also gave time for people around the world to come to Luxor for the event. Egypt hasn't see anything like it- including the opening of the Ikea Store in downtown Cairo."

I starting laughing at my own (bad) joke, while drawing complete blanks.

"What's an Ikea?" This time it was David who vocalized the confusion that all three Cubans shared.

"Never mind," I said. "When they finally got to breaking the sealed plaster wall, everyone crowded around Carter. After he punched this small hole, he stuck a candle in the crevice and peered in. He was worried about the 'canary in the coal mine' scenario."

More blank looks bore holes right through me.

"Do I have to explain *everything*?"

"Yes," came in unison.

"OK." I went on. "Everyone gathered around, just as you all did, to try to see into the tomb of the boy-king. 'What do you see? What do you see?' were the chant-like questions asked of Carter. His reply was, 'Wonderful things.' You all didn't even give me the opportunity to say that!"

"Hmmph!" came from Yoli. "Well, did you see 'wonderful things?' TELL US!"

"Unfortunately, before I could focus on what was there, YOU ALL KEPT HARASSING ME!" I said with a grin. "Now, let's gather our senses, let *me* look first, then I'll tell you all as soon as I can identify anything at all. Clear a way!" They all smiled somewhat sheepishly at their overzealous approach. "Remember, you promised," was a parting shot from Berto.

I returned to the opening, flash in hand. The others were still close, but not stiflingly so. The dim light cast shadows in the tomb. Small chunks of carved limestone littered the floor of the sarcophagus. I could make out engraved lines, but the pieces were so small that only a restorer would have a ghost of a chance at putting them together (did I really say that?!). I relayed the somewhat disheartening discovery to my colleagues. I then played the flashlight beam around a bit more, and discovered a plain pine box, a casket, that was sealed tight. I could see the lid, nailed down with small, hand-cast bronze spikes. I told them about it and Berto immediately smiled. It seems that he was aware of casket-making methods early in Spanish rule of the island, and said that these nails were in line with the 18th century or earlier. I could almost see the wheels spinning in my three friends' brains. I went back into the gap and shined the light all over the casket. On the lid, burned into the wood, there appeared to be very faint words that were incised. I called out to Berto.

"Do you still have that small can of compressed air in your car trunk, just in case of punctures?" He looked perplexed.

"Why on earth…"

"Well, DO YOU?" I demanded, a bit too harshly.

"Yes, of course, I haven't had a flat in a couple of years; that was back when…" I cut him off.

"Please, go get it right away. Nothing will happen until you return. I promise. But leave the cemetery slowly and return as slowly. We don't want anyone to think that something was going on here." With that, he speedwalked back to his car. Thankfully, the caretaker had dozed off and saw nothing. Ten minutes later he was back, with the can of compressed air.

With thanks, and a slap on his back, I stuck my head and arm back into the sarcophagus. I gave a few short sprays of the condensed air aimed at the coffin lid and its engraving. I needed to give it a few minutes to let the dust and debris I blew off it settle. When the air had sufficiently cleared, I turned the light back on. In the dull shadows cast by the flashlight, I could make out a simple phrase. But I asked David to take a look and translate it. After all, it was his community's cemetery.

A moment later he pulled out and turned to face us. His expression was a mixture of disappointment tinged with hope.

"I could read the inscription. And I saw the burn marks; apparently this phrase was burned into the wood. It simply says '*siervo de dios desconocid, o,* 'an unknown servant of God.' That's it I'm afraid."

"Don't be," said Yoli. "This doesn't mean anything one way or another. It only means that we may have to open the box and then see what's inside. Perhaps look at any objects with the body..." I cut her off.

"First, there will be no body, only bone fragments and bone residue. As this is a Jewish burial, there would not have been any embalming or preservation at all. Remember, 'earth to earth, ashes to ashes....' According to Jewish custom, there was to be nothing that stood in the way of returning to the earth as naturally as possible. Even the bronze nails on the lid might have been an exception- perhaps in deference to an important individual. Don't start jumping all over that! At least, not yet. This does seem to be an unusual situation. Second, no ritual items or personal mementos would be buried with the deceased either. So that is a non-starter too. And finally, we now are at a crossroads."

The three of them looked expectantly at me. I went on to explain. "Jerusalem is considered to be the most holy piece of real estate in the western world. It is the heart and soul of Judaism, one of three holy cities to Christendom, and one of three holy cities to Islam. The Temple Mount is the point of convergence; as the traditional location of Abraham's potential sacrifice of Isaac. Consider this- that God is such a jokester. I can visualize it now."

I briefly related the story for Yoli and Berto's benefit. Abraham and Sara were childless. He was approaching 120 years old, Sara was 99. Because of the righteousness of the two, God looked favorably upon them and Sara became pregnant. They were overjoyed. (Until Abraham did the math- *I'll be 135 when he gets his learner's permit for the chariot. I'll be 138 when I have to drive the kid to the prom....*) But the two of them were thrilled at the prospect. The child, Isaac, was born. *Itzhak* in Hebrew means 'he laughs.' So who is the joke on? God then asks Abraham, 'Do you love me?' And Abraham responds with a positive, 'yes!' Then God responds in kind with, 'Kill the kid,' or something along those lines. Just when Abraham (the idiot) is about to do this deed, an angel descends from God and informs him that, due to his unfailing loyalty, God would never ever ask of anyone to sacrifice a human. Abraham was to go on to become 'a father of a great multitude.' And an unfortunate ram whose horns got caught in a thicket would be taken for sacrifice instead.

"And by the way," I added, "that's how humans, according to religious lore, became meat-eaters. For first, the sacrifice was 'God's food,' then we as humans shared in it."

"*Tremendo! Tremendo!*" cried Berto. "It's a great thing, because I love *Ropas Viejas* with *Morros y Cristianos*! Speaking of which, can't you continue your story over a meal? Isn't it time?" For a man who was always hungry with a bottomless pit of a stomach, it was *always* time.

"We can consider our options over a meal, then return to the cemetery should we feel compelled." The always practical head of the community got in the final vote.

"I know just the place. We can go to the *Paladar Hostal Florida*, just nearby at the corner of *Colon y Maceo* Streets. Located in a beautifully preserved colonial building, it serves traditional creole food. The courtyard is open, yet protected from the wind. Your *Ropas* awaits senor!" David led the way to Berto's car; protected, all shined up, and ready to roll.

* * *

The restaurant did not disappoint. Although not a buffet, the menu items were all meticulously prepared with local ingredients. And in spite of the fact that there was no traditional *mojito* as a starter, the *Cristal* beer quenched one's thirst just as well. Once served, I remarked that it was like there was a farmer's market just outside. David replied that yes, it was *indeed* the case. He then asked me to continue the story now that we were full.

"So, back to the potential sacrifice. This story was said to occur on Mt. Moriah. Today we know it as the Temple Mount, for Jews and Christians, and the *Haram es-Sharif*, 'The Noble Sanctuary,' for Moslems. So if the western religious world has Jerusalem at the center of the 'worlds' wheel,' the 'hub' would be the Temple Mount. It would become God's first permanent 'home' on earth, with King Solomon tasked with building a temple to house the Ark of the Covenant containing the broken and copied tablets of the law. After its destruction 26 centuries ago, it would be followed by the start of Zerubbabel's

Temple (never finished) and King Herod's Temple in the 1st century BCE. After its destruction by Rome in 70 CE, a pagan Temple to Jupiter would be built, followed by a Byzantine basilica- only to be destroyed with the Moslem conquest in the 7th century CE. Then the Caliph Omar would be the octagonal Dome of the Rock in 691."

"Quite the history lesson," remarked Yoli. "I never knew… but how does this relate to us? I'm kind of lost."

"OK, here's the parallel. Ever since the city of Jerusalem was reunited in 1967, there have been scholars who have lobbied for exploratory excavations to take place whenever stuff needed to be dug up for the infrastructure. In other words, if a water pipe burst and needed to be replaced, allow the archaeologists a chance to dig preliminarily. They argued that this was in accordance with Israeli law anyway- that should any work be done, and something ancient appear in the process (which in the case of Israel is 99% of the time!) a further survey needed to be carried out before continuing to build. Here's a great example. While the Israeli highway engineers were preparing a new off-ramp for the road at *Tel Shoqet* junction in the desert, near *Tel Sheva*, they came across some ruins. Kati Ben Ya'ir…" I got a look from Yoli. "YES, the same Kati…" She snickered. "The SAME KATI was asked to conduct a salvage operation just to check out what exactly was unearthed. It turned out to be one of the best preserved Chalcolithic houses in Israel, dated to around 3500 BCE."

Now Berto was intrigued. "So what happened?" He was always trying to get the Office of the Historian to preserve more and more of *Havana Vieja*, looking for angles of attack.

"IDAM, the Israeli Department of Antiquities and Museums, *forced* the highway construction to modify the off-ramp in order to preserve and protects the ruins!"

"Sounds great!" Berto was pleased. Here was a precedent he could use in the future. "Seems to be quite reasonable. We are in the process of trying to initiate the same kind of law for *Habana Vieja*, Old Havana, as we restore and preserve the treasured colonial part of the city," Berto added.

"But it had its consequences," I went on. "After the road was finished, there were over a dozen accidents. The off-ramp angle was too severe, and speeding motorists couldn't make the curve and buried the noses of their cars in the sand at the highway edge!"

At this, *everyone* laughed.

"But you don't face the same religious dilemma that Israel does. It is a 'damned if you do, damned if you don't' conundrum. On the Jewish side, what if there is absolutely NO evidence for either of Solomon's or Herod's Temples? And guess what, professionally speaking, because of the detailed descriptions of the destruction, I would not expect there to be any significant remains extant. After all, the current ground level and the paving stones are thought to be almost resting on bedrock as it is- meaning that whatever was there was stripped to the natural ground level. That means that the Jewish community would be torn if work was done."

"I totally agree," said David. 'The sanctity of dreams should be preserved and no work done that might shatter a core belief of our faith."

I went on. "On the other hand, the Moslem hand, the third holiest place in Islam is also sacrosanct. Can you imagine the ire of 800 million of the faithful descending on archaeologists working for the Jewish state? It would lead to the next global war- which could easily put an end to the planet. Finally, in our case here, if we were to fully open the casket and find a few bone fragments and ash, do we run a DNA test? There are descendants of Colon who we could try to type-match. However, what if the tests are inconclusive, or worse, negative? We are no farther along, or better off, than when we started. And even greater turmoil might erupt."

The three others fell silent, staring into their coffee cups as if the grounds held an answer. A few moments later I broke the silence.

"I say that we let the 'unknown servant of God' rest in peace, and not violate the casket in the name of science and discovery. To me, I intuitively feel that I have an answer and am comfortable with that. There would never be a world-wide announcement or publicity regardless. At least I don't think so now that we came this far and got to this point."

David recognized the truth in the statement and added his perspective. "I feel that the island would be torn apart. I feel that a major fight would erupt with the Spanish authorities *AND* the Catholic Church. Cuba would be caught in the middle. And that there would be anti-Semites who would find a way to jump on the bandwagon of continued animosity and use this against us, Jews in Cuba and all over the world. This in turn would benefit the world of terror by perversely recruiting people of Christian faith to support their cause against us."

Berto, the logistician, proposed that we sleep on it.

* * *

Back at the cemetery, the caretaker woke with a snort. He glanced at the battered clock on his makeshift desk and saw that it was going on 1pm. *Time for lunch*, he thought. He packed his knapsack and went out of the hut. He noticed the gardening tools, bucket and rags left outside the door. The visitors had left. A simple note, *Gracias*, was left, along with a 5 Cuban peso note. The note was signed by the president, David Tacher. The old man murmured his appreciation as he stuffed the bill into his shirt pocket, making certain that he didn't put it in the torn one. *That* would thoroughly piss him off. Because this money, outside of his government-based salary, was entirely *his* for his own entertainment. The *familia* would not need to know of this little bonus. He could visit the *taberna* a couple of blocks away on his way home, with no recriminations. As he padlocked the gate, he smiled and made his way out of the *barrio*.

* * *

The three of us made our way back to Los Caneyes. David had been dropped off at the Jewish Center- he said that he had some more thinking to do. The rooftop patio was just the place. He could sit and gaze at the Western Wall painting and try to make sense of everything that had happened over the last couple of days. Yoli decided to go for a swim. The day was hot, the water inviting, and the pool boy was cute. She too needed some space. Although she understood the major problems posed by our quest, she still felt that science and history had lost out in the long run. I don't think that she was upset with us; but rather, felt that her position wasn't taken as seriously as she would have hoped. I sensed that she would come about in time. But in the short-term, there was a deep disappointment. All too often, the idealism of youth casts them headlong into potential disaster; all for a cause, a stance. Its only when we all mature that our impetuousness gets tempered by age, and hopefully, wisdom. Berto, deep down, felt the same as I did; that we both had 'been around the block' several times and could think about ramifications down the road.

I headed over to my room to change into a swimsuit also. That water *did* sent out an invitation. As I walked past the pool complex my phone pinged. It was a text message from Jerusalem. Kati wanted to Skype whenever it was convenient, no matter the time. I picked up the pace a bit. This 'call' would be done inside the room, privately.

I did a quick calculation. It was early evening in Jerusalem. I figured that she would be home by now, using her desktop. I pictured her flat on quiet *Bnei Batira* Street. It was a far cry from the din that marked Havana and her vibrant street life. However, Havana's old city was not that different from old inner Jerusalem city life, like the revitalized Ben Yehuda mall in Jerusalem. Part of the original western city expansion at the start of the 20th century, it was only a ten minute walk from her apartment building. The city of Jerusalem through the 19th century was an out-of-the-way, provincial backwater town that would have been deemed 'worthless' were it not for the religious significance. Even Mark Twain recognized that. *In Innocents Abroad*, dated to 1867, was amazed by the smallness of the city of Jerusalem:

"A fast walker could go outside the walls of Jerusalem and walk entirely around the city in an hour. I do not know how else to make one understand how small it is."

It was only at that time that westerners began to expand the city across the *Hinnom* Valley to the west. This settlement, known as *Mishkenot Sha'ananim*, eventually flourished and set the precedent for other new communities to spring up to the west and north of the Old City. In time, as the communities grew and connected geographically, this became known as the New City. The main street, Jaffa Road, intersected at an angle with Ben Yehuda Street. Elegant European-style colonial houses and shops dotted the landscape. During the period of division of the city, between 1949-67, the area languished due to its position- immediately adjacent to "No Person's Land" of barbed-wire and landmines; separating the Jordanians and Israelis. After the reunification in 1967, a massive redevelopment project known as *Mamilla* would rejuvenate the neighborhood, including the creation of the pedestrian mall.

Called the *Midrachov*, the Pedestrian Mall, the young and young-at-heart in the city would flock here for coffee or ice cream, or their favorite stores to window-shop or, as I put it, 'reality shop' for stuff you needed. I fondly remembered dozens of visits to the area, many with her.

Before the call, I splashed some cool water on my face and cleaned up a bit from the cemetery visit. I took stock of everything that occurred, jotting a couple of 'memory' notes so that I wouldn't forget key points that I wished to tell the IDAM associate director. Her input would be of tremendous value; and have a calm, somewhat detached perspective that would be important in the long run. This was of major importance to the Jewish world, the western world, and the Cuban and Spanish worlds. How we proceeded would impact the 'currently known' record of events.

The phone 'swallowed' once and there was Kati. I could see that she indeed was at home. She laughed when I mentioned my surprise that she *only* must have worked 18 hours that day- amazed that I caught her at the apartment.

"It was actually 16 hours today, Bedouin man!" The smile did wonders for me. I quickly filled her in on our discoveries, thanks to her help, and the help of her colleagues at the Israel Museum. I had emailed some photos to her earlier from the cemetery- showing the sarcophagus and interior of the crypt. She was extremely interested in the wood-burned inscription on the lid of the coffin. When asked about our plans, I was pleased that she seemed to agree with our assessment of how to proceed. But I thought that I heard a faint sense of misgiving in her voice.

"Nu? What gives? I hear a 'but' in your voice."

"Why are you asking about my 'butt?'" She laughed, but there was a slight hiccup there. "I'm torn between the scientist in me and the person of faith in me as well. I agree with you regarding the 'what ifs' of the human experience. We need to explore, to search, to do the Star Trek thing...."

"Huh? Now *I'm* lost." The look on my face caused her to smile. "I thought that you were a real Trekkie! Ah, come on, the old 'go where no man has gone before' *shtick*! Where's Gene Rodenberry when I need him." She made a face then laughed.

"He's dead, don't you know!" I laughed as well. But I understood her dilemma all too well- it was mine also. Then I remembered my friend Sobhy, back in Cairo. "Remember Sobhy?" I said more seriously. "He was faced with the same problem regarding the statue fragment in the museum, remember?" The discovery of Israel's Pharaoh, and the overwhelming urge to destroy the evidence almost destroyed my dear friend and colleague. The thrill of discovery, the tracing of evidence, and the intrigue that involved so many of us nearly did us all in.

"How could I forget all that, and the earthquake on top of it all?" She smiled wistfully, remembering that we all were at risk for a period of time. "I don't know if I care to be a part of all that *balagan*, that mess, ever again. So what's the answer?"

"How about I tell you when I figure it out? We leave for Havana in the morning and I hope, we hope, to sort it out before then." *That's the best you can do?* I thought.

"That's the best you can do?" she said.

"Holy shit! Are you reading my mind?" I was laughing hard. She joined in.

"If so, it's a really short volume!" With that, we signed off and I decided to try to get some rest before meeting the others for dinner.

* * *

A couple of hours later, we met outside the restaurant. The rest had done me a bit of good- I only catnapped, though, because the picture-show of our quest kept re-running the scenario in my head. At best, the evidence had some key pieces fall into place. However, they only amounted to a circumstantial turn of events supported by a short list of intriguing facts.

Yoli looked totally refreshed. The swimming at the pool 'cleared her head' as she put it. And the pool 'boy' was actually a young man her age, and the two agreed to have coffee in the outdoor bar after we met and tried to make sense of everything that had occurred.

Berto, well, is Berto. He was his usual unflappable self. He had taken a short walk around the grounds, checked up on his 'baby' to make sure the Santa Clara 'air patrol' didn't drop any wet and sticky 'bombs,' and then relaxed by the pool with a *Cristal* Beer. He didn't come out and say it, but I thought that he was 'chaperoning from a distance' our younger companion. Working together, educating her in the ways of San Cristobal Travel, had become much more than the usual professional relationship. He looked upon her as a niece that needed a bit of guiding and looking after. Most of the time he got away with it. She was none the wiser. In this instance, she was too absorbed with the pool boy to take note of his lounging a few meters from the pool deck.

David had begged off, citing the need to spend some time with his family. Our unexpected visit and the intensity of our activities over the past couple of days had drained him as well. He promised to see us at breakfast before we left town.

Once inside, it was up to me to secure a table, since both Yoli and Berto made a beeline for the buffet. Apparently they knew something I didn't, that tonight was a shrimp night. Once I got the table and a waiter to bring drinks, I walked over to a three-deep crowd. I peeked around a couple of guests, and saw plates piled sky-high with grilled, breaded or sautéed shrimp.

I made my way cautiously through the throng and got a plate. By the time I moved a couple of feet down the line, the shrimp were sorely depleted. *Maalesh*, '*what can you do?*' I thought in Arabic, then amended it to '*ah bueno*,' the rough equivalent in Spanish. I settled for my standard *ropas viejas* and a couple of sides and returned to the table.

My friends were already digging in. *They* appeared to be the source of the 'shrimp depletion of 2015' (as it would go down in Cuban culinary history) as their plates were Mount Everest sized mounds of crustaceans. I knew that if I commented on it, there wouldn't be a reply- they were stuffing their mouths busily. But I tried.

"You two do know the meaning of 'buffet'?" I asked.

"Hmmmmm…" chomp-chomp-chomp was the sole response that I got. But then came, "please pass another napkin over….."

I explained the notion of the ability to go back again and again (if necessary) as part of the 'what don't you understand about the term 'buffet,' but got a mild rebuke from Yoli.

"Yes, we're not *stupido,* we get it. Did you see us the other night? But 'shrimp night' brings out the best, er, worst, in people. Because we're so far inland here, it's a real task to get the fresh shrimp to Santa Clara. And once it's here, well, it's gone! And in a flash."

"So this is a rare breech of protocol you could say." Berto brought his two *centavos* to the table, between bites.

The meal progressed this way for about 20 more minutes, or two more trips to the food line. And certainly by then the 'decimation of the shrimp' was made complete. It would go down in history.

Once my friends were sated, and coffee was gotten (along with the ice cream! (Where do they put it all?), we 'sobered' up and tried to address the issues at hand- and how to proceed. Unfortunately, we couldn't resolve anything. As we laid out all the facts on the table, giving pros and cons, the 'balance' always seemed to be a 'wash.' No matter what was said, 'on the one hand, yet on the other…' canceled each other out almost equally.

To me it was relatively clear (as mud). We would just have to go to the Archdiocese in Havana and present them with some facts, and get their response.

"Hold on, you want us *to go to the Archdiocese*?" Yoli was stunned. "But they're the, well, they're *the Archdiocese*!" She hurriedly crossed herself. If she wasn't so serious, I'd being laughing. "The Archbishop is probably one of the ten most powerful men on the island who's name doesn't begin with *Castro*." There was another quick 'crossing.'

Berto calmed her a bit. Always the statesman (except when he wasn't), he made it clear to Yoli that no one was accusing anyone of anything. We only wanted to look at some records regarding the Church in the 18th century- and that was all. She needn't be concerned with insulting anyone in the current Church hierarchy. Nor did she need to worry about disparaging anyone in the Church's past as well.

At this point, I tried to lighten things up a bit with, "Only the facts, Ma'am!" Berto laughed as he recalled the old American TV drama, Dragnet. However, Yoli just frowned a bit as she didn't get the reference. The show's reruns had even gone off the air in the States long before she was born. The only stations still rebroadcasting were local independents in a handful of small market towns scattered here and there, mostly just in the U.S. heartland.

My final word was that she'd just have to 'roll with it' and that we'd all play it by ear back in Havana. With that, we adjourned for the evening.

XVII

Back to Havana

THE DAY DAWNED with just a few high level clouds scudding across the Santa Clara horizon. As usual, I was the first at breakfast. I figured that the coming day called for loading up on energy. The buffet beckoned, and with a full plate I made my way to a table as close to the coffee machine as possible. I needed the caffeine fix, because it was a restless night after around 3am. At that point, my overloaded brain forced my eyes open; and from then on the 'picture show' of events kept displaying re-run after re-run for me. Even so, there were no answers presenting themselves.

I was on my third cup when Berto arrived. He, too, looked like sleep eluded him a bit and I remarked on that. I was waved off, as, like me, he immediately 'beelined' to the large urn. However, he was a bit wiser than me. He came back with two steaming cups.

"*Gracias amigo!*" I said as I playfully reached for the second cup.

"Wait jes' one gol-darned minute, pahdnuh," was his response as he blocked my hand.

"Where did *that* come from?" I asked.

"It seems that you're treating this whole thing, especially with the Archbishop in Havana, like a bad Wild West movie, so I was just supplying the dialog." Berto was only half-joking, I could tell. It seems that his sleepless night was focused on the possible confrontation with the Catholic Church later today or tomorrow- and it worried him. "Remember, you get to leave the island after it's all said and done. Yoli and I are still in Havana, and David, well, he will still be in Santa Clara dealing with a very provincial religious clergy. Yes, the Jewish community there has been well accepted, but this rocking the boat could upset the apple cart."

"You really love your American-isms, don't you?" I smiled.

His return smile was still tempered with his serious concern.

Yoli showed a few minutes later. We could all feel a bit of tension, but tried to ignore it by talking about anything but our mystery. I told the others that I had contacted David Tacher at home this morning and said that we hadn't come to any conclusions, and he should stay home with the family and not bother coming to the Los Caneyes. He tried to argue, but I could hear that it was a half-hearted protest. I felt that he was relieved to be free of this burden for a short while. I promised that I would call from Havana if we found out any more information, or had come to any more substantive solution as to how to go on.

We hurriedly finished (which meant another hour, thanks to my friends and their insatiable appetites) and completed check-out in record time. Berto had gassed up the beast the night before because it was the end of the month and he could use the last ration coupon, so we were able to hit the road rather quickly.

Just outside the city limits, we immediately saw dozens of people standing alongside the road waiting for a ride. Since the largest owner of vehicles is the government, and 80% of all Cubans are employed by the government, with nearly 150,000 government vehicles on the road, there are lots of empty places available.

Once more, at the head of the ragged line was the man in a yellow jumpsuit. This was an integral part of government-mandated regulations that arose during the *periodo especial*, the 'special period', that began in 1989, all government vehicles that had empty seats were obliged to pick up passengers. You could easily spot these due to the color of their license plates. Waiting riders were to be picked up on a 'first come-first go' basis. They would pay a nominal fee for the lift, monitored and regulated by the government based on distance. Failure to stop and pick up travelers would be reported and the drivers were to be fined. Of course, this applied only to Cuban nationals; no tourists could take advantage.

I saw an 'I gotcha!' moment and jumped on it.

"Yoli, you really ate too much at the buffet at Los Caneyes these past couple of days. I can feel Berto's car being realllllly heavily weighed down! I hope that we can make it up these hills and then have enough gas for the run into Havana. What do you think, Berto?" I winked.

He caught on, and with the merest hint of a smile agreed with me. "I think maybe, as a government employee of San Cristobal Agency, you might need to join the line with the others here! After all, if we run out, then I need to use a coupon from this month, and it's only the beginning. I can't afford that….."

The look of alarm was priceless! Yoli's eyes were as wide as the heavy chrome hubcaps of the '57 Chevy, and just as shiny. "Berto!" she screamed. "You can't mean this, after all look at those *campesinos* out there! My jeans would be ruined, my blouse!" She was blubbering on and on. The tears started forming in the corner of her eyes. I looked at Berto and indicated that it was time to shut it down.

"You can't, can you? You won't, will you?" She was almost pleading. The chief guide for San Cristobal looked at his best student and started to laugh. I joined in. Yoli's scream was carried well beyond the confines of the top-down roadster, and those along the road for over 100 yards snapped their heads up in amazement. She punched Berto, hard, on his right biceps from the back seat. I was shaking with laughter. She then reached across and smacked me on the left arm. Her embarrassment at 'being had' was clear, and this was her response to get even. I knew that Berto and I would feel it far into the evening to come. She packed a great right and equally potent backhand. I rubbed my shoulder, sat back, and enjoyed the rest of the ride.

It was fairly uneventful until traffic began to build just past *San Francisco de Paula*, the locale of Hemingway's *Finca Vigia*. It remained slow, but steady until the tunnel under the harbor that led to the corniche. From there, it was practically bumper to bumper until we reached the *Malecon* and the approach to the *Nacional*. The long ride was somewhat exhausting. Berto dropped me off and promised to call later to meet up for dinner. I waved to the two of them as they drove off, and took my small bag to the Reception for check-in.

"Senor Flynn is waiting for you in the room," the clerk smiled as he handed me the key to 235; my home away from home in Havana. I hit the shower, then the bed and was out like the proverbial light. There wasn't a peep from Errol, and I slept til the phone woke me as the sun was beginning to set.

* * *

A splash of water, a quick brush of the teeth, and I was downstairs waiting for Berto and Yoli to drive up under the portico. The evening crowd was just beginning to arrive for the dinner and show at *La Parisien*, and the valets were doing a brisk business. So were the CubaTaxis with their tourist fares. I stood off to the side to let these folks by, not wanting to get crushed by the ill-mannered who pushed and shoved their way along the sidewalk to get to the canopied entrance just off to the right and partly around the circular drive.

As always, the '57 Chevy caught nearly everyone's eye as it drove down the long approach that was really an extension of *Calle 21*. With the top down, Berto got his share of admiring looks as well.

I admit, it was an ego thing for me as well as I opened the door and slid onto the vinyl seat. I noticed no Yoli.

"So, where's our young companion? Or is she still pissed that we played such a trick on her along the road from Santa Clara?" I smiled.

"Nothing like that at all," he replied. "Remember that her father lives just a few minutes away from *Habana Vieja*, and she said that she'd walk to the restaurant and meet us there. I decided to call in a couple of favors. I got us a table and a 'comped' meal at the Café del Oriente!"

"Wow!" was all that I could muster. Regarded as one of the finest Spanish/Continental cuisines in Havana, the Oriente was one of the 'in' spots of the old city. It was located on San Francisco Square, at *Calle Amargura*. A few outside tables adorned the façade of the building, with a bar on the ground floor. But it was the ornate dining room on the second floor that was all the rage. The oversized windows in the colonial building at night gave stunning views of the *Sierra Maestra* Boat Terminal, the Commerce Exchange Building, and of course the Cathedral and Convent of Saint Francis of Assisi. I was really looking forward to it.

As always, along the *Malecon* just opposite the boat terminal, a 'parking man' was waiting for us. The notion of *proteccion* followed Berto around like a bad *centavo*. He told me that it was my turn- so I used the lesson learned from my friend and tore a 5 CUC note in half, with the promise of the other half upon our return to a car left in as pristine (or better) shape as when it was dropped off. The man smiled, familiar with the routine, and slid the half-bill into a pocket faster than you could say 'Café del Oriente.' I thought to myself that he should create a magic act for the plaza during the day- the tourists would eat it up.

The air was almost cool, with just a hint of the humidity that plagued the city most of the year. Very few clouds blocked the million or so stars that shone down on the city. All in all, it was a great evening. Since we were a few minutes early, due to the ease of parking, we strolled slowly around the square. I am always drawn to "The Conversation" sculpture. The sculpture itself is a beautiful bronze casting of a conversation between two people in an attitude of serious exchange of ideas! It is mounted on a base of Cuba's finest marble and hidden within this plinth is a box containing French and Cuban coins. In addition, there is a message left for future generations. The importance of verbal, face to face conversation in this age of text messaging and social networking needed to be emphasized, according to the artist. The figures have parts missing from their bodies allowing a clear view through to the plaza beyond. The empty space is probably what makes this sculpture a 'conversation piece' itself. Berto brought this up to me.

"You know, it's not all that different from the things that are left unsaid in a conversation. We need to know how to 'read between the lines' and we really need to understand what people mean to say."

"So I guess that rules out politicians," I replied with a smile.

Since Yoli had yet to appear, we continued to walk around the plaza, passing the white marble *Fuente de los Leones*, the Fountain of Lions, carved by the Italian sculptor Giuseppe Gaggini in 1836. We approached the magnificent façade of the church and paused in front of a more modern statue. It was a sculpture of a famous, or infamous, Havanan, *El Caballero de París*. He was a well-known street person who roamed Old Havana streets during the 1950s, trying to carry on conversations with passers-by; describing his philosophies of life, religion, politics and current events of that day. According to the mythology surrounding this statue, anyone who strokes the statue's beard will have their wishes granted. At that moment, Yoli showed up. She immediately walked up to the figure and tugged on its beard.

"Hi guys! I'm hoping.... Hoping for.....oh wait! I can't tell you or it'll never come true," she smiled that mischievous grin of hers.

"You don't really buy into that story, do you?" I asked somewhat incredulously.

Again, she just smiled impishly.

Since our reservation wasn't for a short time yet, I opted to go back toward the Basilica of St. Francis of Assisi. The Third Order of St. Francis has run the complex since 1842, although the building itself was begun in 1580 for the Franciscans. The building that exists today is 'new' though. Of course, that in itself is a relative term. At some time between 1717 and 1738 the facades and the interior underwent a renovation to reflect the art and architecture of that day- the Baroque. In 1762, the British occupied the island for nearly the entire year. Some say that they used it as a house of worship; while those vehemently opposed to England insist that they used it as a stable and barn for their military horses. Regardless, in 1841 the Spanish government shut it down as a religious institution- fearing the power of the Franciscan order of the Catholic Church. The most significant element of the Church is its bell tower. At 42 meters, it is the tallest in Havana, second on the island only after Trinidad's *Manaca Iznaga* tower; the watchtower of the sugar cane plantation in the *Valle de Los Ingenios* which rises 45 meters in height. Originally a statue of St. Francis of Assisi stood on the top of the basilica's bell tower but it was destroyed by a hurricane in 1846. Today the church is a concert hall for classical and vocal performances. The basilica is said to have the best acoustics in Havana.

Berto glanced at his watch. "Time to go, they hate to be kept waiting." So we completed the quarter turn around the plaza, entered *Calle Amargura*, and walked the twenty steps or so to the door and then up. The somewhat narrow staircase gave absolutely no indication of the luxurious restaurant that awaited. The dark-wood wainscoting and flocked wallpaper were an elegant throwback to colonial days. A beautiful stained glass canopy embraces you from above, supported by classical Greek-style columns. The heavy brocaded curtains, with gold-threaded patterns, gave a sense of opulence. Draw them back, and the view of the plaza and harbor beyond, from the second floor, was really breathtaking; even more so at night with the lights of El Morro Castle on the other side winking and shimmering. It is a view that no one ever forgets. The Maitre D' escorted us to our table, greeting Berto with a hug. *Senor Enciclopedia* seemed to know everyone on the island. I remarked at that again, and he merely shrugged. Yoli winked as if to say that I certainly had gotten that one right. A few moments after we sat down, Angel Roque, the head chef, came out of the kitchen and headed toward our table. He too greeted Berto with a hug and standard kiss on each cheek, and told us to put away our menus.

We deferred to the head chef, and what came out of the kitchen was nothing short of ecstasy. The first thing to arrive were red peppers stuffed with cheese. I remarked that I saw nothing like it on the menu. Berto told me that, for some strange reason, these hors d'oeuvres were called 'crepes.' This was followed by delicious smoked salmon and steak au poivre with grilled vegetables. I told Yoli the next time she went online to Wikipedia and googled "stuffed" she would see my picture.

Chef Roque returned to our table as we were finishing the main courses, in order to make sure that everything was okay. As we complimented the cuisine, he motioned back to the station just outside of the kitchen door. A trolley was wheeled out, laden with deserts- a cheese plate, fruit, and, to top it all off, baked Alaska that the chef personally set aflame for us at the table. Thick, strong Cuban coffee rounded out the meal.

At that point, we decided to adjourn to one of the outside tables in the plaza, in order to try to find our way to a successful resolution of our dilemma.

It had rained a few minutes while we were inside eating. The air was clean, fresh without the usual humidity that accompanied a tropic rain. A slight breeze blew across the plaza from the harbor, and the sea tang was pleasant- not too overwhelming. A waiter wiped down the chairs and we settled in. I had come prepared for this, and pulled a mutli-folded piece of paper from my pocket. I spread it out on the table and explained that these were the main bits of evidence that we had come up with so far.

I read the list out loud, letting each point sink in a bit before continuing to the next.

> 1. Columbus had Jewish crew members and was considered to be at least partly Jewish himself.
> 2. This caused him a bit of difficulty both with his monarch and his family.
> 3. He died in Seville, Spain, somewhat destitute- to some a hero, others not so much.
> 4. The family wished to honor his will in that he wanted to be buried in Hispaniola.
> 5. The Spanish 'rehabilitated' Columbus, wanting to rescue his sarcophagus before the French completed occupation of the island. But did they get there?
> 6. These remains were to be relocated in Havana at what would become known as the Colon Cemetery. Or were they moved?
> 7. *BUT WHERE?!!!!!!*
> 8. Spanish authorities found a sarcophagus inscribed with the name 'Colon' and promptly displayed it in Seville- claiming that it never made it to Hispaniola and then never to Cuba.
> 9. Yet the Church and Cuba believed the remains were still in Cuba.
> 10. Anti-Jewish behavior indicated that some in the Church hierarchy were uneasy with a Jew in their hallowed burials- even a prominent hero like Columbus.
>
> Could they have moved him surreptitiously?
> *__BUT WHERE?!!!!!!!!!!__*
> *__DID WE FIND HIM IN SANTA CLARA?!!!!!!!!!!!!__*

I sat back and looked expectantly at my colleagues. Each was deep in thought, perhaps flashing back to actions that took place centuries ago. I knew better than disrupt them. I took another sip of the strong brew before me and waited. *I won't sleep tonight because of all this caffeine,* I thought. *Or won't I sleep because of this mess?*

The tension was broken as a trio of musicians strolled close by our table. The other two snapped out of their reverie, and looked confused.

"Where did you get the coffee, and why didn't I get one?" Yoli asked, a bit petulantly.

"You were all dreaming away, lost in your thoughts. I *did* put the question out there once, and then chose to let it slide when no one answered."

"Hmmph!" was all she said. That is, until she finally decided that a late coffee was better than no coffee at all. The same went for Berto. I sighed. *'Children' are so hard to deal with!* I thought as I ordered another one to 'keep them company.'

"It seems, at least to me, that the Church here in Havana probably has all the answers that we need." Berto said between sips. "If they can actually find the records is one thing. If they are willing to have a dialog with us about the contents is another. I have never had much luck in dealing with the Archdiocese- even though, I admit, there have been only a couple of instances over the past several years. You know how I am with matters of religion." He smiled ruefully. Maybe this would be a slight turning point for him.

"But do you think that they will open up to us? After all, it may be seen as either intrusion into internal church affairs, or an insult to their integrity and autonomy." Yoli made an extraordinarily insightful comment.

"The one thing *I don't* want to do is step on ecclesiastical toes! Especially on the island. After all, no matter the political and economic status here, the Church still maintains an iron grip on the vast majority of Cubans in some form or another." Berto went on to describe the way that the Church and the State created an alliance early in Cuba's history that allowed each to move ahead in their goals- sometimes dovetailing nicely one to the other. This even continued with the rise of the communist regime in the early 1969s. The Belen complex was the perfect example- and the perfect 'poster-child' for the reason why we needed to tread ever-so-lightly.

In order to create a hospital for convalescents, the Bishop Diego Avelino de Compostela donated his own orchard in *Habana* and a part of his wealth to be used, along with the alms collected for such a charitable deed, on the construction of this convent. The project started in 1712 and finished in 1718.

The convent was given to the first members of the order of Bethlehem that arrived in Havana in 1704. When this order was suppressed in 1842, the convent fell into the hands of the Spanish government that used it as offices, with the exception of the church. The building was occupied by the vice-captain general and by an infantry battalion. In 1854, when the Society of Jesus was reestablished on the island, the Jesuits took possession of the *Convento de Belén* and enlarged it. In the early 1960s, the Church and Castro came to an arrangement that saw the use of the convent converted to meet the needs of social reform for the people.

Today the property is overseen by the Office of Humanitarian Affairs and the Office of the City Historian. Located at *Calle Compostela e Luz y Acosta*, it is in an area of considerable poverty, and, within the convent work is carried out to help those people who are the most vulnerable, weakest and poor. Older adults as well as children and invalids of any age receive direct attention. These are people who can find refuge without stopping to think about the struggle for survival in these uncertain times. A rehabilitation and physiotherapy center, an optician's office, workshops in crafts, singing, poetry, crocheting and physical exercises, group breakfasts and especially human contact allow people to forget the loneliness and sense of abandonment that are usually associated with the elderly. Inside the premises, children and grandparents also interact to bring the interests of the youngest and the oldest generations closer together.

"So, I am loathe to ruffle feathers, roil the waters, overstir the pot..." As always, he *loved* his idioms! I laughed, and Yoli simply gave her trademark "Humpphh" as Berto's attempt at a witticism fell flat on her ears.

"OK, *Senor Enciclopedia*. How then do we proceed? Do we ignore the role of the Church and now just drop it?" I was getting frustrated.

"No, we need to be circumspect in our inquiry. Ask without asking, explore without seeming to probe deeply. And most of all, *flatter* the Church to the *n*th degree! If I know my Catholic prelates, the only thing dearer to them than their faith is their ego!"

At this, even Yoli laughed. By now, the evening was late and we all went to bed. Yoli walked to her father's, Berto drove me back to the Nacional, with the promise to meet me early at the buffet (of course) when he would offer up his plan of attack.

* * *

The next morning broke clear and crisp, just a hint of the fall to come. Errol apparently was sleeping in and I chose not to disturb him. I headed down to the lobby, then down the flight of stairs to the lower level restaurant. As I was approaching the Maitre d's desk, Berto rounded the corner and joined me. The Maitre d' checked my room number off the composite list, and shook hands with the San Cristobal chief of guides. He waved both of us in and I headed straight to the main buffet table to see what was being offered, while Berto 'beelined' it to the coffee machine. I then grabbed a table and got myself a cup also.

After choosing our fare, we settled in and attacked our plates. Small talk surrounded our bites for several minutes, until all that was left was another cup of coffee. We got down to business. Berto said that he would be happy to make an initial inquiry as to whether the Archdiocese would be open to a discrete examination of 'certain records' in their archive. On one hand, he thought that if we narrowed it down to the particular years in question we might have a good shot at getting some data. But then on the other hand, he was afraid that being too specific about years could likely lead to speculation by the curatorial staff. This could lead to a real problem. In addition, I reminded him of Yoli's visit to the Archdiocese just a little over a week ago. Could that set off alarm bells in the halls of the clerical offices in Havana? Before any decision would be made, we needed Yoli's input on how she felt after her interview with the Prelate, Alejandro. I suggested that we head upstairs and wait for her on the veranda overlooking the *Malecon*.

The sun was peeking between the white, puffy clouds over the Straits of Florida, a gentle breeze coming across from the water, making the terrace a lovely spot at this time of the morning. Berto had texted Yoli, telling her where we were. Within a quarter of an hour she came strolling through the double doors from the lobby. A quick glance and she found us. She sat down and immediately called over the waiter. The look on her face said "COFFEE" in bold letters.

"Don't ask," she said. "I'll just tell you. My father asked a million questions, kept me up until, oh, 2 or 3 this morning. *He* doesn't have to get up in the morning! I want to be a pensioner like him. And I want it now!" she growled at us. I looked at Berto, he looked at me, and together we kept our mouths shut until a steaming *café con leche* arrived at the table. I swear that she inhaled it. Before the waiter had walked ten meters she called back to him.

"*Camarero! Otro café con leche por favor!*" The waiter paused and turned back to her. When he saw the look on her face, he practically flew back to the outside kiosk to get the order. After the second cup, Yoli sat back, stared out across the water toward the harbor to the east, and said, "Life is good now." She smiled and Berto and I were able to breathe again.

I quickly outlined what Berto and I talked about the previous evening, and sought her input regarding the options. She, too, was a bit hesitant to go back to the 'well' of the Archdiocesan offices. She felt that, as long as she didn't run into the prelate that she dealt with before, we might have a chance at getting somewhere. The complex was so big that we could get away with it unseen by him. I didn't like the odds too much, and told them so. Yoli had a great idea- she would call and find out if Father Alejandro was in today. If not, it could be clear sailing. It sounded like a good plan, and Berto pulled out his mobile and placed an anonymous call. He sounded like a parishioner who had been counseled by the priest before, and was requesting whether he was in to hear confession. I grinned at that, imagining Berto in a confessional booth. Yoli giggled as well. And Berto, he looked like a Cheshire cat straight out of Disney. After being on hold for several minutes, Berto put his hand over the mouthpiece.

"There's not even any damn music to listen to. No Buena Vista Social Club, no nothing! Just dead air. It's like the Inquisition all over again- creating suffering martyrs upon the pain of death!"

I was about to answer him, when he held up a finger- *Wait!* He mumbled something into the receiver, thanked whoever was on the other end and hit the disconnect key.

"Father Alejandro is away from the Archdiocese, *he went to Santa Clara*! Apparently he took some personal time, and called from there just yesterday to say that he wouldn't be back as he was taking a couple days after his trip to meditate in the Escambrey Mountains."

Yoli was stunned. "Was he following me? How could he possible know anything? I certainly didn't tip him off... did I?" She was questioning herself now. I told her that she needn't worry, and that it could just as easily have been coincidence. We left it at that. Meanwhile, Berto called another extension at the Archdiocese in order to set up an appointment for us.

"*Si, Si, su Santidad*. Yes, Your Holiness. You do understand that he is a world-renowned archaeologist and scholar..... yes, of course, without question.... No, I will make that clear. *Gracias, Padre. Adios.*"

We looked at him expectantly.

"I just got off the phone with the Archbishop's Office. Cardinal Archbishop Jaime Lucas Ortega y Alamino is not in residence in Havana now. He is meeting with his peers from Latin America in Brazil at some sort of conclave. He is not expected for another week. Because of the research visit by an 'esteemed' archaeologist from America (he rolled his eyes), one of his auxiliary bishops will meet us and provide us with whatever assistance we need. But they can only spare some time today."

Yoli looked at him in amazement. "Who is this 'esteemed'.......oh," she said, and began to blush. Once again, her naiveté was charming.

"As I was saying, we will be met by either Bishop Juan de Dios Hernandez-Ruiz or his counterpart, Bishop Alfredo Petit-Vergel. We must get a move on." I threw a few CUCs on the table and we headed out to the car.

We exited the hotel grounds and made a left and another left until we descended to the *Malecon*. From there, it was a short drive east to the area of the harbor and *Habana Vieja*. As we approached the *Sierra Maestra* Terminal, a figure jumped off the curb and waved at us. It was Berto's 'parking protection.' A couple of Cuban pesos sealed the deal. We walked a few blocks into the old city. When we got to *Calle Habana*, we turned right and headed to the area of the Santa Clara Convent. At No. 152 we entered the offices of the Archdiocese. After announcing ourselves at the reception, we only had a few moments' wait until a male secretary summoned us to the inner offices.

After sitting quietly for a handful of minutes, Bishop Alfredo Petit-Vergel was announced to us. A middle-aged man, with the build of a dock-worker, entered the chamber. A physically powerful presence was balanced by a warm smile that was disarming. It was clear that he was a 'people person.' Not quite knowing how to act, I rose and grasped his strong hand. Both of his hands dwarfed mine in their grasp. Although powerful, it was not designed to overwhelm or intimidate by its strength. Rather, it was the power of conviction and support that was conveyed. I was impressed. Berto seemed to sense the same thing, and Yoli was awed in every way. She was more inclined to be one of the faithful than Berto was; and appeared to hang on the Bishop's every action, every word.

He immediately put us at ease as he inquired as to whether or not we would like tea, or coffee. When three hands went up for coffee, it was the Bishop himself who poured us cups- not his secretary (who had previously left the room). I felt that this was a man who came to this calling in mid-life, after working hard at manual labor in his earlier years. I also sensed a man of great intellect as well. This might play out in our favor.

Berto broke the ice with some small talk about the increasing friendship that was now developing with the U.S., and what people on the island were now calling the "Obama Doctrine" of reconciliation after all these past decades. I added my personal take, explaining the several times that I had visited the island as part of the humanitarian and educational programming opened up in recent years.

Bishop Alfredo was delighted at all that was transpiring, and told us that everyone in the Church had been praying for this time to occur.

"It is with a great sense of relief that the normalization of relations with the U.S. is about to come to fruition. I have prayed for the families that were split apart decades ago. And I have also prayed that the leaders *on both sides* would come to their senses and celebrate this reunion."

I knew of the somewhat tempestuous relationship that developed between the Church and the Castro brothers early on. I also knew that a cold truce of sorts was worked out, brokered in part by the Vatican- getting the Castros to look the other way at times in exchange for financial backing of some social institutions by the international Catholic community. But to hear explicit criticism of the Castro regime directly still took me by surprise.

Berto began to gently steer the conversation to the matter at hand- cemetery records and Church documentation that might shed light on tracing the final journey of Columbus. He took the bishop through the more commonly known facts that we had discovered and collated. He took us all back to the last days of Columbus, his 'will' of sorts that told his heirs where he wished to be buried, and the apparent infighting about which location should get 'bragging rights' as the resting place of the great explorer.

The bishop nodded several times- indicating that he was fully aware of the rumors and the facts as presented by all sides. At a couple of points, he would ask an insightful question or two that would clarify things. When Berto pointedly asked about the initial transfer from Hispaniola, and relocation of the sarcophagus in the *Espada* Cemetery, Bishop Alfredo grew agitated, nervous. He wiped his brow as if he was sweating, even though it was quite comfortable in his study.

"How did the Church feel about the constant transfer of the coffin during those turbulent times?" I asked the prelate. "We saw no indication in any of the records of uneasiness or the sense of inappropriateness by Church leaders in Spain, or here on the island. Doesn't there come a point in time when a sense of respect mandates that there be no more activity; and let the great man lie in peace?" I might have gone too far, but the bishop smiled and didn't seem to take offense.

"Your points that you make are clearly coming from a position of respect and honor- that is clear to me. Yet I feel that there is something more than I can hear. Am I right?" The Bishop smiled benignly. (I was reminded of a stupid kid's joke. *When asked the definition of 'benig, n, a young student said, 'that's what comes right after you 'be eight.')*

The three of us sitting across from the bishop now had the tables turned a bit. Yoli seemed more uncertain of things than Berto and I. But I took the lead, which meant that I also would bear the brunt of the 'heat' should it come to that.

I started off by asking about the early days of the *Cemeterio Espada*, the forerunner of the Colon. It seemed to be a safe, neutral starting point. The clergyman outlined the founding and evolution, as it morphed into the larger, bigger complex. He then, without prompting, explored the activity, as officially recorded by the Church, surrounding the movement of the venerated remains of Columbus from one place to the next. When he got to Cuba's involvement, the 'temporary home' and the subsequent 'relocation' to Seville, he faltered and seemed to show a signs of uncertainty with regard to the 'party line.'

Sensing that, Berto jumped into the fray, putting forth a possible scenario that none of us had even considered.

"Your Eminence, maybe out of honor, and a deep sense of respect for Columbus' original wishes to have his body stay in the Caribbean, could his remains have possibly been divided? After all, by that time, several centuries down the road, there would have only been bone dust and some fragments?"

Bishop Alfredo hastily crossed himself and spluttered a response- sending a spray of spittle across the occasional table that separated us. Were it not for the distance, we would have borne the brunt of a saliva shower. Not the most pleasant thing. He turned an unhealthy shade of pink, as his blood pressure rose. But as he collected himself after a couple of moments, his answer was anything but forceful and from the heart.

"Forgive for saying, but I find your claim to be disrespectful, untruthful." His eyes darted about, from Yoli, to Berto, to me and back. Clearly the man was nervous.

"We certainly mean no disrespect, your Eminence. But isn't it possible that veneration and love for 'the hometown hero' could lead to a favorable solution for both nations? After all, with the distances involved, only a handful of people might be aware of the notion of sharing the honor. It really shouldn't be considered to be blasphemy, but rather- 'joint custody.'" Berto surely had a way with words. It appeared to calm the religious leader.

"Yes, yes, of course, I can see that scenario hundreds of years ago. After all, we all are just human, with human responses and actions that we think support our own interpretations of piety. It *could* have been a real occurrence."

The three of us glanced at each other, as the bishop seemed to drift off for a moment. A nerve had been struck- but not a new thought. It was as if this particular church leader had been harboring this hidden notion for a long time, but only was coming to grips with it as outsiders now seem to have stumbled upon it as well. He summoned his assistant and ordered another round of coffee. He said that it calmed his nerves.

We all sat back. I excused myself for a moment, inquiring as to the location of the restroom. As I walked in the direction pointed out, I noticed a set of door leading to the enclosed courtyard. I slipped through them for a couple of minutes, drinking in the cool, shaded air outside. This is what calmed my nerves.

* * *

When I returned, the coffees had been replenished. But in addition, there was an enormous plate of almond cookies. *When did I last hear about these?* I thought. Then it hit me, it was when David was at the Tzarfati household in Santa Clara. I was astonished. *God works in mysterious ways*, was my next thought. I sensed that the time was right now to broach the most delicate of subjects.

As we sat, drank and munched, with small talk interspersed between nibbles, I cleared my throat and set a course.

"Your holiness, thank you so much for the refreshments. It is just what we need after the intense conversation a short while ago. These almond cookies are delicious. The last time I was made aware of this delicacy, it was in Santa Clara. At the house of the Tzarfati family." I saw a look dawning in Berto's eyes.

"You may not be familiar with them," I continued. The bishop shook his head, no. "They are the Jewish family in Santa Clara in charge of the community's burial society, the *Hevra Kadisha*." Now Yoli smiled a bit as she, too, saw the direction I was heading.

"I am familiar with the practice of our Jewish cousins," replied the prelate.

"Well, this family has had leadership of the society for many generations- in fact, one could almost say that it was hereditary!" I laughed at this, and everyone smiled. The really thin layer of ice that had formed was now broken. I briefly outlined our recent visit there, and described in detail the nature of the Jewish cemetery, and the incredible Holocaust Memorial. Bishop Alfredo became very animated when he mentioned that he had been there, and prayed with members of the Jewish community there. He seemed extraordinarily thoughtful in his description of the event- it struck a real chord with him apparently.

I thought this might be the moment to change direction of the conversation, so I outlined the work that we had done in our research in both Havana and Santa Clara, with Berto filling in any details that I may have left out. Berto also supplied the necessary translation when the Bishop's English understanding became unclear. In addition, I described the new scientific technology that we employed through the kind assistance of the Israeli Department of Antiquities and Kati Ben Ya'ir. I gave glowing praise to her work. The prelate broke in and said that some day he would like to meet this tremendously capable woman. At that point, I felt that the time was right.

"Your Holiness, if I may ask, when did the exploration of the Jewish ancestry of Senor Colon begin for the Church?" I asked. Yoli gasped. She apparently didn't think that I would be so abrupt and direct with a man of the cloth. He merely sighed, smiled, and set down his coffee cup from mid sip. He looked at his watch.

"It is noon now. Do we dare drink a toast with something more, well, 'toastable?' *I* certainly welcome it!" He didn't look troubled in the least at the question. "You know it's only a rumor," he said as he went on to describe the official Church stance on Columbus' supposed heritage that focused on his

Jewishness. Church records were so vague in the 15th and 16th centuries, he continued, as a bottle of Havana Club rum miraculously appeared on the low table with four shot glasses. The Bishop poured a dram into each of them, and took his glass.

"*Salud*! To the memory of Cristobal Colon, may he rest in peace, *wherever* that may be!" He winked at us and threw back the glass. We all followed suit, Yoli spluttering a bit as the liquid burned its way down her throat.

"Where was I, oh yes, his ancestry. I should be indignant, after all, you have just implied that a great Catholic hero isn't so, well, Catholic. But I'm not. After all, doesn't *Catholic* really mean 'universal?'" He was smiling broadly now. "I have long been aware of the notion that he had Jewish blood, based on very scant, and somewhat obtuse, statements found in early biographical texts. It was a turbulent time in Spain, what with the *Auto-de-Fe*."

Yoli broke in, "I'm not so sure that I follow, your Eminence." She was unaware of the direction that the conversation was heading. The Bishop went on.

"The *Auto-de-Fe* consisted of a Catholic Mass- prayer; a public procession of those found guilty; and a reading of the sentences of those accused. They took place in public squares or esplanades and lasted several hours. Both ecclesiastical and civil authorities attended; not to mention the masses. Artistic representations of the *Auto de Fe* usually depict torture and the burning at the stake. However, this type of activity never took place during an *Auto-de-Fe*, which was in essence a religious act. Torture was administered during the trial, not after it concluded, and executions were always held after and separate from the *Auto-de-Fe*. The first Spanish version of this event took place in Seville, in 1481; six of the men and women that participated in this first religious ritual were later executed."

Even I was unaware of some of these details, and I thanked Bishop Alfredo for the education. He continued.

"I can easily see why the Church would try to suppress any records regarding the possibility of Columbus being a Jew- he then would have had to have been subjected to the religious inquiry and, if found 'guilty,' I hate that word in these circumstances, would have had to suffer the consequences. Which then would have meant no discoveries, etc."

"So what *are* you saying?" Yoli's directness was a sign of her youth, but the Bishop took no offense.

"What I am saying is that I, personally, believe that the Church, in its practical wisdom, knew of Columbus' Jewish roots, yet chose to hide them. The Church is its members, its clergy. For most of them, they aren't as rigid or dogmatic as many make the body of the organization out to be. Yes, just as is the case for everything, there are those of uncompromising conservatism who view it as a means to stand up to the onslaught that anti-religion attackers bring to the 'battlefield' against all people of faith, regardless of their particular spiritual system. But practically speaking, it shouldn't matter which path one takes as long as the goal is the same- a life leading to the center, to Godliness. I say that it doesn't matter whether Columbus was a Jew or not- he led a holy life in search of God; the same God for Jews, Christians and Moslems. But you know, if this perspective ever got out to both the Church leadership and Cubans, I would be finished. I consider the works and deeds to which I have dedicated my life of utmost importance. And I will not do anything, *ANYTHING*, to jeopardize that work in mid-stream.

"So if word of this meeting gets out, I will deny it ever happened. I will be righteously insulted by the allegations and work without rest to destroy the rumor, that has circumstantial proof at best; and in turn, you will suffer the consequences as well. Don't consider it a threat, just a fact. And frankly, I don't see what good it would do to release this 'rehashing' of old theories. But I will do one thing to show that we are on the same page.

"With your permission, I will write a tract on the next anniversary of Columbus' death- describing the great man's contributions to the advancement of science and discovery, working on behalf of *all* of God's children. Plus, I will revisit the 18th and 19th century episodes surrounding the uncertainties of the transfers from Hispaniola to Cuba to Seville. I will point out the assertions of our Dominican brethren who insisted that the wrong sarcophagus came to our island and then on to Spain. That keeps the controversy 'in-house' so to speak. People will turn their attention elsewhere. I believe that American lawyers refer to it as 'misdirection.'" And should the explorer still be on *La Isla*, not far to the east of here, no one of us shall reveal that secret".

All of this was said with a wink … and a smile.

We were astonished. But, finally had our answers… so to speak.

* * *

Outside, as promised by the street urchin 'responsible' for Berto's 'baby,' not a speck of dust, and nary a 'bird bomb,' marred the immaculate surface. A couple of CUCs exchanged hands with a smile, and top down, the cruiser headed west along the *Malecon*, into the setting Caribbean sun.

*"Clear the road of straws
'Cause I want to sit down
On this trunk that I see
And I can't arrive there that way

From Alto Cedro I go to Marcané,
Then to Cueto, I go to Mayarí"*

Printed in the United States
By Bookmasters